# After the
# Crash

## BOOKS BY EMMA DAVIES

Published by Bookouture in 2021

An imprint of Storyfire Ltd.
Carmelite House
50 Victoria Embankment
London EC4Y 0DZ

www.bookouture.com

ISBN: 978-1-80019-428-1
eBook ISBN: 978-1-80019-427-4

# After the Crash

EMMA DAVIES

*bookouture*

# CHAPTER ONE

The window is dimmed with dust up here in the attic, and I have to rub a hand against it to clear a circle on the glass. But the picture-postcard view is worth it, even if it is blurry with rain that has streaked the buildings and set the pavements aglow. Only moments before, the sun was beaming down from a clear sky, but angry clouds have forced their way in from the sea and let loose another of the squally showers that have marked the weather of the last few days. Still, in another half hour they will be gone, and the brilliant white light will return, so different from the much softer, golden rays that cover the rolling green hills of home.

I push the thought to one side. Whatever the beautiful countryside around Marwood Holt had been in the past, it certainly isn't home now – but I promised myself there'd be no comparisons, no longing for what my life had been before. This is different, that's all.

I'm perched at the top of a whitewashed building among a jumble of crooked, narrow streets, where everything and everyone jostles for space. There isn't a spare inch to be found, at least not in the town anyway. Atop the cliffs the land is beautiful, wild and free, although sadly barren of my beloved trees, but down here, beside the bay, the place will be teeming with life again in a matter of moments once the rain blows away. It never seems to stop moving, as continual as the tide itself.

I've never lived by the sea before. Or with my daughter and son-in-law. But then the last eighteen months have seen a series of firsts. Being widowed for one. I lift my chin a little, fighting back the tears that threaten; no more, there's been enough already. It's just the change that's bringing them back, I know that. Once things are a bit more settled, I'll be fine.

I return my attention to the room, to the bed where I've been sitting and my suitcase that stands beside it. It holds the last of my things to be unpacked and, once they are, I will be fully installed as a guest of the Lobster Pot, its first incidentally. I have a bed-sitting room that doubles as my study and, just through the connecting door, a tiny bathroom, which is all I need for now. I've even managed to bring one or two pieces of furniture with me from my old home, things I couldn't bear to be parted from. What was left, those things that didn't need to be sold, have gone into storage until such time as I can retrieve them.

A soft knock sounds at the door. I know it's Robin. Leah had to dash out earlier to pick up some materials she'd ordered for the hotel. She looks tired, as if she's been doing too much, or hasn't been sleeping. It worries me, but she'll only think I'm fussing if I mention it.

'I thought you could do with a bit of something to keep you going,' says Robin as I open the door. He's balancing a cup of tea and a plate of sandwiches in his hands. 'Breakfast was hours ago.'

I smile, feeling instantly a little guilty. He's been so kind, bringing me regular cups of tea that he really hasn't got time to make, and trying to ensure that I eat something. I haven't the heart to tell him that I don't have much of an appetite. It's a reminder to ask Leah what she'd like me to do about food while I'm here. After all, it's not like I'm a guest. She hasn't got time to be waiting on her mum hand and foot.

'Thanks, Robin. I probably should have come down, it's just that this is…' I trail off to look around the room. 'I'm finding it all a little strange. I'm very grateful but—'

'It's not home, is it?' He smiles in understanding. 'But things will settle down, Louisa, I'm sure of it. It's early days, after all.'

I nod, taking the plate from his hands. That's just what people said when William died. *Don't be so hard on yourself, Louisa, it's still early days...* I *wouldn't worry about that just now if I were you, it's early days...* Except that, very soon, the harsh reality of my life without William made it clear that those early days of grace were well and truly over. The time had soon come to stop crying at the slightest little thing, and start planning for my future. It's been eighteen months now since he was killed, his life cut short by a drunk driver; moving here is simply another addition to the growing list of things I've had to get used to. And get used to them I must.

Robin is hovering, clearly at a loss for something to say. I smile again, taking the mug from him this time, a signal that he's free to return to whatever he was doing.

He backs away and is almost at the door when he pauses. 'I'm going running later tonight,' he says. 'When it's cooler, and a bit quieter, but I don't mind walking instead if you'd like to come with me. I can show you around the town and the best paths to take up onto the hills. There are some spectacular views.' His long ginger hair hangs over one shoulder, tied in its customary band to keep it out of his face. One that has more freckles than the night sky has stars. You can tell he's a runner and likes to keep fit; he's tall and rangy, with not an ounce of fat on him so that his baggy shorts hang low on his hips and his tee shirt hugs his flat stomach.

'Thanks, Robin,' I reply, touched by his gesture. 'But perhaps on another day. I'm planning nothing more strenuous later than a long bath followed by an early night. Besides, I'm sure you'd much rather go by yourself. You can have a proper run then, instead of dawdling while you wait for me.'

Robin looks as if he's about to say something else, but instead simply nods and, raising a hand in farewell, slips from the room.

I look at the plate of sandwiches in my hand. Great thick doorsteps cut from fresh bread and overflowing with filling. They look beautiful but I'm very afraid they'll feel like dust in my mouth. I put down the plate on the little table beside my bed and take my mug back to the window, lifting it to my lips. Despite the heat of the day, the tea's warmth is still comforting.

The clouds are already beginning to break, and I know the pavements will start to steam as soon as the full force of the sun shines on them once more. But the hot, humid air won't last. Within minutes the ever-present breeze off the sea will sweep it away. I wonder what wintertime will feel like here, and shiver at the thought of the biting cold I imagine.

I should go out and explore, because the longer I leave it, the harder it will feel, but right now my desire to crawl under the bedcovers and stay there is proving hard to resist. Which has perhaps been the strangest thing of all about this period of time. I'm not normally like this. Before William died, I was independent and spent much of my day alone too, happy in my own company. But my days had also been filled with industry. My job kept me busy, as did my hobbies, and I couldn't bear to see time wasted. I tut and stop my train of thought from going any further – that isn't what I'd been running through my head at all. Rather that, given my previous abilities, I now can't understand why the sudden absence of William in the world should change me into someone who wouldn't mind if she never sees another soul again.

And there I am, thinking about William, once more. The celebrations for our twenty-fifth wedding anniversary only a few months before his death. And people had said it wouldn't last. I purse my lips, remembering all too well the comments my mother had made. *The pair of you with disastrous marriages behind you and yet you're willing to do it all over again. You hardly know him,*

*Louisa, and you're no age at all. For heaven's sake, take your time with this one...* But I hadn't wanted to and neither had he, so our whirlwind romance turned into a spur-of-the-moment wedding, but it had worked. For all these years it had worked beautifully.

It had been hard in the beginning perhaps, when we'd had no money. William had a child, Simon, and his ex-wife had certainly not been backward in coming forward anytime she'd wanted anything. It hadn't been his fault that the relationship fell apart, but he'd done the right thing, supporting his son right up until his eighteenth birthday. For a long time, it had meant that we couldn't buy a home of our own, or go on holidays, or buy nice things, but neither of us had cared. Leah had come along by then and we were happy; our family was complete and nothing else mattered. A few more years went by and then William's career had suddenly taken off, everything he did turning to gold, and we were finally able to buy our own home and become accustomed to some of the finer things in life.

The last ten years had been nigh on perfect and, despite being in my late forties, I hadn't viewed my age as any barrier to happiness, in fact, quite the reverse. I'd assumed that if my fifties were going to be anything like my forties then I would really enjoy them. But now I'm forty-nine and the thought of the next big birthday simply fills me with despair.

It wasn't as if William had let the payments on his life insurance policy drift deliberately. He'd just been busy, preoccupied by the new project he'd taken on at work. Grateful that he'd still been given the opportunity and not been passed over for a younger colleague. He'd been determined to make it the massive success I knew he could and, although I'd wanted him to slow down, I'd had to support his decision – that was William all over; he could never say no to anyone. He was generous to a fault, one of the reasons why I loved him so much. And why he'd lent Simon all that money, of course, only I hadn't found out about that until after he'd died. It was a huge chunk of our savings that William had obviously assumed he would get back with dividends. Except that Simon's business had gone bust four months ago so now there was no hope of my ever being repaid. Simon felt bad about it, he'd told me often enough, but that didn't really help me from a practical point of view. The money was gone, and no amount of wishing would bring it back.

I swallow another mouthful of tea. So here I am, my worldly goods in storage and, for the time being at least, lodging in a seaside hotel with my daughter and son-in-law. It isn't how I had imagined my life at all. But I am, finally, and most importantly, debt-free. And I must remind myself of that. Without William's huge salary coming in, I'd been in trouble within three months. The fact that I'd managed to keep everything going for a few more was a miracle or, rather, foolish, as I now know. My bank account had been haemorrhaging money, but it hadn't seemed right to move away from the home we had shared together, and my blinkered grief had only made things worse.

I put down my mug and cross to the bed, heaving my suitcase up onto it. Sinking down on the mattress, I lift the plate of sandwiches, closing my eyes briefly before taking a large bite of one half. It takes an age to eat, chewing and chewing, trying to find enough moisture to swallow the mouthful of food, despite the tea I've just drunk. I'm very much looking forward to the time when my body no longer views food as something I have to take in to survive. Then I might be able to enjoy Robin's excellent culinary skills.

I'm halfway through my unpacking, hanging up my clothes in the single wardrobe, when I lift a pale-pink linen shirt from my case. I put out a hand to steady myself as the room begins to spin and I sink back down on the bed. How could I have forgotten this was in here? William's shirt. The last one of his I have, soft, and still unwashed. I bring it to my face, the scent and feel, so, so familiar. And the near constant ache of longing deep inside of me rises once more.

My phone rings and, glancing at the display, I snatch it up, glad of the interruption.

'Barbara!' I exclaim. 'Oh, it's so good to hear from you. Please tell me you've got something nice and juicy for me. Something I can really sink my teeth into.'

There's a slight pause from the other end of the line. 'Well, it's lovely to hear you sounding so keen, darling, but how are you, Louisa?' she says. 'Are you moved in yet?'

'I am, it's...' I look around the rather faded room as I speak. 'It's lovely here. Different, but lovely all the same. And I'm sure I'll get used to it. I'm just unpacking the last of my things, but my laptop is already charged and raring to go. Barbara, what have you got for me?'

My editor gives a nervous laugh. 'Hold your horses a moment, I want to know how you are, Louisa. You. Not your furniture, or your cardigans, but you. It's still early days, you know, and I'd hate for you to rush back into things before you're ready. You've had the most enormous upheaval...' She breaks off. 'It's lovely that you're trying to sound so keen, but this is me you're talking to, Louisa, and we go far enough back that you don't have to kid me you're feeling okay.'

Her words bring a sudden sting of tears. Barbara and I do indeed go way back. She'd been the first person to give me a chance, back when I was a young and ambitious journalist with no credits to my name, and I've worked for her ever since. Not continuously; I had some time off when Leah was born and Barbara has moved magazines on more than one occasion, but our paths had continued to cross and for the last five years I've been a features writer, albeit freelance, for *Your Life*, an upmarket glossy publication that caters for the needs of intelligent successful women – people like me, I'd thought.

'I've tried so hard to keep everything the same, Barbara,' I reply, gently laying William's shirt on my pillow. 'I knew I couldn't, not really, but it was important to me, and William. You know how he felt about that house, it was all he ever dreamed of and he worked so hard for it. We had everything planned for our future, we…' I trail off. There's no need to tell Barbara, she's heard it all before, more than once. 'I feel like I've let him down.'

'Oh, Louisa…'

There's sympathy in my friend's voice, but just beyond it I can hear the same whispers I hear in everyone's voice. *It isn't you that's let William down… but the other way around.*

'But,' I add firmly, 'I'm here now, and getting myself settled. And the one thing that's going to make me feel better is work.'

'I know that's how it seems, Louisa, but don't underestimate how you're going to feel; this is another massive change in your life. Why don't you take a little more time for yourself? I know you haven't written for a few months, but you could have a bit of a break and enjoy the seaside. Besides, you'll be fit for nothing if you don't start looking after yourself.'

I can feel the thought of all that inactivity wrapping its cold tentacles around me. I mustn't let myself be pulled in.

'Thanks, Barbara, but, honestly, I'm much better when I'm working. And if you think about it, that's going to make me feel far more settled than lazing around all day, doing nothing. I couldn't bear it. No, I need to work. I want to work.' I think for a second. 'I could do an exposé on… oh, I don't know… but something local. It's lovely here, but there must be miscarriages of justice and dodgy dealers the same as anywhere. I'm sure I can come up with something. Just give me a couple of weeks to have a snoop around and I'll have a list of potential articles lined up for you.'

'I've no doubt that you would but, actually, Louisa, if you're absolutely set on starting straight away, you could do me the biggest favour.' She clears her throat slightly. 'As you know,

Erin is just about to go on maternity leave and I need someone experienced to hold the reins while she's gone. Now, I know her cross-section of the magazine might not seem like a good fit for you, but it's a hugely successful area for us. It would make me feel a lot better knowing that I've got you to look after it in Erin's absence.'

I have to put my hand over my mouth to stop from swearing out loud. 'Homes and Gardens? Me…? Barbara, are you *mad*?'

'Listen, it's not as daft as it sounds. I know you think that kind of thing is beneath your skill set, and in a way you're right, but it takes a really good eye to spot the potential in something. You have such a great sense of style. You only need to look at… Well, anyway, I think you could bring something amazing to it, Louisa. You're certainly not lacking in imagination, and I know we've done a few coastal features before, but not for a long while, and very few during the winter months. It could be a real breath of fresh air.'

*You only need to look at your old house*, that's what Barbara had been about to say. And yes, I did have a beautiful home, and a gorgeous garden, but that's because it was so important to William. And to me, of course, but I don't have a practical bone in my body, not really.

'Think about it,' adds Barbara. 'Please, that's all I ask.' She pauses. 'Look, something came across my desk the other day, and I think it could be a really great story. Why don't I ping you over the details and you could take a look. Have a think about it for a couple of days and get back to me.'

My stomach sinks in disappointment. I understand exactly what Barbara is saying. 'Sure,' I say. 'Yes, do that. No harm in looking, is there? Oh, hang on a sec…' I lower the phone and press the mute button, deliberately waiting a few seconds before reconnecting the call. 'Sorry, Barbara, that was Leah at the door. She needs my help for a minute. So, yes, send over whatever it is and I'll have a think. Anyway, everything is all right with you, is it? The boys okay? Jack?'

'They're fine. Keeping me on my toes as usual. Listen, you take care, okay, and I'll speak to you soon. And thank you, Louisa, I know you'll do a fabulous job. Love to the family…'

She hangs up before I do and I'm left looking at the phone, wondering if what just happened is what I think just happened. And a little frisson of nervous energy flickers through me. I'm a champion of the underdog; I right wrongs and fight against injustice. I'm not sure I know how to write about anything else.

I sit down at the small desk Leah has set up in one corner of the room for me. It's positioned directly under one of the skylights, so the overhead lighting isn't ideal, but I'll manage. My laptop lies there, primed and ready to go, just like I told Barbara, and I open the lid and wait for the screen to spring to life. The email lands in my inbox before I've even finished typing in my password. Barbara never wastes any time, she'll already be on to the next item on her list and, rather ironically, her ability to juggle so many things at once is one of the qualities that I admire in her. But today, I can't help feeling as if her efficiency isn't that at all, but rather something else.

The message is brief:

*See what you can do with this, Louisa. There are so many angles you could come at this one from, and to start with you're going to need all your old investigative skills. I don't know who the artist is, but he must be local – and it could be a brilliant feature. A great excuse for a walk on the beach!*

*B x*

Attached are two photos, each of brilliant blue sky, with a wide curving arc of sand beneath. The pictures have been taken

from a clifftop, the whole sweep of a bay in focus, right down
to the sparkling silver of the sea. And there below, in the middle
of the huge expanse, is an intricate mandala design, somehow
drawn onto the sand. And, judging by the distance from which
the photo has been taken, its dimensions must be enormous.

I move my thumb and forefinger apart on the touchpad, the
gesture enlarging the image. It's extraordinary. And beautiful.
Every line that makes up the circular pattern seems perfectly
placed, the execution flawless. It's hard to comprehend how it
could even have been drawn but, after another second or two, I
close the photos and stare at Barbara's message. Everything she
put in her email is true; I can see that there's a wonderful feature
here, just waiting to be written. Except not by me. This isn't what
I do. I'm an investigative journalist, but this… this feels horribly
like I'm being put out to pasture.

I tut, shaking my head. I'm sure that's not true. I heard what
Barbara had said. Erin's going to be away for a few months and
Barbara needs someone to step into her shoes for a while, that's
all. It's not permanent; I'm just being touchy, seeing shadows that
aren't there. But the thought is in my head now, that it's take this
assignment or nothing, and I can't remove it.

I get to my feet, closing the lid of my laptop and moving back
to the window to stare at the street below. I'd asked Barbara for
something I could sink my teeth into and that's exactly what she's
given me. The fact that it's different from what I expected isn't a
bad thing. It's a challenge, I tell myself, that's all. A new challenge.

And it's probably exactly what I need.

# CHAPTER TWO

I wake the next morning bathed in sweat, my hair hanging in limp strands and stuck to the side of my face. It's my own fault. I'm simply not used to noise at night and had got up around four in the morning to close the window and since then the heat has built steadily. It feels like a heavy cloak I have to fight to be free from. At home… *before*, I correct myself, the night was a place of deep, quiet dark that soothed and slowed the mind and senses. But the gulls here, so stereotypically the right thing to hear at the seaside by day, at night never seem to cease their raucous shrieking.

I rub absently at my skin. It feels slightly gritty and, sighing, I swing my legs over the bed, padding across the floor to the window, throwing it open once more. A dull sunless day stares back at me, but there's a breeze blowing at least, and I breathe it in, feeling the fresh air flood my face. The street below is just coming to life, the beginning of a new day, and the first of my new future.

But it isn't excitement that awakens. Instead, it's grief that rears up at me, and I swallow, putting out a hand to steady myself. It takes a moment before I'm able to move; the mornings are always the worst, the waking up alone. I had a routine before, even on my own. I knew what to do and when to do it. Now, I feel adrift, and the raw pain I'd first felt when William died has somehow renewed itself. Perhaps it's just the shock of moving, the sheer newness of everything that's bringing it to life again. I turn away from the window. Time to get myself going.

Half an hour later, I'm almost ready to face the day. My room, like all the others in the hotel, hasn't yet been renovated, but I shower and wash my hair in surprisingly hot and copious water. I dress carefully, picking out a soft blue shirt to go with my pale-yellow cotton jeans, and, once I've dried my hair and styled it, I stand for a moment, observing my reflection with the attention to detail that one only ever reserves for oneself.

I'm lucky that my clear skin requires relatively little attention, and the small amount of make-up I wear is enough to bring a slight pink blush to my cheeks and lips, which complements my hair. Golden-blonde, it falls to just below my collarbone, its soft waves bouncing gently around my shoulders. I peer closer, grey roots just beginning to show on top of my head while around my ears, where my hair is naturally lighter, it shines white instead. I'd always kept it perfectly coloured when William was alive, and since his death for that matter, but I wonder if now might be the time to finally let nature take its course. Or is that just giving up? I slip on the rings William gave me and, satisfied that what I'm feeling on the inside doesn't show too much on the outside, prepare to go downstairs.

It's much later than I'd realised, but when I open my bedroom door the hotel beneath me seems quiet, even though Leah and Robin will already be up and busy somewhere. They have an enormous task ahead of them, much bigger than I had originally thought before coming here. Buying this place fulfilled all their dreams, but renovating it is going to require a huge amount of work. They've already begun to strip the rooms, all except for this small attic floor which Leah had plans for before she offered it to me. But the whole hotel is almost unusable after years of neglect and lack of investment. Stripping it of its furniture and fittings has only revealed the extent of its sorry condition.

It's a Monday morning, just before ten, in the middle of July, but the season hasn't quite reached its height yet. The schools don't finish for another ten days or so, but in any case the Lobster

Pot won't be open for a while and certainly not for this year's holidaymakers. Christmas, Leah said they're aiming for. That way they can start slowly and iron out all the niggles and teething problems while they're quiet. Then, they'll be well and truly ready for next year. But even so, six months seems a very short space of time to achieve all that they need to.

I pause at the foot of the stairs, stepping onto the terracotta tiles of the entrance hallway. It's a gleaming, airy space, coloured by the light which spills into it from the stained-glass panels beside the front door, specially commissioned by Leah. It's the only area of the hotel that's been finished, apart from the kitchen which lies beyond the reception area, along a corridor away to my right. To my left are two interconnecting lounge rooms, plus a dining room and conservatory. I check my watch and turn right.

The sight of my daughter always makes me smile in slight amazement. In between the times when I see her, I forget just how alike we are, and now, watching her as she stands in the kitchen chatting to a man I don't recognise, I'm struck again by just how much of a mini-me she is. Her golden-blonde hair is natural, just as thick as mine, and today it's drawn into a high ponytail, the wisps of her fringe feathering her forehead. With an apron over a cornflower-blue dress decorated with vibrant pink peonies, Leah could easily claim first prize in an Alice in Wonderland lookalike competition. She even has William's piercing blue eyes to complete the fantasy.

I hover in the doorway for a moment, unseen, watching as Leah continues to chat. She peers into a large cardboard box that stands on a table in front of her, before nodding and giving the man a wide smile. He makes a quick note on a pad he's been holding at his side and, returning her smile, he raises a hand in farewell as he heads for the door. It's as she turns, lifting the box in her arms, that she notices me. She slides it back down again and comes forward, smiling.

'Mum! Did you sleep well?'

I wait until she reaches me before drawing her into a quick tight hug. 'I think I must've done,' I reply. 'I woke a little hot, but it was my own fault. I don't think I'm used to the noise of the seagulls yet, and I closed my window.'

Leah frowns. 'Maybe we could get a fan, or…' She grimaces. 'You get used to them, but I admit they do make a racket.'

'They've got chicks at the moment,' says Robin, appearing from a room just off the rear of the kitchen. He wipes his hands on a rag he's carrying. 'That's why they're so noisy. Squabbling for food and fighting off potential marauders.' He smiles. 'Morning, Louisa.'

I dip my head at his greeting.

'I'd leave your window open though if I were you. It's not even hot at the moment, not really. But you'll cook otherwise.'

'I didn't think,' adds Leah. 'Sorry. I've hardly been up in those rooms since we've been here. I knew they were a bit musty but…' She trails off, looking at Robin. 'We'll get a fan.'

'Leah, it's fine, there's no rush. I'm just not used to the noise, that's all. By the end of the week I probably won't even notice them. And at least it's cooler today.'

'Don't you believe it,' says Robin. 'Ignore the cloudy start; it's often like that here. In another hour it will boiling again.'

Leah frowns at him. 'That's not helpful,' she says, rolling her eyes, and then, 'Did you fix it?'

Robin pulls a face. 'No. The joint's corroded, I'll have to get a new one.'

'But I need the water on in there,' answers Leah.

'Well you can't have it. Not at the moment.' He smiles, and I recognise the look in his eyes. 'I'll go now,' he says. 'And with any luck you'll have it back on just after lunch.' He wipes at a damp patch on one leg of his shorts. 'And meanwhile, don't use the sink or we'll have water everywhere.'

He grins at me as he departs the room, leaving me looking at the tightness around Leah's mouth.

'It sounds as if you're having a trying morning,' I say.

She raises an airy hand. 'No more than usual,' she replies. 'The sink is blocked. Again. And leaking scummy water everywhere. You think you'd be able to buy a hotel and still have working plumbing five months later, but no, apparently not.'

I'm not sure what to say.

'Is there anything I can do to help?' I ask.

But Leah doesn't answer, her attention caught by some other thought. 'Oh…' She stares at me. 'I've just realised, you haven't had any breakfast, have you? We were up really early, you see, and I said that Robin should let you have a lie-in, but then I forgot and—'

I hold up my hand. 'Leah, it's *fine*,' I reply. 'I don't expect you to wait on me hand and foot. In fact, you mustn't. You've got far too much to do without worrying about someone who is perfectly capable of looking after herself. Plus, if anything it's my fault, I'm ridiculously late.'

'Yes… No…' Leah seems distracted and I realise that she is no more prepared for this than I am.

I gaze around the kitchen and the professional catering equipment that fills it – everything on a much bigger scale than I'm used to. 'Perhaps I could just have a cup of coffee? And a piece of toast? I don't want much, I don't normally bother.'

Leah frowns. 'No, you've got to have a proper breakfast. I should have sorted something out for you, I'm sorry, Mum. Maybe you could have a toaster and kettle up in your room. Oh, but no, that wouldn't work, would it? Where would you keep the bread? Or the butter for that matter?' She pauses. The conversation is becoming more awkward by the second.

'Maybe just show me where things are for now,' I offer. 'And we can work out everything else as we go along. Just point me at the kettle.' I give her a reassuring smile.

'Right, yes.' She points to the far corner of the room where there's a small hand-washing sink. 'The kettle's over there, and all the other stuff you'll need is in the cupboard above it. I can put the grill on and make you some toast, if you like?'

'That would be lovely, darling, thank you. And then I can get out of your hair.'

Finally, Leah smiles. 'Have you got any plans for today?' she asks.

'Not really,' I say, standing by the kettle. 'I thought I'd just take it as it comes. I'll go out and have a wander around town to start with, maybe go for a drive.' I reach up to take down a mug from the cupboard above my head, holding it aloft for a moment. 'Can I make you one while I'm here?'

Leah wrinkles her nose. 'Maybe I'll just have some tea, I don't really fancy a coffee just now.'

I add another cup to stand beside mine. 'Is there anywhere you recommend I should go?' I ask.

'Well, the town itself is lovely. There's plenty to see, some beautiful shops. And the beach of course. There's a path that takes you up onto the cliffs if you feel like a proper walk.' She busies herself with the grill.

'I've got to have a think about work as well,' I add. 'I had a quick chat with Barbara yesterday and she'd like me to write some pieces for the Homes and Gardens section. I'm not quite sure how I feel about that.'

'Oh, but I think that sounds wonderful. Much more fun than what you used to do.'

Past tense, I notice. But what I do, did do, isn't really meant to be fun. And it certainly isn't for the people I've tried to help. People who've been on the receiving end of miscarriages of justice, for example. I write about consumer issues, political policies, human rights too, not how to choose between brands of strawberry jam. I'm finding the shifting emphasis rather difficult to get my head around.

'I think I might have had enough change in my life just recently,' I say. 'I'm not sure I'm really ready for any more.' I add some coffee and a teabag to the respective mugs in front of me and pour on boiling water. 'Although… Maybe now *is* the perfect opportunity for a change. Maybe I should have a drastic rethink about what I do. Now that I have the chance that is; no responsibilities, no bills to pay—' I come to a sudden halt, embarrassed at my lack of tact.

Fortunately, Leah doesn't seem to notice.

'No, don't give up your writing, Mum. You've always loved what you do. Write about different things certainly, maybe that would suit you better, but don't give it up altogether.' She catches her lip in the corner of her mouth. 'You know, you're welcome to stay here for as long as you want to, Mum. Robin and I don't mind. You probably won't want to. You'll be itching to get yourself settled and find somewhere of your own…' Her voice fades as reticence creeps in. 'But there's no rush, is there?'

I catch her eye just before she looks down and I know exactly what she's thinking. How can I want to find a new home of my own when it will be one without her father in it?

*

By eleven, I'm standing on the pavement outside the hotel, looking left and right. In front of me is another row of buildings, much like on this side of the street, a hotchpotch of styles, some tall and thin, some low and wide, whitewashed or natural stone, roofs at juxtapositions and chimneys jostling for space. It's what gives the street its pleasing appearance; that and the now bright-blue sky which sets off the colourful bunting as it flutters, criss-crossed down the road. The town can't surely be on holiday all of the time, but that's what it seems to be saying.

To my left, the shops and tearooms stretch away up the hill towards the church and its spire which stands atop the rise, dead centre, filling the horizon. Like a lone finger, pointing to heaven amid the fluffy white clouds of the picture-postcard view.

The sea lies to the right, the road giving rise after a short distance to a pedestrian causeway filled with tiny shops; some of them seemingly no bigger than a shed. An array of buckets and spades spill out onto the walkway, bright colours inviting in the sun. I turn left, saving the sea for later.

It takes all of thirty minutes to work out the lie of the land. Immediately surrounding the Lobster Pot are the kind of places you find in every coastal town. Shops that don't really sell anything but memories; things which here seem desirable, but which back in your home never quite seem to fit. Out of place, or out of time. And when you've been in one shop, you've been in them all – nick-nacks and rock, fudge and flip-flops. Squashed into the meaner streets, sandwiched between the others, and much further away, are the shops that cater for the people who actually live here all year round. Places to buy bread and lightbulbs, meat and pet food. And lastly, in one very grand row of elegant Victorian buildings, are the art galleries and craft shops, selling ceramics and glassware, handmade jewellery, textiles and expensive woollens. And it's here that I spend most of my time.

Even so, there's only so much to look at before the thoughts, which at first flitted vaguely through my mind, gradually coalesce into a vague unease at what I can see around me. I feel exposed. Different. As if separate from everyone else... And then I stop dead in the middle of the pavement as a single thought pushes to the front of all the others. I don't just feel alone, I am alone.

I scan the figures around me: husbands, wives, children, an elderly couple still holding hands after all these years. They smile, they laugh, they squint in the sun, they bicker, they tease. They play-fight, they mop up tears, they walk unspeaking, they wander, wonder, but they do it all together. Why hadn't I realised that it would be like that here? That, above anything else, the seaside is a place for people, not somewhere to be on your own.

The threat of tears sends me scurrying into the nearest shop. It's primarily a sweet shop, the front half given over to jars and packets, novelties and handmade chocolates, but in the back it's more akin to a newsagent, with cans of drink and packets of crisps. I walk straight to the shelves and pluck a glossy magazine from the selection at random. It's a measure designed to distract me, to stop me from dwelling on my thoughts, but, as I turn the pages, I'm struck by something else. The articles are probably just the kind of thing Barbara has in mind for me. And, as yet, I have absolutely no idea how to approach writing them.

Ten minutes later I leave the shop with a stack of seven magazines under my arm and retrace my steps up the hill. I spied a small cafe earlier, much further off the beaten track than most, and possibly the only place I'll find a space, given that it's now lunchtime.

The cafe is busy, but there's one space free in the window. It's not the most comfortable of places to sit, but I squeeze onto a stool pushed against a waist-high countertop and survey the plastic menu card in front of me.

After I've ordered I look at my stack. I've read hundreds of these kinds of magazines of course, who hasn't? Even if it's just at the hairdresser's or the dentist's waiting room. But the language is so different from what I'm used to employing, and the tone warm and friendly. I use much more forceful language when I write, to make an argument or voice an opinion, and it's usually in quite bold terms. These kind of articles are ones in which the photography is just as important as the words to sell the message, if not more so. In fact, do people even read these? I confess I never have, I just skim through them and look at the pictures.

Despite the lack of choice on the menu, when my coffee arrives it's rich and fragrant, full of flavour, and the scone I ordered to go with it at least three inches tall and still slightly warm. It crumbles slightly as I slice it, plump sultanas glistening with juice. I've also been provided with two dishes, one full of thick jam and the other clotted cream. I stare at my plate, slightly overwhelmed. My body is telling me I need to eat something and a scone seemed a good choice, plain and not too filling. But I'd forgotten I'm in Devon now, home of the cream tea, and, with so much competition from other cafes and tearooms, I guess large is the standard portion. I duly load up one side of the scone and take a bite.

The first taste is far too sweet, cloying, but after a second or two during which I wonder how I'm ever going to finish it, my brain suddenly responds and a rush of saliva fills my mouth. I haven't been starving myself but my meals have been bland and lacking in thought or care. To all at once taste something, really taste it, has awakened something within me, even if it is just a survival instinct. I finish one half of the scone quickly, eager to satiate my thirst for the heady sweetness cut through by the silky mellowness of the cream.

I push away the plate after a moment and sip my coffee, staring out at the street. Because it still feels odd. Like I don't belong here. I don't normally sit about in cafes, eating scones and drinking coffee like I haven't a care in the world. I shouldn't really be doing it now because apart from anything else I have work to do. The voice in the back of my head pipes up again, loud and clear: *If I don't write, I don't get paid.* It matters now I have no one to look after me.

So I open the first of the magazines and read from the beginning, starting with the editorial. I finish my coffee and, after a few minutes, eat the remains of my scone, but it doesn't feel quite so pleasurable now and leaves me feeling uncomfortably full.

As I leave, a little while later, a waitress catches my eye and thanks me for coming. 'See you soon,' she says, and it surprises me. The sincerity of her smile for one, and the invitation to return. The place is packed; I wouldn't have thought they'd need to drum up more custom. I'm back out on the street before I realise that perhaps they do. Competition for business must be fierce here, and I guess they're only as good as the next customer. It's the middle of summer too, what must it be like in the winter?

I've taken several steps before I realise that I'm already looking for the angle, looking for the way to pitch a story, because I'm sure there's one here. And I can't help it, it's just the way I think. I'm far more interested in the plight of the people who own the business than I am the quality of the scones.

I peel the magazines away from my arm. Robin was right: the cloud has lifted, the day has been transformed, and the heat is making them stick to my skin, leaving patches of colour where the print has transferred itself from the paper. I'm tempted to throw the whole lot in the bin. But I know I can't. I can't afford to.

# CHAPTER THREE

The hotel kitchen is quiet as I enter. In fact there are no signs of life anywhere on the ground floor, but all that changes as I climb the stairs, heading for my room. As soon as I push open the door to the first floor I can hear bursts of hammering coming from directly ahead of me, and voices too, I realise. It's Leah I can hear, and she doesn't sound happy.

'But I didn't say to go ahead and build it, I said I wanted to wait.'

'Then why did I order the wood,' asks Robin, 'if it wasn't to go ahead and build the bloody thing?'

'I don't know, maybe because you weren't listening…'

I pause on the landing, not wishing to eavesdrop, but to get to the next flight of stairs I have to pass right by the room they're in and all the doors have been taken off. It's going to be impossible to walk past unnoticed. The room is completely empty, stripped of all its furniture – even the carpets have been taken up. Robin is standing in one corner, a length of wood in one hand, while Leah stands in front of him, her hands on her hips. I've seen my daughter in that pose before and, looking down, I walk on by.

'What?' I hear her say as I pass, and I know it's in response to a change of expression on Robin's face. He can't have missed seeing me. She tuts and then her voice comes closer, from directly behind me.

'Hi, Mum. Is everything okay?'

She's not stupid, she'll know I've heard their altercation. So, do I maintain the pretence that I haven't, or make reference to it?

'Hello, love, I'm just on my way back up to my room to get a bit of work done. Well, make a few preliminary notes anyway, just ideas really.' I smile as if there's nothing at all amiss. 'So, how's it all going then?' I ask, looking about me. 'These are such beautiful rooms.' And it's true, they are. Big and airy, with high ceilings and enormous windows.

'Yes, well they will be when they're finished,' replies Leah. '*If* they ever get finished.'

'There's rather more work here than we first imagined,' explains Robin, keen to soften his wife's words. 'I think the previous owners simply papered over the cracks. Quite literally. We're having to strip everything back much further than we banked on before we can even begin to start work.'

'That doesn't sound good,' I agree. 'But once it's done, you'll have something that's not only beautiful, but has a sound foundation as well. It will last for years.'

'Exactly,' says Leah. 'Which is why we shouldn't skimp on the fittings. That's just what I've been trying to tell Robin.'

I groan inwardly. I seem to have taken sides unwittingly, and that wasn't my intention at all.

'I've seen the most beautiful antique armoires,' continues Leah, 'which would perfectly match the sleigh beds we like. They're authentic too, from a French brocantes. They'd look stunning.' She pouts slightly.

'I see,' I reply neutrally. 'They do sound nice.'

Robin grimaces. 'What Leah is trying to tell you is that several weeks ago we discussed my making some built-in wardrobes for these rooms because it would save on space, and money. And being the dutiful husband that I am, I went ahead, ordered the wood and made a start, because I didn't know that in between times my wife had been scouring the French countryside for hulking great lumps of furniture.' He finishes with a smile but it's obvious how irritated he is.

'Well, maybe you can do half and half,' I suggest. 'Have your armoires in some of the rooms and fitted wardrobes in the others.'

'No, they have to be the same,' replies Leah. 'Everything has to be uniform so that when a guest books, and hopefully rebooks, they know exactly what they're getting, the same impressively high standard throughout.'

I consider her words. 'But it could also be interesting to have rooms which are different, unique even…' I pause while Leah raises her eyebrows. 'Not that I know anything about it,' I add quickly. 'It just struck me that having an eclectic mix of styles might be quite nice for the jaded traveller, you know the one who spends most of his or her life in hotel chains, where everything *is* the same.'

'Which is precisely why they *are* so successful. The customer recognises the quality of the brand and they know exactly what they're paying for.' Leah's expression leaves me in no doubt that I'm right in one regard only: that I don't know what I'm talking about.

I flash a quick glance in Robin's direction. As if things weren't awkward enough, now I'm in grave danger of straying into rocky territory, smack bang in the middle of their relationship. 'Well, I'm sure whichever look you decide upon will be gorgeous; I can't wait to see everything when it's finished.' I rearrange the pile of magazines still in my arms. 'I'd best get on.' And then I turn and scuttle back out to the corridor.

Except that once I get back to my room, the relief I expected to feel at having escaped a tricky conversation has morphed into something approaching claustrophobia. By not wishing to become caught in the middle of Leah and Robin's relationship, this hot and airless space at the top of the house now feels more like a prison.

I'd never even considered coming to the Lobster Pot before Leah suggested it. And while it was true that my financial situation had left me with little choice, I still persisted in the belief that there would be another answer to the mess I was in. But as soon as she mentioned it, relief had flowed through me and, suddenly, possibility, a thing I had thought closed off to me, had miraculously opened up.

But even knowing it was a lifeline I had to grasp, it had still thrown up some difficult emotions. Not least that I was having to turn to my own daughter for help when surely, as a parent, that situation should be reversed. So there was guilt, shame and a certain degree of embarrassment too in accepting her offer, but I've tried to view it with positivity; as a much-needed period for reflection, not only on a practical level, but also to adjust to the changes in my life, physically and emotionally too. While I was still living in the house that William and I shared, my grief might have seemed ever-present, but it had also been held in check by much of my world remaining as it always had been. Now, surrounded by change, I feel as if I've had the rug pulled out from under me, that I'm free-falling.

However hard it is for me coming to live here though, it's equally hard for Leah, I remind myself. And for Robin too. Having me land in their midst when they're both so busy is awful timing and I've been worried about Leah enough as it is without causing her any more stress.

Perhaps I need to make some decisions about my future much sooner than I'd first anticipated. And highest up the list of these has to be my work. It's currently the only form of income I have. And what little I'd recouped from the sale of the house after I'd paid off all my debt isn't going to last long if I keep dipping into it.

The trouble is that, although my work for the magazine is regular, I'm only required to submit one or two articles a month, occasionally more if Barbara's particularly pushed, but that doesn't happen often. I'm paid well for these, and I'm proud of the work I've produced, but it's nothing compared to what I could earn from a full-time job. I never had to worry about this before and I realise how spoilt I've been; well and truly having my cake and eating it. I physically couldn't write for months after William died and Barbara had simply accepted it, just as I knew she would. *Whenever you're ready is fine*, she'd said, but what I hadn't realised, and perhaps she hadn't either, was that things were moving on without me in the time I was away. And I hope I'm not about to pay the price. Whatever I decide to do in the future, in the here and now I do have an offer of work and one that I need to figure out how to approach.

It takes just over two hours to finish reading and, when I'm done, I stand and stretch before walking a circuit of the room, returning to stare at the notes I've made. I realise that I'd finished adding to them after the third magazine – there was no need. Because the one abiding thought I'm left with, after reading pages and pages of articles, is that everything I've read is more or less the same. That's not altogether surprising; a lot of these magazines are part of the same overall publishing group, and so if one prints an article on which essentials to pack for the best summer beach bag, then several of them do. Even the titles that are less beauty and fashion and more countryside and rural affairs share similarities. Canal boats seem to be the flavour of this month's selection. So where does that leave me?

Most of the notes I've made comment on the language used and the form of the articles. They're factual, but not in the way I would write them. The style is flowery, appeals to the senses and invokes a strong feeling of desire. In a way they're just like this little seaside town; they wear their colours on their sleeve and sell a dream, inviting people to believe that their lives would change if only they did this particular thing or bought that particular thing. But there's no depth to anything here; nothing to inform or challenge and, in short, it all just seems… I wince. Even inside my head the word seems uncharitable, but I can't help how I feel, and to me it just all seems trite, pointless nonsense.

I blow out a puff of air from between my cheeks, wrinkling my nose. Maybe it's just the mood I'm in.

I glance at my watch. The afternoon has crept past and the hotel beneath me now seems quiet. It's getting towards the time of day when I would normally start thinking about what to have for dinner, even if it's just beans on toast. Tonight though, we're going to have dinner together. One of Robin's specialities, I gather, which we'll eat al fresco on the pretty little terrace at the back of the hotel. First I think there's just enough time for a little fresh air. The beach isn't quite as busy as earlier, but still thronged with people, alive with the sound of children calling and shrieking as they play. A burst of music reaches me as I walk, the excited bark of a dog somewhere, but I move past them all, walking to the shoreline and following it until I'm far beyond them. Now, there's only the sound of the sea, washing over the line of pebbles that lie there, dropped by an outward tide. A gust of wind blows the carcass of a tiny crab across the sand, its shell hollowed out, the skeleton paper-thin.

The cliffs behind me have risen higher the further I've walked and I cross the sand to sit beneath them, clambering over a pile of rocks to perch on one, a rock pool still full of water in a hollow beside me. I wriggle myself comfortable and then I sit, letting the wind blow through my hair, as my thoughts seem to move with it, this way and that. It's quite some time before I inhale a deep breath of the salty air and push myself off the rocks to walk back. I will go and enjoy dinner with my daughter and son-in-law, the first of many in my new home. And then tomorrow… tomorrow, I will start looking for the man who draws pictures in the sand.

# CHAPTER FOUR

I always feel better when I have a plan. It isn't necessarily a good plan, but it's a place to start and that's half of the way to being a plan. I'm hoping that today will allow me to fill in the rest of the blanks.

I'd gone to bed last night filled with an even greater resolve than I'd had in the afternoon. Dinner with Leah and Robin had been lovely but, as relaxed and pleasant as it had been, I'm only too aware of the amount of work that lies ahead of them, and how easily my stay with them could sour. There's a lot of truth in the old adage, two's company, three's a crowd, and I don't ever want them to feel that way about me. No, I must use my time at the hotel wisely; do what Barbara has asked of me, bank the money and, while I'm doing that, try to decide what I want my future to look like.

I root around in my handbag, checking that I've got everything I need. I filled a water bottle from the sink this morning and I've slathered myself in sun cream too, so I'm as prepared as I'm ever going to be. I can't start to think about how I'm going to write this article unless I find the very man it's supposed to be about, and with any luck the answer will present itself.

The photos of the beach Barbara sent have already been saved to my phone and I have another quick look at them now. It isn't the beach I walked on last night; even though there are cliffs above, the shape just isn't right. So first I need to find out where it is. And hope to God it's fairly close.

*

Despite the fact it's only ten in the morning, the shops along the causeway are enjoying brisk trade and, after a moment's hesitation, I decide that it doesn't really matter where I start. I duck my head under an array of hanging plastic buckets and spades and enter the first shop I come to. It's dark inside, and it isn't just because of the sudden contrast from the bright skies outside. The only window is the one at the front, and if sitting under a wide awning weren't enough to cut off most of the available light, the rest is obscured by more paraphernalia hanging from the ceiling just in front of it. The rest of the room is also crammed to the gills with everything you didn't know you could possibly need for a day at the beach, and a pang of nostalgia fills me.

Right at the back, a young woman stands behind a till, her eagle eyes trained on the room. She looks vaguely annoyed when she sees me approaching empty-handed.

'Hi,' I say brightly. 'I wonder if you can help me?'

Her eyes swivel briefly in my direction, flick back out to the view beyond my shoulder and then come to rest on my phone which I'm holding out towards her.

'I'm trying to find this beach and I wondered if you knew where it was? I can see it's not here but…'

The woman is shaking her head.

'I'm not local,' she says. 'Sorry.'

'Oh…' I widen my smile. 'I thought seeing as you sell everything for the beach, you'd be bound to know.' She barely even glanced at my phone.

'I'm from Leeds,' she adds. 'At uni. I'm just staying with my aunt for the summer 'cause she offered me a job.'

'Oh, right… Not to worry then, thanks. I'll try somewhere else.'

'Nigel might know,' she offers, turning to serve a woman clutching an inflatable ball. What little attention she was giving me disappears entirely.

I step forward slightly.

'Who's Nigel?'

She smiles at her customer. 'Fish and chip shop,' she replies, our business concluded.

I thank her and leave. I'm just about to go and find the place she mentioned when I catch sight of a stand of postcards hanging amid the buckets outside. My eye is drawn to one in particular, the blue of the sky impossibly bright, and underneath it is a perfect semi-circle of pale sand. I fish my phone back out from my handbag and compare the two images. They're shot from different angles, and the one on my phone taken from a greater distance away, but the shape of the bay looks to be identical. I flip the card over but all that's printed there is the name 'Garrards' who I take to be the producer of the garishly coloured image. But if the card is here, then the beach must be close by, surely.

Looking up, I can see the fish and chip place about three shops down but, when I reach it, it's closed. They don't open until half eleven. I check my watch but there's no point in hanging around, someone else must know. The shop next door holds a stand of maps. It's a small second-hand bookshop, I realise, and I go inside, smiling at the instantly recognisable aroma of warm, musty book paper. The shopkeepers here must take lessons in how to cram as much stock as possible into their shops, because there isn't an inch of wasted space in here either. I almost daren't move for fear of tipping over one of the precarious stacks of books that are piled on the floor.

A bearded man calls a cheery hello from where he's perched several steps up a small wooden ladder. 'If you want a look at anything, just go for it. Don't worry about moving things around,' he says. 'That's the beauty of our system, you see. The customers take care of the stock rotation. You wouldn't believe the things that come to the surface sometimes.'

I can't help but smile at his easy manner. 'Actually, I'm looking for some information, sorry.'

He pulls a face but comes back down to ground level. 'Well, you're in luck,' he replies. 'We have a special offer on today. Instead of the usual three-book purchase you only need buy one today to claim your free piece of information.'

His smile doesn't falter and looks so genuine I'm not sure whether he's actually being serious or not, but then he laughs.

'I'm just joking… What is it you need to know?'

I hold out my phone again. 'Someone recommended this beach to me, but I'm not sure where it is. I thought it might be easier to ask someone instead of trying to work it out from a map.'

'Elliot's Cove,' he says, looking back up at me. 'It's certainly beautiful.'

'Oh, so you know where it is then, that's brilliant. Is it easy to get to?'

His face falls. 'Not exactly.' He holds up a hand. 'Just a sec.' He rummages for a moment on a small desk at the rear of the shop before grabbing hold of something and bringing it back to me. He opens out the map he's brought and I hold one side of it for him so that he can better explain.

'So, this is us,' he says, pointing to a dip in the coastline. 'The cliffs run up here… and just along, the next proper bay is Elliot's Cove. That's not its real name of course, but it's what the locals call it.' He gives me a searching look. 'Never mind, it's a long story.'

He directs my attention back to the map and I can see a variety of lines; the main roads are coloured yellow, the tracks white, and some are dotted, which I take to be footpaths. But surrounding Elliot's Cove… nothing.

I look back up and the man can see the query in my eyes. 'I can see you've spotted the problem,' he says. 'There's no proper access. Not a road, not even a footpath. The only way to it is across the sand, then over a jumble of rocks and around the headland. All of which get cut off by the tide at regular intervals.' He looks me up and down. 'Or you can swim or take a boat…'

He raises his eyebrows and I laugh, acknowledging his correct assumption that neither of those options is open to me.

'Sorry,' he says. 'It is beautiful, and quite unspoilt... but now you know why.'

I grimace. 'Ah well. Thanks anyway, you've been very helpful.'

He smiles again. 'Sure I can't tempt you to buy a book?'

I look around me. 'I don't need tempting,' I reply. 'But could I come back another time? I'm not just saying that – I will – it's just that I'm going to be out for much of the day and don't want to carry more stuff than I need.'

He nods, a mischievous light in his eyes. 'I'll see you tomorrow then.'

I hold up a hand in surrender. 'Okay, tomorrow it is.'

I help him fold up the map and he's about to stow it away again when instead he reaches out a hand towards my phone.

'Course, if you're desperate to get to that beach, you could always ask Isaac.'

'Isaac?'

'Yeah, the guy who does the drawings.'

I stare at him. And I'm sure my mouth drops open. 'You mean the ones on the sand?' I ask, careful to check I'm not jumping to conclusions. 'Do you actually know him?'

'Everybody knows Isaac.' He grins. 'He's a local artist,' he explains. 'The sand thing is just a bit of fun, whimsy if you like. But then that's Isaac all over, he's somewhat of a character.'

I could kiss this man. It's exactly what I want to hear. 'I don't suppose you know where I could find him, do you?' I ask, feeling my heart beat faster.

He looks at his watch. 'At this time of day, probably on the beach.' He points at my phone again and smiles. 'Not *that* beach, this beach.' And he gestures outside. 'You'll know him when you see him... flowing white hair and he'll likely as not be carrying a canvas sack.'

I hardly dare ask. 'What's the sack for?'

'Litter,' he replies. 'A regular Womble is Isaac, cleans up after us all. Hates waste.'

'Oh, I *see*…' I'm not sure whether that makes him more or less desirable from my article's point of view, but it will certainly provide some raw material. 'It's good to meet you…?'

'Francis,' he supplies.

'Good to meet you, Francis,' I say. 'You really have been very helpful. And I won't forget, I'll be back tomorrow to buy a book or two, I promise.'

He grins. 'Enjoy the beach.'

The sun seems even brighter back outside, and I pause for a moment trying to adjust to the sudden change in light. I slip my phone back into my handbag and grope for my sunglasses, which always seem to sink to the bottom no matter what I do. But, despite fishing everything out, I still can't lay my hands on them. And then I remember: I took them out for a moment back at the hotel to better wedge my notebook inside my bag – they're still lying on the bed. My eyes are already beginning to water. I swipe a finger underneath them, but I'm not going back for them now, not when I might miss finding Isaac. I'll just have to manage without.

It's not far down to the beach from here. On the other side of the causeway is a small car park, and on the other side of that an area of hardstanding filled with picnic tables and benches. Two cold-water taps have thoughtfully been added to a low retaining wall, perfect for filling dog bowls or swilling off sandy toes. From there it's just a short walk down a flight of steps onto a wide strip of beach which runs in either direction, seemingly for miles. So where to start?

I wonder on any given day how many people on this beach will have flowing white hair and be carrying a sack. My guess is not many, but that still leaves the task ahead of me akin to searching for a needle in a haystack. There's nothing for it but to pick a spot, start walking and hope to get lucky. And while I walk, I can try to think of what to say when I do meet him.

The pitch of the article will depend largely on what sort of a character Isaac is. I have an image in my head of a druid-like figure, which is probably nothing like the reality, but for some reason the flowing white locks have also acquired a flowing robe to go with them. It's green at the moment. He's probably incredibly ordinary, if a little on the hippy side; he is an artist, after all. But to make the article work successfully he'll need to have just enough about him to make it interesting in a stand-out, unique sort of way, but not so much quirkiness that he turns into a ridiculous caricature.

With all these thoughts running through my head, it takes me a few minutes to realise that I haven't actually been looking at the people I've passed by at all. I started walking the opposite way to that of yesterday evening – I'm thinking that someone picking up litter would probably head for wide open spaces, the stretches of beach which are quieter. You probably wouldn't want to walk in among everyone and be subject to their comments and, besides, how could you tell what was rubbish and what had just been put to one side to take home at the end of the day?

I pause for a moment and scan the scene in front of me, but I can see no one matching the description of Isaac I've been given. And yet something keeps me walking. The beach isn't just a flat space, I realise, it's filled with things; some that should be here – pebbles and seaweed, bits of wood – and some that shouldn't – tangles of string, ripped plastic bags, a crisp packet. Even the bits of wood that are weathered and eroded might look part of the beach, but they're not, they're just as alien to this environment as I am.

Ten or so minutes later, I become aware that a rocky outcropping has appeared in my field of vision and, thinking about the map Francis showed me in the bookshop, I realise this must be the way to Elliot's Cove. And for now, it is indeed cut off by the tide. I squint into the distance but there's no one else on that section of beach apart from a few lone walkers, and none of them look to be my white-haired wizard.

I'm wasting time so I turn on my heels and begin to trek back the other way until I'm among the crowds once more. This time I do stand and stare, a hand shielding my eyes from the sun as I systematically scour the figures ahead. But my patience for the task is beginning to desert me and my calf muscles are aching from trudging on the soft sand. I make my way back up onto the causeway, where I have one last look around before retracing my earlier steps into the town. If Isaac is on the beach, I certainly can't see him.

I stand for a moment, indecisive, but then remember that, apart from the fact that Isaac likes to pick up litter, Francis also told me that he's a local artist. What he creates apart from drawings in the sand I have no idea, but if he sells any of his work locally there are a few other places that might know of him.

A few minutes later I'm peering into the window of one of the elegant buildings I'd been in yesterday. This particular shop sells all manner of artwork – paintings, sculpture, glassware – and, judging by the subject matter, I'd say most of it is local. I push open the door and begin a slow circuit of the room, but I can't see anything bearing Isaac's name. Some of the paintings are signed, but a good proportion of the other items don't have anything to identify them. I'm still hunting for clues when an assistant approaches me.

'Are you looking for anything in particular?' she asks.

I smile gratefully. 'I am actually,' I reply. 'Although, I confess I'm not exactly sure what. I saw some designs recently, drawn by someone who I believe is a local artist and they were really rather intriguing. I just wondered whether he sold his work commercially.'

'Do you have a name? Or perhaps if you describe the designs…'

'It's Isaac, but I'm afraid I don't know his last name.'

She holds up a hand. 'Ah, then I think I know who you must mean. I don't have much of his work in at the moment, but here, let me show you.'

She selects a piece from a display cabinet a little distance away, one I admit I'd rather skimmed over, and brings it back to me. 'What do you think?' she asks.

I gaze curiously at the object that she's given me – a sculpture, but with no uniform shape or discernible up or down either. The colours are all of the same palette though, muted powder blues, soft sage greens, a splash of stronger pigment. At the centre is a piece of driftwood, gnarled, but at the same time worn smooth by the tide and pieces of sea glass tumble over it. Some are big, some much smaller. One is a smooth pale oval of green with white flecks that glint from within. It's beautiful, and incredibly tactile. I hold out my hand to take it, feeling its weight, running my finger across the surface of the wood. I turn the price tag, flinching as I see the cost, and hand it back rather quickly in case I drop it.

'Quite extraordinary, isn't it?' says the assistant, and I nod politely.

'Do you sell many of them?' I ask.

'Oh yes…' She pauses. 'I'd sell more but Isaac isn't always that prolific,' she explains. 'To start with I'd get three or four a month, but then it became two or three, then nothing for a couple of months. He's only just started bringing them in again. But I think that's just the way he is. I'd rather have them in small quantities than not at all.'

I'm nodding, trying to process what she's saying. 'So, you haven't been selling them for all that long then?'

'No, only since last… November, I think it was. He's new to the area.' She narrows her eyes slightly. 'Sorry, I didn't catch the reason you were looking for him,' she says, clearly having deduced, quite rightly, that I'm not interested in buying one of his pieces. It's quite possible she thinks I'm a rival gallery, looking to poach him.

'I should have explained,' I say quickly. 'I'm actually down on holiday at the moment, staying with my daughter and son-in-law, but I'm a features writer for a women's magazine. You know how it is, never off duty and always with ideas running through my head. I saw a photo of an incredible design that he drew on the beach, and when I mentioned it to my daughter she thought he might be a local artist.'

It's obviously not the whole truth, but even though it's not too far from it, it doesn't matter, I can sense a wariness about her. She isn't going to tell me anything useful now.

'I get the feeling that Isaac's a very private person,' she adds, and my suspicions are confirmed.

I'd like to point out that whether Isaac is interested in being the focus of an article is his decision, not hers, but I don't. Instead, I give her a broad smile. 'I was just curious, that's all,' I say. 'I've covered a lot of stories about artists, but I've never come across anything quite like this; I just wanted to show my appreciation. But thank you for your time anyway. Maybe I'll bump into him around the town, he might even live here.'

But the woman's not going to fall for that one either and gives me a tight smile. It's time to go, but no matter, there'll be someone else I can ask. Isaac's sculpture is already being returned to the shelf where it had been displayed and I head for the door. A younger assistant is there, polishing some glassware from the window display, and she leans in as I pass, directing a furtive glance back towards her employer as she does so.

'Try the allotments,' she whispers. 'Isaac's often there.'

There's no opportunity to say any more, but I beam a smile at her, nodding my thanks before slipping through the door.

I feel a bit like a ping-pong ball being batted from one place to another, but I'm getting closer, surely? I rummage for my water bottle in my bag, feeling hot, and thirsty too. In fact, I can feel the first stirrings of a headache above one eye. It's probably from squinting against the sun, but I know from experience that there's only one way it's going to go, and that's downhill. The water helps and I rub my hand around the back of my neck, trying to ease the muscles there before pulling out a little street map Leah had given me from my bag.

The allotments aren't specifically marked, but there's an area off to one side of the road leading up onto the cliffs that is coloured green, with lines bisecting it. For now, it's my best bet and I can always ask someone on the way there.

In the end I don't need to. At the bottom of the cliff road is a helpful sign pointing upwards and as I begin walking up the steep hill I can feel months of inactivity catching up with me. I wonder who on earth had the crazy idea of locating the allotments in such an inconvenient place.

Yet, once I get there, I see exactly why. The view is spectacular in whichever direction you look. From the beach on one side and the sparkling silver-blue of the sea, to the majestic sweep of the cliffs on the other. I imagine that when you stand up, trying to ease an aching back from a hard digging session, this must more than make up for the pain.

I pause inside the gate. It's taken me only ten minutes to walk here, but my shirt is stuck to my back and my headache has morphed into the kind that sits over one eye and thuds with each and every movement. I really hope my journey hasn't been wasted.

Despite the heat of the day, it's quite busy too, and my arrival has not gone unnoticed. People who were bent to their tasks look up, smiling as I pass, and several bid me good morning before returning to their job in hand. An elderly man sits reading a newspaper and he lowers it, watching me quite unashamedly as I pick a path and carry on walking, feeling very self-conscious.

The allotments are shaped like a fat upside-down 'L' and as I turn to make my way around the final corner a black cat, fur warmed by the sun, approaches and winds its way sinuously around my legs. A loud purring vibrates in its throat before I've even bent to stroke it.

'Samson, you are such a flirt.'

The amused voice comes from slightly behind me and I turn to see a man coming out of a brightly painted shed, carrying a gardening fork.

His white hair isn't flowing, it's smooth and sleek and tied back in a band. His soft smock-style shirt sits over stone-coloured linen trousers and his feet are clad in sandals. A leather bag is slung across one shoulder.

But there's no mistaking who this is. I've finally found Isaac.

# CHAPTER FIVE

'Hello,' he says, his mouth curved upward into a smile, the sun glinting off the bright blue of his eyes. 'Just push him away if you're not fond of cats. Samson persists in the belief that he's utterly adorable and that no one can resist his charms.'

I stare at him. And then I realise that I should say something, that I'm standing here with my mouth open. But my throat feels glued shut and the effort required to force words past it superhuman.

And all the while Isaac stands there, smiling. Because he has no idea what I'm thinking. How can he? He can have no idea that the shirt he's wearing is the same as William's. The one I bought on our last holiday together; the soft salmon-pink linen that he thought would look ridiculous, but didn't. He'd looked gorgeous. It's how I still picture him when I'm alone with my dreams at night, leaning casually against the bench where he was sitting, one arm stretched out across the back, grinning up at the camera. It's what I'd thought of as I'd lifted his shirt to my nose only the other day.

I bend down, trying to hide my reaction, and run a hand along the cat's warm back. He's beautiful and I scoop him into my arms, pulling him close. He rolls his head up under my chin, pushing against me, his whole body vibrating as it purrs.

'Have you come to see Miriam's patch?' Isaac asks, indicating an overgrown rectangle on the opposite side of the path from his. 'Although it's not Miriam's now, of course, but she was the last person to have it.'

I shake my head. 'No, I… I was looking for someone,' I manage. 'I was told they might be here.'

'Oh…? I know most folks on the allotment, I think. Who were you after?'

But I can't answer.

I crouch down and place the cat gently back on the path, where he walks away as if suddenly bored of all the attention.

'It doesn't matter, don't worry.'

His brows knit together. 'Okay,' he says simply. 'If you're sure.' He pauses for a moment. 'I was just about to dig up some potatoes, would you like some?'

I stare at him.

'They're only tiny,' he says, mistaking my silence for reticence. 'Salad potatoes, but a gorgeous flavour. A little butter on them, maybe cooked with a sprig of mint… I can give you some of that too, if you like.'

'No!' It comes out more forcefully than I'd intended. I soften my voice. 'No, thank you. That's very kind, but I…' Besides, who gives potatoes to a complete stranger?

He smiles again. 'No problem.' And I can see it isn't. He doesn't seem to mind whether I have his potatoes or not.

I begin to back away and then, aware that he's still watching me, I turn to walk hurriedly towards the road. My face feels scarlet, my pulse beating painfully just below my temple. And it takes quite a few moments to lose the sensation that I'm about to be sick.

*

I don't remember the walk back into town or picking my way through the tourists to get to the hotel. And I don't even care that I'm hungry and thirsty, or that my room still feels almost unbearably hot. I dump my bag on the floor beside the bed and lie down upon it, turning to face the wall, where I pray for the oblivion of sleep.

The pain has gone when I awake – the physical pain of my headache, that is. The emotional pain still sits like a hard lump in my chest, one I cannot swallow. It's assumed the position it had before, in the first few days after William's death, and I'd only just felt that I'd got rid of it too. I swing my legs around and sit on the edge of the bed, wondering what to do with myself now.

A door slams beneath me and it's a sudden reminder that I'm not alone. That I don't have to be alone. I rise from the bed and stand in front of the mirror, looking at my dishevelled hair and creased face. I roll my shoulders and let them drop, opening my mouth as wide as it will go and closing it again, trying to inject some life into my features. My eyes stare back at me and I cast them downward, wary of the sorrow I can still see in them.

Leah's in the dining room when I find her and, although I'm longing to talk to her, I can see she's bristling with anger. She's standing bolt upright, staring out the window, with her arms wrapped around herself, clutching her elbows. There's no sign of Robin and I immediately think of the slamming door I heard and wonder if that was him on the way out.

'Hello, love,' I say. 'How's it going?'

I can see her shoulders drop straight away. She turns around. 'It's not going anywhere just now, and if Robin has his way it won't ever.'

I know from past experience that it's better not to give my opinion – the mood she's in, she'll get cross with me even if I agree with her. Besides, my silence will hopefully give Leah the opportunity she needs to have a vent.

'Look at this room,' she says, holding up her hands in an expansive gesture. 'And what do you see?'

I take a moment. She doesn't mean literally what do I see, because at the moment it's far from its best. For a start, years of inch-thick flock wallpaper are in the process of being removed and the floor is littered with debris. What Leah's asking instead is for me to cast my mind into the future, to see the room transformed and what my impressions of it will be then.

'Beautiful light,' I reply, truthfully. It's the thing that struck me most about this room when I first saw it. There are three huge bay windows overlooking the garden and I can well imagine the style that Leah has in mind for it.

'Exactly!' She crosses to a pasting table that stands in the middle of the room and picks up a sheet of paper. 'Look,' she adds, handing it to me.

On the front is a watercolour scene which, if I'm not much mistaken, is of the town itself.

'Turn it over,' Leah instructs.

I do as she asks and see that the rear carries information for a local painting group – not a professional group, just like-minded people who paint for a hobby. It's interesting but I'm not sure what point Leah's trying to make.

'I picked that up from the local library this morning. Not that there's anything special about it, it's just one of about thirty very similar. And everywhere you look you see the same thing. The whole bloody town wants to paint or draw or weave or make jewellery.'

'Okay…' I say slowly. 'But I'm not sure what that has to do with you. Unless you're thinking of joining one.'

She rolls her eyes. 'Chance would be a fine thing. But no, that's not the point here. All these clubs, societies, gatherings, whatever you want to call them, they all have to meet somewhere. And just look at the light in here, Mum, the view… Wouldn't it be the most amazing space to paint in?'

'Well, yes, I suppose it would…' I break off at the thunderous look on her face. 'No, it definitely would but, maybe I've missed something here, only isn't this still going to be your dining room?'

'Jesus, doesn't anybody in this family have any vision?' She sighs, and I know I'm in for an explanation of her insight, one so obvious she can't figure out why no one else can see it.

'I want this hotel to be one of the very best, if not *the* best hotel in Eastleigh, but even that won't be enough. Look around, Mum, hotels here are ten a penny and to survive we've not only got to be good, we've got to have something that no one else has. In fact, the Lobster Pot is a prime example of exactly what I'm talking about. It was a family-run hotel for decades, but each and every year saw a decline in business, with the result that each and every year there was less money to reinvest and so the place became shabbier and shabbier, the customers fewer and fewer, and so on. It was a vicious circle and, in the end, it couldn't even be sold as a going concern. It was priced at next to nothing because the whole place needs gutting before anyone can start again.'

I'm beginning to wonder why she and Robin took it on in the first place if she's as pessimistic as she sounds about their chances of succeeding.

'Most of the business we do will be concentrated around the summer months,' she continues, 'and just about the only other thing that goes on here during the winter months are the infamous turkey and tinsel breaks. The whole thing makes me want to heave, it's all so staid and unoriginal.'

She pauses a moment to check I'm still following her, and I nod quickly.

'If you look at any of the minutes from residents' meetings here, you'll see that the one thing they constantly moan about is the lack of facilities for local people. So, I want us to straddle both areas of the market, catering for visitors to the town, but also providing a warm and welcoming space for the folks who actually live here all year round. There are so many possibilities… We could have artists in residence, workshops, retreats, day-long courses, or even just an open space for people to come and do whatever they want. We just need to be a bit more creative with how we use this room, that's all.'

Looking at my daughter's face, it's easy to see why Robin might not have been quite so enthusiastic about the plans as Leah; she's getting more and more carried away by the minute. But her habit of throwing herself into something up to her neck is often a symptom of trying to avoid whatever else might be going on in her life, and I can't help wondering if this knowledge is what has made Robin so reticent.

'So, what do you think?' asks Leah, putting me on the spot.

'That it could be absolutely wonderful,' I reply. 'Incredibly inspiring… but rather a lot of work too, I would imagine.'

'Yes, but we already have a lot of work ahead of us, Mum. Isn't it better to try to do it now, when we're still at the whole concept stage, than plan out all our fixtures and fittings, soft furnishings and the like, and then have to change it all in the future to accommodate new plans? It would work out to be twice as expensive.'

'I see. Well, I can understand your point of view but… is this where you and Robin have disagreed?'

At the mention of his name she scowls again. 'He thinks I'm trying to run before I can walk,' she says. 'And that we should do things gradually; get one thing under our belt before we start to expand into new areas.'

I nod. 'There's merit in that opinion too,' I reply. 'There's nothing wrong with wanting to be a bit cautious, particularly where finances are concerned. I would imagine incorporating new ideas into the plans at this stage will mean exceeding the budget you originally set yourselves. Maybe Robin just feels that's a little bit too risky.'

'He's so… complacent at times. So happy to leave things as they are. Urgghh, he makes me want to scream.'

I smile. And he provides a balance which is exactly what you need sometimes, I think, but don't say. 'You know, when you're in full flow, Leah, you can be a little bit scary at times, and—'

'I am not!'

I hold up a hand. 'Just let me finish. And while you have the most amazing energy, imagination and drive, not everyone has those qualities to the same degree. It takes them out of their comfort zone, that's all. And people don't like it when they feel out of control.'

She narrows her eyes, but I can see she's thinking about my words. Maybe even recognising a little of the truth about her own behaviour.

'You'll probably find that Robin comes around to your way of thinking, simply because he knows full well that it's a really good idea. But maybe what he's not so good at is going full flow with an idea when it's just been sprung on him and he's been asked to commit to it straight away. Perhaps he just needs a little more time to get used to the idea first.'

Finally, I can see her expression begin to soften. 'I just want this to succeed, Mum. We have to get it right. There will be no second chances if we don't.'

I smile wistfully at her. 'You're so like your father at times, you know. So full of ambition, and so impatient to achieve all that you desire. But you'll get there, sweetheart. Just don't forget that not everyone works at the same speed as you do. And you'll never get there at all if you burn yourselves out. There's time enough to make things happen, don't worry.'

But instead of taking heart from my words, she frowns again, an anxious look crossing her face. 'That's just it, Mum, there isn't time. I have—' She breaks off. 'It doesn't matter. Anyway, how about you? Have you had a good day?' Now that she's paying attention, I see her eyes narrow as she looks at me. 'Is everything all right?'

'Just a bad headache, love. But it's okay, it's going now.' I look down again at the leaflet that's still in my hand before passing it back to Leah, feeling her scrutiny. She's spotted the drawn skin and tired eyes.

'Actually, I met an artist today,' I say. 'It's something Barbara wanted me to follow up. She'd come across some work of his, quite unique and…' I stop mid-sentence. I'm rambling now and I need to get to the point. 'Anyway, I've spent a good part of the day looking for him, and when I found him…' I stop again, aware there's every chance I could start crying again. 'It took me by surprise, you see, but he was wearing a shirt… identical to the one I'd bought your dad on holiday, the linen one, remember? The one I kept after he died. I think it was just the shock of seeing him there, out of the blue and—'

'Oh, Mum…' She opens her arms to me.

'I probably made a complete fool of myself.'

'I'm sure you didn't,' she murmurs. 'Besides, what would it matter, even if you had.'

I pull away from her. 'But that's just it, it does matter. Barbara wants me to write an article about him and… he actually isn't anything like your father… but I don't think I can, not now. Not when every time I see him it's going to make me think…' I stare up at her face. 'I'm being stupid, I know but…'

'Mum,' says Leah firmly. 'It's not stupid. You've had a huge upheaval over the past couple of weeks and you haven't even settled in here yet, not properly anyway. Everything is bound to feel strange and a bit up in the air.'

'But I should be over it by now. Crying like a lovesick teenager, it's ridiculous.'

She doesn't reply, but pulls me into a hug again. And I can feel the tension in her arms, across her back.

'Are you okay, love?' I ask, remembering the direction in which my thoughts had previously been heading. I hadn't wanted to upset her.

'I'm absolutely fine,' she replies. 'Why wouldn't I be?'

This time it's my turn to scrutinise her face, but she just flashes me a bright smile. 'Come on, let's go and get a drink. There's a tin of big fat brownies too. They're going to help no end.'

*

My head is still reeling as I open the door to my room. The tea and a huge dose of chocolate have certainly helped, but I'm now convinced that my worries about Leah are justified. She tried to disguise it well enough, and her concern for me gave her plenty of hiding places, but she's my daughter and I know her too well.

And the worst thing is, I think it's my fault. That my outpouring of grief smothered any opportunity she had to do the same, filling all the spaces where she could have let hers loose. And now maybe it's too late. When I think back to when William actually died, she went to pieces the day we found out, but after that a quiet solemnity grew. Grew and never went away. I don't think I saw her cry more than once, just a stoic silence… even through the inquest. As if her grief had become stuck fast, and now I'm not sure she's ever going to be able to let it out.

My laptop chimes softly in the corner of the room, announcing the arrival of a new email, and it's a welcome distraction. I wake the screen and see that it's from Barbara, straight to the point as usual.

*I've been thinking… I'm sure you have loads of ideas yourself, but it struck me that you might not have much understanding of the current trends in this area of the market, so here are a few ideas that have been in circulation recently and might help you to get started. Any one of these will reflect the current zeitgeist perfectly. Let me know what you think? Any news on our mystery sandman?*

I stand back from the screen, suddenly aware of a new sensation. Fear. Because knowing Barbara the way I do, she isn't going to let this go, and her casual enquiry isn't casual at all, that's not how Barbara operates. She isn't going to be satisfied until I have delivered an article to her, whether I want to or not. And I suddenly realise that this is a test. Whatever leeway Barbara has given me before has just expired and I have only one choice left to me now. Except it isn't a choice.

I must write about the man in the salmon-pink shirt.

# CHAPTER SIX

'Good morning,' says Francis. 'I'll be honest, I wasn't sure if I was going to see you again, but here you are.' He grins at me.

'Here I am,' I reply. 'As promised.'

I hadn't really intended to come to the bookshop this morning, and certainly not this early, but a sleepless night disturbed by tumultuous thoughts of what today might bring propelled me from my bed not long after dawn.

Not surprisingly, given that it's only a few minutes after opening time, there's no one else in here but me. A situation I'm not entirely comfortable with, but, it has to be said, of my own making. I look around, wondering whether the placement of books is just as chaotic as Francis described, or whether there is a system for locating things. As if sensing my thoughts, he lifts his head from the desk.

'So, loosely, fiction on this side, non-fiction on the other.' He begins to point like an air hostess aboard a plane giving emergency-exit directions. 'And supposedly, crime and thrillers, general fiction, romance and a teeny-tiny bit of sci fi and fantasy. Then cookery, gardening, history, sports and biographies.' He gives an apologetic smile. 'At least that's how it was when I first opened about three years ago. Now the subject placement is a little… looser.'

I return his smile. 'That will do for me,' I say, moving over to the area where crime titles should live. Happily, Francis says nothing further, knowing full well when to leave a customer to browse, and returns to his paperwork.

I don't really have any expectation of what I might find, or would like to find, but after ten minutes or so I've already picked up a couple of titles by authors whose books I've previously read and enjoyed. There are several more I could choose, but as my list of people with who I can at least pass the time of day, inclusive of Francis, currently stands at one, I'd rather come back more often than take too many now. There is of course another reason why the odd chat with Francis might prove useful. And as luck would have it, as I'm paying for my books, he raises the subject himself.

'So, how did you get on yesterday? Did you find Isaac in the end?'

His name whispers through my head as I hand Francis a ten-pound note. 'I did actually, although when you said flowing white hair… I think I was looking for Gandalf for half of the morning.'

Francis grins. 'You know, that's not a bad description.' He fishes in a box on the desk for some change. 'So, what did you think to Elliot's Cove then?'

'Oh, I didn't actually get there, I…' I pause, frantically trying to come up with a reason why I didn't go. At a noise from behind me, Francis's smile grows even wider.

'Talk of the devil… Good morning, Isaac.'

A wave of heat travels over me.

'We were just talking about you,' he continues, looking at me as he pauses. 'I'm sorry, I don't know your name.'

I'm not sure I want to give it just yet, but I can hardly refuse.

'It's Louisa,' I supply.

'Louisa was in here yesterday asking for information on Elliot's Cove and I pointed her in your direction. She had a photo of one of your drawings. I thought you might be able to show her how to get there safely.'

And then Isaac comes forward, away from the bright light of the doorway to better see me. 'Hello again…' His eyes meet mine. Curious. 'So, it *was* me you were looking for yesterday,' he says. 'I did wonder. No offence, but you didn't look like the type who'd be interested in taking Miriam's plot. But why ever didn't you say?'

A surge of embarrassment rises in me at his comment, embarrassment tinged with panic. 'I think I was... I don't know really... I wondered if you'd think I was being rude.'

'Why would I think that? Particularly as you'd just walked all the way up the hill to find me.'

I look at Francis, stricken, although why he would be of any help I don't know.

All too predictably he smiles. 'That worked out well, didn't it?'

My heart is beginning to thump in my chest. I'm not ready for this. It's too soon to go anywhere with Isaac, but I'm very afraid that's exactly what is going to happen.

Isaac is studying me. 'What did you want to go there for anyway? Elliot's Cove isn't really somewhere you should think of going. It's not safe.'

'I'd just heard it was nice, that's all. And the drawing intrigued me.'

'Did it now?' he replies. He tilts his head to one side, flicking his eyes to Francis who suddenly looks distinctly uncomfortable. The silence grows and, just when I don't think I can bear it any longer, Isaac draws in a breath. 'You know, I wasn't planning a day on the beach, but why not? The conditions are perfect today.'

'There you go then,' says Francis, recovering himself. 'See how perfectly that's worked out. And I'll even hang onto your books for you while you're gone so you don't have to carry them. Just call in on your way back and pick them up.'

I manage a tight smile and hand them over. I feel like a fish out of water, drowning in air.

Isaac finally focuses his attention away from me. 'I'll just collect my own book and then we can be on our way,' he says, turning to Francis. 'Thanks for finding that for me.'

Francis returns to his desk and picks up a rather battered paperback. 'Like I said, it's not in the best condition but...'

'As long as it's readable,' replies Isaac. He holds out his hand for the book, smoothing a thumb across the front cover before fishing in his trouser pocket. He pulls out a five-pound note. 'I shall enjoy this,' he says. 'It's been a long time. And keep the change, Francis, I appreciate it.'

Francis looks as if he's about to argue, but then changes his mind. 'I should give it to you for free, but…'

Isaac's smile is suddenly warm. 'But nothing. You've got a living to earn, just like the rest of us.'

He lifts the flap of a leather satchel that's slung across his body and pops the book inside. The rich-coloured hide of his bag is soft as butter through use and I have just a second to see the title before it disappears; it's a copy of *Moby Dick*.

I follow Isaac down the steps from the causeway and out onto the sand in silence. I'm glad of it, my mind is in turmoil. I'm here under false pretences and now I have no idea how to extricate myself. Turning the clock back would help.

We turn left, retracing my steps from the day before.

'So, Louisa, are you new to Eastleigh, or just visiting?' His smile is warm, his face angled to the sun, and all I can see is the blue of his eyes, lit from within.

'Just visiting,' I reply. 'Staying with relatives.'

He nods. 'So, you're kind of local then.'

'Not really. None of us are from around here originally.'

'Us?' he queries.

'I'm staying with my daughter and her husband. But he's not local either.'

'Fair enough,' replies Isaac evenly. 'So, you're here on holiday then. How long are you staying for?'

This is all wrong. I need to start this conversation again; properly. Tell Isaac who I am and why I want to talk to him. But I missed my opportunity my first time and now this conversation seems to be running away with me as well. I aim for vague.

'I'm not sure yet. A couple of weeks maybe, we'll see how it goes.'

Perhaps I should just stop him. Explain there's been a misunderstanding, and start from the beginning. But even as I think it, I hear the voice of the assistant from the gallery in my head. *I get the feeling that Isaac's a very private person...* There's every possibility this could go disastrously wrong, and I can't take that risk. Perhaps a softer approach might be better after all.

'How about you though?' I ask. 'You're local, I take it?'

'I live locally, but I'm not local, no.'

I look across at him, but he's focused on some point in the distance.

'Oh, I get it, one of those unless-you've-lived-here-for-four-generations-you're-not-local things, is it? So where is home then?'

'Here, for the moment,' he replies with a soft smile. 'I'm not big on roots, really, I've lived in too many places.'

It would appear that Isaac is just as reticent as I am when it comes to answering questions about himself.

'Francis mentioned that you're an artist,' I say.

'I like to be creative, certainly. Whether that makes me an artist I'm not sure. I turn my hand to various things.' He stops so suddenly that I end up several paces ahead of him. He stoops to pick up something from the sand and opens his palm, holding it out to me.

'Look at that,' he says. 'Have you ever seen anything more perfect?'

It's a whelk shell, pearly white and soft brown in colour, but just like hundreds of other shells.

'Are you familiar with the golden ratio?' he asks. 'The most beautiful building block there is, and these little shells have perfected the art of it effortlessly.'

'I've heard of it,' I reply. 'Wasn't there something about the *Mona Lisa* that's connected with it?'

He nods. 'It has perfect proportions. So do a lot of things in nature.' He opens his satchel and takes out a small fabric drawstring bag and pops the shell inside. 'I meant to say… if you spot any shells, whole ones, would you mind picking them up?' He turns to look at me. 'So, what do you do when you're not on holiday?'

'I'm a writer,' I say without thinking.

'Oh? What kind?' He smiles. 'Obviously I don't literally mean what kind… I'll rephrase the question. What do you write?'

My reply stutters in my head. 'Non-fiction mostly,' I say without elaborating.

'Books? Articles? Copywriter?'

'Oh yes, books,' I reply, grasping at the opportunity he gives me. Has he noticed the sudden bloom of heat on my cheeks? I can't tell him I write articles because from there it's only a short leap to my being a journalist. But I know nothing about writing books and Isaac strikes me as the sort of person who would instantly deduce this for himself. 'I'm a ghostwriter actually. Biographies mostly.' I bend down to pick up another shell. 'So, what do you want these for?' I ask, changing the subject.

'It's a project I'm working on,' he replies. 'Rather a long-term project and some days I wish I'd never started but, if I ever do get to finish, it will be the most amazing thing you ever saw.'

Despite myself, I smile. Partly at Isaac's words, but partly at the realisation that he's not going to give away anything about himself either. Evasiveness has always triggered my determination to find out more in the past, and I can feel my natural investigative instinct beginning to stir.

'That's a very big assumption to make.' I say it lightly, I don't want to antagonise him too much. That won't get me very far at all.

'Maybe it is,' he says, turning to look at me, his eyes catching the full glare of the light off the sea. He's clearly amused. 'Although, I can sense you're doubting me. So, go on then, tell me, what's the most amazing thing you've ever seen?'

My response is immediate. 'My daughter,' I say. And instantly regret it. I should have thought of something else, something much less personal. William and I travelled to some far-flung and exotic places, I've seen quite a few things which would have been far more appropriate.

Isaac's step falters a moment.

'When she was born,' I add. 'Red-faced and furious, but still the most incredible thing I've ever seen; her fingernails, tiny toes, every single one of her eyelashes…'

At first, I think Isaac hasn't heard me but then he halts completely and I see him swallow. His face looks oddly hollow.

'Okay, maybe my project isn't the most amazing thing you'll ever see.' He indicates the beach ahead of us. 'It's not too much further now.'

We walk in virtual silence the rest of the way, pausing occasionally for one of us to pick up a shell, but it's not a particularly pleasant silence. After ten minutes it's beginning to feel awkward, and after fifteen I'm desperately trying to think of something to say. But we're coming up to the end of the bay now, cliffs rising vertically above us, and just in front of them are a series of large boards, fixed on posts and sunk into the sand. We're too far away to see yet what's written on them.

'What are those?' I ask.

Isaac frowns. 'In some cases, the difference between life and death.' His words sound harsh, not solely for what they are, but the way he says them. 'For some very foolish people,' he continues. 'Who don't realise that the sea isn't something you can cheat or tame. The sea will have its way no matter what.' He pauses, eyes fixed on mine. 'I will show you the safe way to get to Elliot's Cove, but if you ever come here again you have to promise me that you'll follow my instructions. If something looks off, do not ever think to yourself it will be okay. Chances are it may be one of the last things you *do* think.'

He sounds so overly serious I'm tempted to make a joke, but something in his eyes tells me not to. When we finally reach the barrage of signs, I see why.

My first impression is of the colour red. Bold block lettering covers the boards as does the letter 'X' in several places. Isaac walks straight past them.

'Hang on a minute, I need to read these.'

'No, you don't,' he says, coming back to me. 'I will tell you what you need to know.'

He walks away again and I stare at his back, irritated by his arrogance. But after a moment I follow him until we're standing at the first outcropping of rocks.

To my surprise, he gives me a bright smile. 'The first thing you need to understand is the geography of the place… And the fact that Elliot's Cove sits much further back than this beach does.' He picks up a pebble from the sand and drops to his haunches. 'So, this is us,' he adds, drawing a gently curving line in a wide arc. The right-hand side of the line is considerably higher than the left-hand side, so that the whole thing sits at a tilt. 'When you're on this beach it's hard to see that it's angled in this way, and that these rocks here are a promontory, quite a large headland actually.' He draws in the rocks stretching out far beyond the original arc he drew. 'And on the other side of these rocks, Elliot's Cove angles quite sharply backward but you can't get any sense of that from here. It's only from up on the cliffs that you can see.'

He pauses to check I'm following.

'And what this means is that the tide hits the beach we're currently standing on much earlier than it does on Elliot's Cove. So, when you're there it's very easy to be fooled into thinking that the tide still has a way to go before it comes in, when in actual fact these rocks here will already be underwater, cutting you off. It also creates a very strong rip tide. Even the strongest swimmer can find themselves dragged under off the tip of these rocks and then thrown back against them.'

'Okay,' I say, swallowing, as a very vivid image fills my head of just what a person would look like if that happened. 'Well, I'm not a strong swimmer, so…'

'Good, then you won't be stupid enough to try it.' He smiles again. 'The other thing to be wary of is that in certain weather conditions, even if the tide is out, you can still get freak waves; big enough to knock you off the rocks. The easy way to tell is if the beach on this side is crazy-full of surfers. If it is then there are some huge waves out at sea and Elliot's Cove is out of bounds.'

'Okay, got that.'

'And that's it. Bear all that in mind and you're perfectly safe. There's a list of up-to-date tide tables printed on the boards back there. Memorise them or, better still, check them any time you come here. If there's any margin for error, don't risk it.'

I look back towards the boards. 'So, are we okay then?'

He nods. 'Tide's on its way out at the moment. It's perfect timing. And don't worry, I won't let you stay any longer than is safe.' He crosses to the foot of the rocks. 'This line of red paint marks the easiest place to cross, where the rocks are the flattest. Still want to go?'

'What, now you've put the fear of God into me…?' But I nod.

'Okay then, follow me.'

I eye the sea warily, but it's barely washing the rocks some distance away and, climbing up onto the first boulder, I begin to follow Isaac. The rocks aren't huge, and our path isn't particularly steep, but I'm not used to clambering over such things and I can feel the burn in my thigh muscles as I take each step upwards. However, it doesn't take long before I can see that we're almost there and, as I pull myself up onto the final slab of rock, I get my first proper glimpse of Elliot's Cove. And my body comes to a sudden halt, hand flying to my mouth in awe.

'Oh my goodness…'

# CHAPTER SEVEN

I like words. When I write, each one is a tool at my disposal and I particularly hate it when their meaning becomes diluted. And never more so than in the case of the word that fills my head right now. Because Elliot's Cove is awesome. Not in the throwaway, trite, millennial way it's come to mean, but in the actual sense of the word: capable of filling with awe. The photographs I've seen of it don't do it justice, neither does description, but looking out across the sweep of the sea and the sand before me, it's as if I've seen the world created anew.

Beside me, Isaac stands quietly. He doesn't feel the need to say anything, and I'm glad. I want to drink in the silence as much as anything. Of course, it isn't silent. There is the relentless crashing of the sea, both around me on the rocks and further in the distance onto the wide arc of sand. And there is birdsong, the gulls and others too, I realise, but there is still silence. No, not silence, a stillness that is as palpable as the wind on my skin.

After a moment Isaac carries on, and I follow him, stepping down off the rocks and onto the broad expanse of sand to walk side by side.

'So why don't people come here then?' I ask. 'I'm glad they don't, but it's extraordinarily beautiful. I would have thought more people would.'

'Some do, plenty do in fact, but word has got around that it's not a good idea to be here, and that sticks. It's mostly families that come to this part of the country and they just want to be somewhere safe with their children, not take risks. After all, there are plenty of other places to go. And I think the council have taken the view that keeping people away from this beach is considerably cheaper than trying to rescue people from it.'

I look at the beach in front of me, at the depth, the line of dunes that slopes a little distance before the bank steeply rises to meet the cliff.

'So, I understand that the cove gets cut off from the other one when the tide is in, but it surely doesn't come in far enough to be a danger to anyone on the beach?'

'No, it doesn't…' He sighs. 'But people are impatient. And as soon as they see their passage out has gone, they panic and that's when they start to take risks. If they simply waited until the tide went out again then there'd no problem, but if night is coming or the weather is bad…'

'They'd have to spend the night on the beach.'

Isaac doesn't reply but instead gives an almost imperceptible nod. He's thinking about something, but whatever it is he isn't going to say.

'So, who's Elliot?' I ask. 'Only, when I mentioned this place to Francis, he told me that it's only the locals who call it by that name. A long story, he said.'

There's a much firmer nod. 'Who *was* Elliot,' he replies. 'Past tense. Elliot was… hard to describe what exactly, but a hermit, loner, homeless man, guardian, saviour… any of those labels are accurate. He died about ten years ago, with no discernible family and with very little known about him. That is to say that most folks knew *of* him, many spoke with him on a regular basis, but no one had ever troubled to find out who he was.'

'And do you know?'

He shakes his head. 'No, I wasn't living here then, so I only know the stories. But essentially, Elliot was in his seventies when he died – probably, no one knows for sure – but he made this beach his home, and he cared for it as if it was his own back garden. He lived alone, although he shopped at the local market by all accounts so certainly wasn't without money. And always well enough dressed too, despite having seemingly few possessions.'

'You said he was a saviour?'

'There are a few people hereabouts who potentially owe their lives to him. Who got caught on the rocks and were given safe passage. Or, in one case, taken into his camp to pass the night, given food and kept warm until the tide turned and they could return home next morning.'

I bend down to pick up another shell. 'So, what happened to him? It obviously didn't have a happy ending.'

Isaac shrugs. 'An early morning walker found his body washed up on the beach just around the bay. He'd drowned and his body showed signs consistent with being thrown against the rocks.'

I turn away as a sudden wave of grief comes perilously close to the surface.

'That's so sad,' I manage after a moment.

'Do you think so?' Isaac looks up at me, the slight tilt to his head familiar somehow.

I stare back. This man is not William, I remind myself; he wore his shirt, but he's nothing like him.

'Yes,' I answer back. 'The loss of anyone's life is sad. How can it be anything else?'

'Most people say it was a tragic accident, but I don't think of it like that,' replies Isaac evenly. 'I think Elliot had what was, for him, the perfect life. He lived exactly the way he wanted to – perhaps not the way others would choose, but to him it was the only way to be. And I think his death was the same. He was getting old and the post-mortem results showed that he had lung cancer. Not advanced, but I think Elliot knew what was ahead of him. So, he chose his death. He chose what was right for him, and I think that, one day, probably when he felt particularly at peace, he simply let the sea take him. The damage his body received from the rocks was after his death, so I think he'd drowned long before the tide brought him back to the shore. Knowing the way he lived his life, I think there's a tremendous courage and "rightness" about the way it ended. And if you consider that in other cultures they celebrate death just as much as life, they—'

'You can't celebrate death, that's… horrible…'

Isaac's eyes roam my face. 'I meant more that they celebrate life, all of it, even its end. Death is just another part of life. It all has meaning.'

'Well, I don't care what they do in other cultures. In my world, when someone dies it's sad, it's…' I break off, furious with myself for being unable to go on.

Isaac pauses. 'I'm sorry, I didn't mean to upset you.' His voice hardly carries above the sound of the waves. 'Would you like to go back?'

'No,' I reply. 'No…' A little softer this time. I have a job to do, I remember. I have to tell people about this man, and his story. 'But I think perhaps we should change the subject.' I indicate the sand ahead of me. 'This is where you draw those pictures, is it?'

At first I think Isaac isn't going to answer at all. A cloud comes over his face at my words and he stares down the beach, blinking furiously into the wind. But then he suddenly turns back to look at me, studying my face. His eyes searching mine.

'Would you like to make one?' he asks.

I'm so surprised by his question, my mouth hangs open. 'Oh, I hadn't thought…' Do I really want to do this? But then I nod; however reluctant I am, activity of any kind is better than being alone with my thoughts.

We're still following the line of the cliff and, after another minute or so, Isaac walks closer to the wall. 'Just got to fetch the tools out of the shed,' he says.

I frown, but then, as I watch, he reaches a fold in the rock face and, taking his bag from his shoulders, hangs it over an outcropping. Then he slips his hand behind the fold and… disappears.

I march over and see immediately that there's a small opening here. Isaac appears carrying two garden rakes, one rather much smaller than the other, which he hands to me.

'Have a look,' he says. 'It's a jolly handy cupboard.'

I do as he directs, holding the rake aloft, and to my surprise find myself inside something almost exactly resembling what he described. It's a small cave, about eight-foot high by six-foot deep and four-foot wide, perfectly light. I can see a few other things that presumably also belong to Isaac, stored here until he needs them.

'Great, isn't it?' he says. 'It's virtually hidden from the other side so almost impossible to spot by the casual observer. I found it a few months after I started coming here and decided to use it for my tools. It certainly saves fetching them with me every time. Besides, if anyone really feels the need to steal a garden rake and then hike over the sands with it, they're welcome to it.'

He holds his own rake aloft like a shield and takes off, striding towards the centre of the sand. I have to skip a little to catch up with him.

'The conditions are perfect today,' he says. 'Usually the surface is far too soft, but the heavy showers of late have slicked it down a bit. And even though the top layer has dried, underneath, well, you'll see.'

We walk in silence the rest of the way, until we're standing almost smack bang in the middle of the cove. The tide is going out and the beach is a vast empty expanse of space.

'Do you have anything in mind to draw?' he asks, as we come to rest.

But I shake my head. I haven't given it a moment's thought. And I'm beginning to feel rather silly.

'Then we'll just go freestyle, shall we?' He smiles as if what we're doing is nothing out of the ordinary at all.

'You'll have to show me,' I say. 'I don't know…'

Isaac places his rake on the ground and draws a smallish circle, the teeth leaving dark trails in the sand. 'The trick is not to worry too much if things aren't even, or accurate. Every one of these is unique and even mistakes become an embellishment. Besides, what looks like a massive problem down here, from up there, at a distance, fades into insignificance.' He points at the cliff behind us and grins. 'Now there's a metaphor for life if ever I heard one.' He lays the head of the rake back down on the ground. 'So, what now? You choose.'

I look at the sand, at the pale length of his hair that has tipped forward over his shoulder. What I am doing here?

'It doesn't matter what we do,' he adds, mistaking my silence for indecision.

'I don't know… petals?' I suggest. It's the first thing that comes into my head.

'Petals it is,' he replies and proceeds to draw a series of ovals attached to the central circle. Now the whole thing resembles a daisy.

He stands back to have a look. 'Your turn.' He indicates that I should carry on.

I heave a sigh, beginning to feel very self-conscious. I don't know what to do, or what will look right. On a whim, I drag the rake out in a straight line from the tip of one petal and then do the same to the other five, so that the lines resemble spokes on a wheel. Then I join the end of each line to the next so that the whole outer line becomes another circle. Pushing the rake through the sand is much harder than I imagined.

'Yes!' says Isaac. 'I like it. Now let's colour some of it in.'

He drags his rake across one of the segments that now surround the inner flower. By doing so he turns the whole patch of sand dark. It really is like colouring in. Now there are three dark segments and three light.

Without thinking I walk to the edge of one of the divisions and, locating what I think is the middle of the line, this time I draw a spiral, much like the shells we collected earlier. Isaac follows suit, working from the other side, and before I know it I'm adding another set of spirals, each facing the first. Isaac stands back.

'Tricky...' he says, and looks up at me, grinning. But then he simply draws a triangular point atop each row of whorls and almost immediately I can see where the next stroke needs to go.

Ten minutes later the pattern has almost trebled in size. And my arms feel like they're about to drop off. This is much harder work than I imagined, but I'm loath to let Isaac know that I'm struggling. I catch a breather as he draws in the next round of the design and try to think of some questions I can ask him, details that could put the flesh on the bones of my article.

'So how long have you been doing these drawings?'

Isaac doesn't even look up. 'Not long,' he replies.

'What, you just happened to have a rake in your hand, did you?'

'No...' He rolls his eyes. 'I made the first one with a stick... and I've honed the method since then.'

'But why do you do them here? Why not where everyone can see them?'

Isaac stares at me bemused. The rake comes to a halt and then starts again. 'Really?' he asks, as if I'm a child. 'I would have thought that was a little obvious.' His tone is intensely irritating.

'Humour me,' I reply bluntly.

He stands the rake upright, pushing his weight against it. 'Because I don't draw them for other people to see,' he replies. 'I draw them for me. I don't want crowds gathered around, oohing and aahing, trampling all over the thing, making noise... When I draw, it's just me, the sun, the wind, the thoughts inside my head – and that's all I need. The fact that other people might see them from time to time is a... side effect, that's all.'

I almost laugh. 'You draw whacking great pictures in the sand and you don't expect people to see them.' His naivety is incredible. 'Well, if you don't mind my saying, that's a little hard to believe given that the best place to see them is from up on the cliff. They're *made* to be seen from a distance.'

'Yeah, and you know what? If someone does spot one, then I couldn't be happier. One, because maybe it might bring a smile to someone's face. And two, because if they're up on the cliff, then they're not down here on the beach with me. I don't want people coming here. I don't advertise what I do, I don't tell anyone when I'm going to do it. Sometimes I don't even know myself.'

'Then why did you ask me to help you?' I'm goading him now, but I can't help it, his attitude is really beginning to annoy me. And I can see any possibility of an article slipping further and further away from me.

Isaac looks directly at me, his face flushed with anger. 'I don't know, I thought you were interested.' He pauses. 'But maybe I got that wrong. You know, if you're going to ask me questions about why I do this, you should at least respect my answers.'

'Okay then,' I say, throwing up my hands. 'I *am* interested, so tell me, if it's not for other people to see, why do you do this? What does it bring you?'

He glares at me and the seconds tick by with no response. I'm about to ask him if he even knows when he heaves a sigh and closes his eyes.

'Peace,' he replies softly. And then he opens his eyes and his look is a challenge. 'It brings me peace.'

I look away for a moment, uncomfortable under the weight of his gaze.

'And I don't need you to understand it, but I would like you to accept it.'

I nod slowly, suddenly aware of the space around me. 'Okay, I get that. But I'm sorry, I still think you're kidding yourself if you can't see that these are for other people too. You're an artist, isn't that what it's all about?'

'Sometimes,' he admits. 'When I want it to be, when I have bills to pay the same as everyone else. But sometimes no. When I create it's not the end result that's important, it's the process, the connectivity I feel when I'm doing it. It doesn't matter that they might only be visible for an hour or so. It's that they were created in the first place.'

I squint across at him. 'Sorry… Why are they only visible for an hour or so?'

Isaac's answer is to stride away from me, walking inland. He stops after a moment and draws a straight line in the sand. And then he marches back.

'See that,' he says. 'That's the tideline.'

I look at the pattern we've made, then at the line he has drawn, a line that's behind us.

'They get washed away,' I say, incredulously. 'You don't even draw them further back, do you? You just let them get washed away, destroyed.'

'I let the slate be wiped clean,' he replies. 'Ready for a new day.'

'How can you even bear it?' I stare down the beach, turning to the sea behind me, knowing that it will soon rush in and claim whatever it wants. 'I don't know why you even bother.'

'Maybe that's why you don't understand,' he replies, sadly. 'Nothing lasts forever, Louisa, but we don't have to mourn something just because it's gone. Instead we can choose to celebrate that it was here at all.'

I shake my head. 'No, you're wrong.'

I look at the rake I'm still holding, at the patterns of light and dark in the sand. I can't be here.

I hand the rake back to Isaac, unable to meet his eyes. 'I'm going now,' I say. It's all I can manage.

For a moment I think he's going to try to stop me, but then I see a look of disappointment come over his face. Disappointment tinged with resignation.

'Retrace your steps,' he says. 'And take the path we took in coming here, it's marked, don't forget.'

I'm a few feet away when his words come again.

'Go and see it, Louisa. Go up onto the coast road heading towards Evercombe and, where you see the sign for our town, walk out towards the cliffs. Look at it and then you'll see.'

More words follow but I can't listen, I have to get away. I barely remember my passage over the rocks, almost holding my breath as I put one foot in front of the other, concerned only with creating distance between where I am and the things I don't want to think about.

I heave a sigh of relief once I'm back on the main beach, when I can see crowds of people once more, hear the shouts of children at play. Even though I'm out of breath when I make it back to the causeway, I don't even think about stopping. I pick a road at random and walk it, knowing that I'm not going to slow down until I've outrun my thoughts.

I barely even register where I am until I realise that I've been walking in a curving arc and am now coming around the top of the road where the Lobster Pot sits. But I don't want to go back there either, and cross over as I reach the turning to the small car park at the rear. But then I stop, my hands fumbling in my bag. Keys…

Even on an overcast day like today my car is boiling hot, but I open all the windows before carefully pulling out of the tight parking space and navigating the sharp turning onto the narrow street beyond. Then I'm free, pulling away up the hill, wind buffeting through the windows. The church rises up ahead of me and I steer towards it for no other reason than it's something to aim for. I turn right when I reach it, blindly following a sign, and it's only when I've gone a little way that I realise it's the name of the village that Isaac mentioned, the one further along the coast. At the thought of his name, I push down harder on the accelerator and, with a burst of speed, leave the town behind, relishing the open road ahead of me.

But no sooner have I the countryside in my sights then I slow down. Where am I going? Am I simply going to keep driving until I can do so no more? And if I do, what will it achieve? My thoughts will still be waiting for me at the other end. I can't outrun them; past experience has taught me that.

The back of a sign flashes past me, lodged in the grass on the other side of the road, and I dip my head to read what it says in the rear-view mirror. It's back to front, of course, but I don't really need to check, I know exactly where I am. Maybe this is where I intended to come all along.

The sky is a wide open space to my right as I slow to pull into a small parking area alongside the road. It's only long enough for two cars, but there's no one else in sight as I come to a halt. I rest my hand on top of the steering wheel for a moment, making sure I really want to do this. But I already know I'm going to get out of the car before my fingers are on the door handle.

I walk slowly across the road and step up onto the scrubby grassland. There's nothing to separate it from the tarmac and it's the only thing that stands between me and the sea. It pulls me forward like a magnet.

I gasp when I see it. Even the tiny portion of the drawing that I helped to create is clear from up here, but now the shape of it is so much bigger. And it's beautiful, just like Isaac said it would be. From just lines in the sand, a work of art has been created, intricate and entwining, and yet so simple. Each individual element combines to make a whole. And every part necessary, built on the last, nothing existing in isolation.

My hands rise to my head, seeking to catch the ends of hair which are being whipped around by the wind. I flatten them down to tuck behind my ears where they're instantly tugged free. So, I let them go, watching strands ripple past my face, blowing one way and then the other as I sink to my knees.

The beach is empty so no one sees me watching as the waves creep up it. The minutes drift past, like the bloated clouds that cross the sky above me, casting shadows onto the sand below. And, finally, when I can bear it no longer, I hear Isaac's words. Words flung at me as I walked away from him. Words that were meant to make me understand what he was trying to say. A message of hope.

'You'll see it,' he'd said. 'You'll think it beautiful, incredible, and even when the tide has gently removed it from the sand, you'll still know it. Maybe then you'll understand that just because something of beauty can no longer be seen, it doesn't mean it no longer exists.'

But as I sit, watching the waves ripple over the fragile grains of sand, I cannot see hope. Only ruin.

# CHAPTER EIGHT

*And so Isaac keeps watch over the beach, its unofficial guardian, looking out for the unwary walker or the plain foolish who take no heed of the many signs which spell out the dangers of Elliot's Cove.*

*And yet there's a huge irony in this. A way of being that clashes head-on with…*

I pause and delete a few words… No, that's not quite right yet…

I frown and straighten up from the keyboard, arching my back against the ferocious ache in my shoulders. It was good of Leah to find this desk for me but it's just slightly too high, or else the seat is too low. Either way it isn't ideal for spending hours sitting and writing.

I refocus my attention, trying to regain the thread of the point I was making but, just as I get to the end of the paragraph, the loud whine of a saw starts up, scrambling everything in my head. The shattering sound stops momentarily and then starts again. I find the beginning of my paragraph once more and wait for another pause, quickly reading as soon as it comes. My hands lift, poised over the keyboard as the link to the next phrase begins to form in my mind, but no sooner have I got the words in the right order inside my head than they scatter again, cut through by the strident noise.

I glance at my watch; it's a little before one in the afternoon. Which means I've been sitting here for the best part of three hours, and I've precious little to show for it. I've started and restarted this article so many times I've lost count. Because, no matter which way I look at it, so far everything I want to say can be communicated in about four paragraphs. It's not an article in any way, shape or form, it's just a collection of ideas. I simply don't know enough about Isaac yet, or what he does. And the stupid thing is I probably realised this within about ten minutes of sitting down to write this morning but I ploughed on regardless, trying to ignore the fact that if I want to know more about him, then I'm going to have to see him again. There's no other way to do this.

I search for the last email from Barbara, scanning some of the other suggestions she made for potential articles, but none of them immediately grab me and there are certainly none I can make a start on straight away. An empty mug sits on the desk beside me and I pick it up as I get to my feet.

There's no need to wonder where Robin is, I just need to follow the sound of the electric saw, which, as my hearing had already deduced, is in the room right below me. I stand in the doorway and wave until I catch his attention.

'I'm just going to make a drink and some lunch,' I say as soon as he stops and looks up. 'Can I get you a sandwich or something?'

He pulls off the goggles and mask he's wearing, wiping a hand across his face. 'I'd love one,' he admits. 'Anything will do… and something cold to drink if you can find such a thing,' he adds. 'Just water would be fine.'

'Will do. Shall I shout you when it's ready?'

There's a nod and a wave; the goggles are already being pushed back into place.

Leah is still busy stripping the dining room of its hideous layers of wallpaper, but she too looks hot and decidedly bothered. Her hair, and actually most of the rest of her too, is covered with bits of sticky paper. I'm pleased when she nearly bites my hand off at my suggestion. It will be good for them to stop and have a proper break.

Twenty minutes later I carry a tray piled with sandwiches and a jug of iced water through onto the pretty terrace at the rear, bright with geraniums. It's shaded by a huge umbrella and there's just enough of a breeze blowing to make it pleasant. Robin inspects his hands before picking up a sandwich.

'MDF might be cheap,' he says. 'But it gets everywhere when you cut it. I'll be much happier when I can get my hands on some real wood.'

Leah frowns gently. 'Well, you were the one who wanted to use it,' she says. 'We could have had solid wood.'

'Which makes no sense at all financially,' replies Robin, with a smile. 'Once I'm finished, no one, least of all our punters, will be able to tell the difference.'

'What are you making?' I ask, pouring all three of us a drink.

'The fitted wardrobes,' he replies.

'Oh, so you're not having the armoires then?' I say, handing Leah a glass. I scrutinise her expression. 'Sorry, is that still a sore subject?'

She shakes her head. 'Not really. They would look stunning… but Robin's right. We don't need to be that extravagant. I just hope the wood looks as good as he says it's going to.'

Robin raises his eyebrows. 'It's only the carcass that's MDF, the parts that show are reclaimed oak, that doesn't mean it's rubbish.'

'Yes, but I don't want rough rustic… I want…'

'Expensive rustic. Yes, I know.'

I chew my sandwich, watching the conversation bat back and forth between the two of them. Leah doesn't look particularly upset over the decision but I'm not sure she's totally convinced. I think Robin is going to have to pull something quite remarkable out of the bag to meet her exacting standards.

'And the other downside, of course, is that making our own wardrobes takes much longer than simply buying some. Plus, while Robin's doing that, he can't be getting on with anything else either.'

'So, let me help with something then,' I say. 'I know I'm not skilled labour but I can certainly do some of the more basic stuff.'

Leah is examining her sandwich, lifting one half of the bread to peer inside. 'I know, Mum, and thank you, but you have your own work to do. And after having such a long break, it's probably important to try to get back into it.'

'I'm sure I could manage both,' I say, frowning with exasperation as Leah continues to peer at her food. 'It's just cheese and salad.'

'Yeah, I know, but something tastes weird.' She sniffs and then pulls out a round of tomato and drops it onto her plate. 'Anyway, let's see, shall we? We're not in dire straits yet, but don't worry, we'll soon rope you in if we need to.' She pauses a moment to chew thoughtfully, seemingly satisfied now. 'How's it all going anyway?'

'Slowly,' I reply. 'Barbara sent me some suggestions for the kind of articles she'd like to see but I've no real idea how to go about writing them; they're so different from what I'm used to. Plus, they're for the Christmas and winter editions, don't forget – nine million ways to cook a turkey or dress a tree, which is really hard to think about when it's boiling hot.'

'So, what kind of thing is she looking for then?' asks Robin. 'Presumably something a little different.'

'Not necessarily. A Devon Christmas,' I reply. 'All things seaside, traditional, old values, proper Christmas spirit…' I roll my eyes.

'Well how about local customs then?' says Leah. 'I'm sure there must be some.' She takes another mouthful of food and then waggles her fingers as she chews and swallows. 'You should ask Prim, she's bound to know.'

'And just who is Prim when she's at home?'

'The local florist… Prim-*rose*, would you believe. Anyway, she's also chairwoman of the local history group. If she doesn't know, no one will.'

Which is exactly how I find myself pushing open the door to the florist forty minutes later. Unfortunately, it's rather busy. And rather small. The shop is tucked between two others in a smaller street off to one side of the main road. It's almost as if it's an afterthought, carved off from the other much larger shop next door, perhaps in an effort to maximise the investor potential, but it doesn't really work. It looks gorgeous, with buckets of blooms spilling onto the pavement outside, and it smells gorgeous, but with three other people inside there's almost no room for me.

I'm about to go when a woman who looks anything but prim comes through a doorway at the back of the shop. She's wearing an electric-blue pair of dungarees with neon-pink boots and is carrying a shallow tray filled with flowers: buttonholes and an unmistakable bridal bouquet. Roses. I can smell them from the doorway, heady and sweet. I carried them in my wedding bouquet, and I know just how their velvet petals will feel against my skin. Her face is animated, wearing a huge smile for her customers, and for me, I realise, as she signals with a nod that I should wait. My plan for escape has been thwarted.

Prim's arrival is greeted by a round of cooing, particularly from the eldest of the three women who I assume to be the bride's mother, and I wait patiently while Prim checks through their order with them. After a good deal of gushing praise, I hold the door open for the family as they leave, with best wishes for the happiest of days tomorrow echoing in their ears. And then there's just me, my sense of loss so profound I can hardly speak.

'Wedding season,' says Prim. 'Don't you just love it?' She stares wistfully after the family who have left. 'If only life was as simple as organising a few flowers and living happily ever after.'

Despite myself, I smile at her words.

She shakes her head as if to remove the thoughts from it. 'Sorry, don't mind me… If you've come in here to order wedding flowers, I've probably just shot myself in the foot, haven't I?'

I shake my head. 'No, nothing like that, don't worry.'

'Oh, thank God,' she says. 'My mouth runs away with me at times. I really am my own worst enemy.' She grins at me and I get the feeling that not much in life gets Prim down. 'Anyway, never mind me, what can I help you with?'

I pull a face. 'Sorry, but I didn't actually come in to buy flowers. My daughter suggested I come and talk to you.'

'Oh, okay… a bit intriguing… Do I know her?'

'Possibly… It's Leah, from the Lobster Pot. She and her husband bought it earlier this year, they're renovating it.'

She smiles. 'Of course.' She cocks her head to one side. 'In fact, I can see the family resemblance, now you've mentioned it. But yes, Leah has kindly asked me to supply them with flowers once they're open, although I gather that might be a while yet…'

'Mmm… there's rather a lot to do.'

'That doesn't surprise me one little bit. The previous owners were… how can I put it? Lazy, rude, and thought so little of their customers I'm surprised they stayed in business as long as they did.' She grins. 'Their son is also my ex-husband…'

'Oh, I *see*…'

'So I'm very happy that Leah and Robin have bought it. And they'll be sitting on a goldmine if they get it right, it's such a beautiful old building. And quite prominent in the history of the town too.'

'Actually, it's for historical reasons that Leah suggested I come to talk to you. She said you run a local history group.'

'I try to,' Prim replies. 'Although, we're rather less of a group of people, more like a smattering. Oh, did you want to join?' Her face falls as she sees my expression. 'No… obviously not.'

'Sorry,' I say. 'But I *was* hoping you could help me. I'm a features writer for a magazine and I'm looking at writing an article on traditional Christmas customs here in Devon. Leah thought you'd be the person to ask.'

Her eyes light up again. 'I'm organising one actually, so yes, definitely the person to ask. Once upon a time nearly every household in Devon, and Cornwall too, would burn an Ashen Log in the fire on Christmas Eve.' She raises her eyebrows. 'It's essentially a yule log, but one made from a bundle of green ash which is then bound with seven withies, that's willow stems, before being burned in the grate. Each of the withies represents something different and there are various traditions that go with it. Is that the kind of thing you mean?'

'It's exactly what I'm after,' I reply. Finally, I seem to be getting somewhere. 'And are there other customs too, even some which might be very specific to a certain area?'

She nods as another customer comes into the shop. 'Quite a few. Mostly variations on a theme, but it's quite interesting to see the regional differences. It's a bit like the long-running cream-tea argument we Devonians have with our Cornish neighbours. You know, whether it's cream first, then jam on the scone, or the other way around.'

'Which everyone knows is the only way to have them. Scandalous putting the jam on first.'

Prim smiles at the elderly woman who's just spoken. 'Hello, Eileen.' She plucks a card from the small counter behind her and turns to me. 'Why don't you give me a ring and we can meet up if you like? Sometime outside of work though, I'm madly busy with weddings at the minute, but I can find a free slot somewhere.' She hands me the card. 'And you should go talk to Isaac as well. He's providing all the ash we'll need, and the withies, he's quite clued up on local customs too. Do you know who I mean? About your age, longish white hair tied back, he's a local artist.'

I nod wordlessly.

'He's often on the beach,' adds Prim. 'Or up at the allotments most afternoons.'

I glance at her waiting customer, glad for the excuse to leave. 'Yes, I know where that is.' I wave the card. 'I'll give you a ring then, shall I? And we can arrange a time to meet. Thanks, you've been really helpful.'

Prim waves an airy hand. 'No problem. Say hi to Leah and Robin for me.'

'I will, thanks.' And then I'm back outside, breathing deeply in the fresh air. But I can still smell the roses.

*How hard can it be? You're going to give Prim a call later on, so why not just pop up to the allotments and speak to Isaac while you have the time. What's the difference?* Easy as pie, and yet here I am, struggling to put one foot in front of the other. *Except you will go, you know you will... because however much you don't want to see him, there's also a part of you that is very intrigued by him.*

# CHAPTER NINE

I see him as soon as I turn the corner, not on his own allotment but the one that belonged to… some woman whose name I can't remember. The one that's come free for rent. He's digging, his back to me, but it's unmistakably him; his long lithe form is bending and straightening, seemingly without any effort at all. A pale-green shirt clinging to his back.

I pause. I could turn and walk away now, and he'd never know I was here. And yet… So I put one foot in front of the other until I've moved past him, enough for him to see me if he looks up.

'Don't tell me… You regret not taking me up on my offer of potatoes and are wondering if I've any left?' He straightens, leaning an arm on his fork.

He looks entirely happy, not only in himself, but to see me. As if my outburst of two days ago never happened. But however I feel about *him*, I can't just ignore it. I couldn't have stayed on that beach a moment longer but I ran away and was probably very rude; I have to say something.

'The other day, when I left, I'm sorry, I was—'

But he holds up a hand to stop me. 'No, don't apologise. My opinions are sometimes better kept to myself. Anyway, no harm done, at least not by you, and I'm sorry if I offended you.'

I swallow. I don't know what I was expecting, but it wasn't a heartfelt apology.

'I finished the pattern though,' he adds. 'It turned out well, I think.'

'I know, I... I did go up onto the cliff, like you said. I think it looked beautiful.'

He gives a slight bow. 'Then I'm glad.' His eyes hold mine for a moment. 'So, what can I do for you today? Is it potatoes after all?'

'No.' I smile. 'It's not the potatoes. I've just been talking to Prim actually.' I break off to squint at the sun. 'It sounds daft, but I was asking her about local Christmas customs. I'm going to fix up a time to talk to her about it, but she mentioned that you're helping her with some wood or something.'

'Ah yes, the Ashen Yule. I own a small area of woodland not far from here so I offered to provide the raw materials, that's all.' He raises his eyebrows at me. 'Maybe I'm missing something, but that seems an odd thing for you to be talking to Prim about, given that you're just visiting.'

'I was after some information, actually. My editor has asked me to do a few seasonal features and one of the suggestions was local customs. My daughter recommended I ask Prim, that's all.'

Isaac processes this information for a moment, looking puzzled, and too late I realise that as far as he's concerned I write books. I can feel a slow flush working its way up my neck. There's another slightly long look and then Isaac rubs his palms together as if to loosen dirt from them and drives the fork further into the ground with one foot.

'Would you like a brew?' he asks. 'I'm going to have one.'

I look around me, surprised, although a little relieved by the rapid change of direction and the question.

Isaac's response is to laugh and point at the brightly coloured shed that sits at the back of his space. 'Come on, let's get the kettle on.'

He leads the way and motions for me to wait while he disappears inside, returning seconds later with a fold-up deckchair. He opens it up with a flourish, setting it on the path.

'Won't be a sec,' he says, as he ducks back through the door. I can hear sounds of industry coming from inside and then his voice, slightly muffled by the confined space. 'Is tea okay? Milk and sugar?'

'Just milk please,' I call, as I take a seat.

He's back moments later with a chair for himself which he plonks down beside mine. I have to fight the urge to move a little further away.

'I have a little gas Primus stove,' he explains. 'Can't get through the day without several cups of tea, and it's not the same from a Thermos.' He pulls a face. 'So, what's all this with Prim then and talking about seasonal features?'

My heart sinks and I could kick myself. It was stupid to think that he'd ignore what I'd said.

'My editor's kind of like my agent as well,' I reply. 'So, if I'm in between projects I write the odd magazine article for her. It depends what she can sell, but Christmas is always a good opportunity.'

'I see. So that's what you're doing now, is it?'

I nod, casting about for what to say. 'I have a bit of time before the agreement for my next book is finalised.'

'But I thought you were on holiday.'

'Yes, that's right.' I can feel my face burning. Does he *know* I'm lying?

But Isaac smiles. 'Your editor a bit of a whip-cracker, is she? I thought you meant you were on a holiday holiday, not a working holiday.'

I'm digging myself a bigger and bigger hole here and my own smile feels tight in reply. 'You know how it is, needs must and all that. I'm freelance, you see, self-employed, so I can't afford to turn down a job. I work from wherever I can plug in my laptop.'

Isaac draws in a steady breath, nodding in agreement. 'I see… So, what can I help you with?'

I make a loose gesture with my hands but his eyes never leave mine. 'I'm not exactly sure, but Prim seemed to think that you know something of the local customs here. That's what I need: more detail about what goes on, and maybe some background information too.'

'Okay…' He pauses. 'And when do you need all this by? Only…' He gestures towards the mass of overgrown weeds he'd been busy digging up when I arrived. 'I'm on a bit of a mission, and I really need to get that lot dug over and planted up during the next few days. How long *are* you staying here for?'

I clear my throat, wondering whether I can fudge the issue without giving too much away. 'I'm actually not sure at the moment. My daughter and her husband are renovating a hotel which they bought at the beginning of the year. I came for a break originally, but they need so much help, I might stay a little longer than I first planned. Just to help them out with a few things.'

Isaac nods and I can feel his eyes straying to my hands. I know exactly what he's looking for, but I'd rather he thinks I'm married than not, and the rings William gave me are never leaving my fingers.

'So, if I crack on with the plot over the weekend, I can probably spare some time early next week. Would that suit you?'

'Yes, perfect, thank you.'

'And you might like to take a look at the woodland too. It would be great for photo opportunities—' A high-pitched whistling comes from the shed. 'Ah, tea.' He gets to his feet. 'Hold that thought.'

My head fills with an image of a snowball rolling downhill, getting bigger and bigger with every turn, and the irony of this perfect seasonal metaphor makes me want to groan out loud.

I get to my feet and wander over to look at the vegetable plot while I'm waiting. It feels too uncomfortable just sitting waiting for my drink and I should have refused really. I probably would have if I didn't need Isaac's help.

'So, you've decided to take on the other plot then,' I say when he returns carrying two mugs. Anything to forestall further conversation about a trip to the woods.

'Utter madness,' he replies. 'But yes. I've been umming and aahing over it for weeks, ever since Miriam gave it up. It's too much to take on really, but…'

He hands me my mug and I take it, looking around me in confusion. 'You must have a huge family,' I comment. 'You've all that space and now this lot as well. Just how much veg does one man need?'

A look crosses his face that's hard to define and his head drops a moment. For a second or two I think he's not going to reply at all, but then he takes a few steps away from me, heading towards the far end of the plot. I get the distinct feeling that he's buying time but, just as I'm wondering what I could possibly have said to upset him, he looks back and smiles.

'Now you know why I've been trying to give away my potatoes,' he says. 'Seriously though, it's not all for me. There are far too many people in need, and although what I do doesn't make much difference, anything is better than nothing.'

'You mean you give it away?'

He nods. 'Not all of it. But you're right, I can't eat it all. So I give what I can to the local food bank. That's the trouble with seaside towns. On the surface everything is all sunshine and smiles, but a lot of people hereabouts rely on tourism to make a living and that's not what it was. There isn't a huge amount of work elsewhere either; a problem that's hidden away of course, because poverty doesn't fit with the message the town council try to sell about the town, but it exists just the same.'

I take a sip of my tea, mentally storing away his words. Another story, another time. 'And now you've taken on a second allotment as well.'

'I know. Like I said, probably madness. Still, at least it means it will be put to good use rather than lying neglected.'

'But don't you have to pay for them?'

'Yes, but the council were keen to get it rented so they dropped the price. And on that basis I couldn't pass it up. None of what I grow will go to waste, don't worry. Sadly, there will be more than enough willing takers.'

He catches sight of my expression. 'What? You don't approve?'

'No, sorry, I absolutely approve. I'm just... surprised, that's all. Most people wouldn't do what you do; if they wanted to help at all, they'd just donate money to a charity.'

'But there's no sense in that; the help wouldn't go where it's needed. Doing it this way means I know who benefits.' He pauses a moment to look at me, searching my face. 'What?'

I blush furiously. 'Nothing. I—' He thinks I don't believe him, but I can't help my incredulous expression. I'm genuinely shocked to find someone who thinks the way I do. I've spent half my working life writing articles and fighting cases for the very people that Isaac has set out to help and I can't tell him any of it. But, oh, how I'd love to. 'I think it's a remarkable thing to do,' I manage.

Now it's his turn to colour. 'I sell some of the produce as well, to one or two hotels in the town. For a fraction of what it would cost to buy, but it's enough to pay for the allotments and in return they get a good supply of locally grown fresh food, while I get plenty of fresh air and exercise, plus food on my own plate. Then any excess goes directly to those who need it most.'

'So that all works out wonderfully then.'

'Yes,' he insists, firmly. 'It does.'

He holds my look for a moment, and I wonder if he thinks I'm being sarcastic. It's quite possible I'm just about to be forcibly evicted from the allotments, but then a rogue smile flits across his face. He turns away and goes to sit back down and I've no choice but to join him if I want to carry on the conversation.

As if reading my thoughts, Isaac takes a slug of his tea and then turns to me. 'So then, Christmas customs. I bet you're of the opinion that the Christmas tree came to this country courtesy of Prince Albert, aren't you? Whereas in fact, legend has it that it was the invention of an eighth-century Devon saint, St Boniface. He travelled to Germany where the local pagans celebrated the winter solstice by worshipping an old oak tree. But once old Boniface had chopped down the oak, a fir tree grew in its place and henceforth all the pagans, now converted to Christianity, started to hang decorations on the tree and began to celebrate Christmas.'

'*Really?*'

'That's what they say…' He grins at me over the top of his mug. 'He's now the patron saint of Devon.'

'Okay… well I guess that's the kind of thing I'm thinking of. The article is for the Homes and Gardens section of the magazine so will need to focus on how the local customs and traditions are upheld; food, drink, crafts, and so on. So that the reader feels they could take some of the ideas and incorporate them into their own celebrations.'

Isaac drinks his tea, eyes narrowing as he ruminates on something.

'So, which do you prefer, writing books or articles?'

'Oh…' I can feel my cheeks begin to redden again. 'I haven't really thought about it.' Of course I haven't, because we're discussing something that isn't true.

'But presumably, when you write an article for a magazine, you at least get your name beside it. Whereas with ghostwriting, I don't know… If I had a talent for writing, I'm not sure I'd want to remain anonymous. I think my ego would have quite a lot to say on the matter.'

For God's sake, he's making me feel defensive about something I don't even do. 'But there's also the security of knowing how much you're going to be paid and not having to worry about royalties, et cetera. And good ghostwriters are very much in demand,' I add. How the heck would I know?

'Are they?' He looks surprised. 'And you're a good one, are you?'
I stare at him. 'Well, I…'

But then he breaks into a wide grin. 'Relax, Louisa, I'm just teasing. But seriously though, fair play to you. If I'd written a book, I'd want my name up in lights.'

'Would you though?' I counter. 'I mean, take all this.' I indicate the riot of growing things in front of us. 'Who knows you do this?'

He looks puzzled. 'This?' he queries. 'Plenty of folks. I'm not dressed in disguise if that's what you mean.' He plucks at his shirt. 'This *is* actually what I look like.'

I tut. 'I don't mean growing the stuff, I mean your giving most of it away; your charitable enterprises. Who knows about those?'

His silence is my answer.

'Exactly. Your light's already under a bushel. I don't think you'd be all that comfortable in the limelight.'

'No, perhaps not.' He looks down at his upturned palm for a moment, rubbing at a callous beneath his middle finger. 'You weren't thinking of writing anything about me, were you? Only I know what you writerly types are like. Always on the lookout for a story.'

I ignore the sudden flicker of shock that fires in my stomach. 'Why would I want to write an article about you?' I ask, as evenly as I can manage.

A wry smile crosses his face for a moment. 'No reason,' he replies. 'Just checking.'

'Well I'm not,' I lie. 'I have enough to do.'

Bugger.

He looks up and stares across the open space, turning his head towards the sea. 'So, would you like to write a book one day?' he asks. 'As you, I mean. One of your own.'

'I've thought about it, yes,' I reply, truthfully. 'But I'm not sure now is really the right time.'

'How come? I thought you were in between contracts at the moment.'

'Yes, but…' How on earth do I explain? 'I just don't think I'd be able to concentrate. For one thing the hotel is being renovated and I had to work to the strains of a hammer and electric saw this morning as it was. That's not too bad when you're undertaking research, or writing a short piece, but writing a book under those circumstances…' I shake my head. 'Not going to happen.'

He nods several times, considering what I've said. 'You could find somewhere quiet,' he says, after a pause.

'I work in coffee shops sometimes,' I reply. 'But the ones back home are quiet during the week, not like here. I'll find somewhere; I haven't exactly got my bearings yet.'

Isaac fishes a small fly out of his tea and flicks it away. He looks as if he's about to say something but then drinks instead, finishing what's left with several loud swallows.

'Don't take this the wrong way,' he says, still staring at his mug. 'But you could come and write here if you wanted to. Well, not here exactly but…' He gets to his feet, standing a little awkwardly. 'I could show you.' He breaks off as my eyebrows rise, a wary expression on his face. 'Just… Well I know how it feels when things are stifled. It's not a coincidence that there's a proliferation of painters here, the light is wonderful, but it's not the only thing.'

I shouldn't go with him, I know that, but there's something about the expression on his face. I push the thought aside.

I give a slight nod and Isaac begins walking along the path leading out onto a main, much wider one, which loops its way around the whole allotment. We're heading to the very far end and I can see nothing ahead of me but a low-lying hedge and blue sky above. Below us will be the sea. It's only as we get much closer that I spot a small stile, almost hidden, tucked into the space between the hedge and the boundary.

'It's not far,' says Isaac, making light work of the step up. He offers me his hand which I pretend not to see.

Once I'm over I'm surprised to find myself on a much gentler slope than I'd imagined. An expanse of tufty grass stretches away from me, disappearing to the horizon, and I soon spot the sea, revealed inch by shimmering inch as we walk. After only forty metres or so there is a more pronounced drop, but not dangerous, and as we draw closer I realise it's like a series of terraces. Closer still, and I can see that rough steps have been dug into them, allowing for ease of passage. And all around scrubby bushes cling to the hillside in clumps, growing denser and taller the lower we descend, thriving in the areas less scoured by the wind.

The view is incredible. Unobstructed. Stretching out on either side to the furthest edges of my vision. And it's different here. In the town, the sea looks painted onto the scene – undeniably picturesque, but with a manufactured air to it. Here, there is wildness and rugged freedom. I much prefer it.

I look over to where Isaac has come to a halt, like me, gazing out at the point where the sea meets the sky. I step forward, signalling my intent to carry on, but Isaac doesn't move, and I see his chest expand as he fills his lungs.

I almost don't see the building at all until I realise that's because we're at roof height, looking out over the top of it, where a flash of sunlight on metal reveals a chimney, glinting through the shrubbery ahead. It's taken us no more than two or three minutes to get here but, sheltered as we are by the hillside at our backs, the sound has dropped away. Or rather, it's as if it's been concentrated into a dense stillness that is nothing except the air around us.

'Watch your step here,' says Isaac. 'It's a little steeper.'

He moves to the right and I see another set of steps, proper ones this time, made from boards, with a knotted rope handrail slung alongside them. And then I really begin to understand where Isaac has brought me.

Sitting pressed against the back of this much steeper terrace is a wooden building, with long windows down each side, two to the front, and a slightly raised veranda encircling it. Smack bang in the centre of the side looking out to sea is a door. And around the building… nothing, but the land itself.

To my astonishment Isaac removes a rock lying in the sandy soil, lifting out a jam jar that has been sunk into a hole beneath it. He fishes out a long-spindled key and saunters over to the door as if he owns the place. The thought sticks in my brain as I watch the key turn in the lock with ease and see Isaac push open the door and disappear through it. *He* does *own the place.* Incongruously, almost impossibly, and rather unbelievably, this extraordinary building nestled into the hillside belongs to Isaac.

I realise I'm still standing, unmoving, almost unblinking, as Isaac sticks his head back around the door. 'Well? Are you coming in?' He grins. 'Welcome to my studio.'

I know my mouth is hanging open. I shut it, only to find it hanging open again seconds later. If it's possible, the inside of the room is almost as incredible as the outside and it suits Isaac perfectly. His rumpled linen clothes, his satchel slung low over his hips, his sandals, even the shoulder-length white hair drawn back into a ponytail, blend seamlessly with this rustic space.

There are gauzy lengths of fabric at the windows, diffusing the otherwise bright light which floods in. The wooden boards lining the walls are painted white, as is the floor. But not a brilliant white, instead they gleam with something softer, almost pearlescent. A small pot-bellied stove sits on a hearth in the middle of the rear wall, while to the right a truckle bed has been pushed into the corner, a wooden frame providing a rail on which a pair of red woollen curtains hang to close it off. To the front left, a rough wooden workbench spans the corner, extending along the wall. It's piled with assorted – I peer closer – flotsam, and a similarly rustic cupboard stands to one side of it. Filling the rear wall behind is a second bench, longer and thinner this time. A single-ring camping stove, flask, portable radio and a row of books all jostle for space on its surface. An open packet of biscuits lies on its side, an apple come to rest against it. On the floor, a deckchair piled with colourful cushions completes the furnishing.

What's even more surprising than finding this place here is finding it full of things. Things that would have all had to be carried down by following the exact same route I've just taken. There's no other way of getting here.

'What do you think?' asks Isaac. He moves from the centre of the room to stand in front of the workbench, signalling at the view from the window.

'I don't know what to think, but it's safe to say I've never been anywhere like this before.' I look around the room again. 'How on earth did you come by this place? What even is it, a house? A big shed?'

'You like to put labels on things, don't you?' He's smiling again. 'It doesn't really matter what it is, it's just here.'

'I'm curious to know how it came to be here though, halfway down a hillside, with no proper access, no amenities. Do you own it?'

He nods.

'Then how?'

'Because, like many coastal areas, there are beach huts available for sale in a number of locations and when I came here I intended to buy one if I could. That proved to be much harder than I thought until, one evening, when I was in conversation with an elderly gentleman in the pub, we got chatting about it and he mentioned this place. Knew it from when he was a lad but had no idea whether it was even still in one piece. So I came to investigate. It was unloved, broken, but still undeniably here and, after some pretty exhaustive enquiries, I found record of its purchase by the local council who bought it at the same time as the allotments. I did a deal with them, simple as that, and I've spent the last few months making it habitable again.' He raises his eyebrows. 'I can see you think I'm crazy.'

'I'm just surprised you even managed to do it, considering there's no way here except the way we came.'

'I didn't say it was easy and I've had to be pretty inventive, but that was half the fun.'

'But there's nothing here.'

'I know, isn't it wonderful? Just listen…' He holds up a hand to suggest I do just that. 'It's so quiet here, the stillness just seeps through you.'

It's a little unnerving actually.

'Yes, it's peaceful,' I say, 'but what I meant was more that it's so tucked away from everything. Doesn't that make you nervous? I mean, anyone could just walk in.'

'Well, I guess they could, but why would they want to? That's supposing they even found it in the first place. As you so rightly said, the only way down here is through the allotments, which are perfectly secure, and apart from the folks who rent them, no one else really goes there anyway. There's no reason to. Besides, if anyone found this place, I don't suppose they'd be hell-bent on creating trouble for a perfect stranger.' He gives me an amused look. 'I think you've been reading too many thrillers. No, they'd more than likely just be curious. In which case, they could come in and have a look around before going on their way again.'

'And you said this is your studio? You actually work here?'

He nods, looking pleased with himself.

'And so you come here and, what? Create stuff?'

'Sometimes. I call it my studio but, actually, I don't try to define what I do here. I do whatever feels right at the time. So some days, yes, I might create something from what I find on the beach, other times I might read, or draw. A lot of the time I just sit and think. It's a good place to just be.'

'But there's nothing here, no electricity, no water…'

'I know. That's what makes it so perfect.' He gives me a curious look. 'I admit it wouldn't be for everyone, but it's the way I live my life, Louisa. Whatever I take, I try to give back in equal measure.' He raises his hands in an expansive gesture, a broad smile lighting up his face. 'So, do you think you could write your magnum opus from here? You'd be very welcome to.'

I stare at him. At the space. And then back at him, utterly thrown by his words.

'No,' I say. 'No… I can't come and work here.'

'Why ever not?'

*Because it's a ramshackle, glorified shed. Because there's no internet. No loo… Because I'm pretending to be something I'm not.*

What on earth do I say? I'm aware that my fists are clenched by my side, that my stomach is churning. 'Just no,' I repeat again. 'It's…' I throw my hands up helplessly. 'Sorry, I have to go.' I turn and rush to the door, lurching through it, feet sliding somewhat on the wooden boards outside.

'Louisa!' The voice is shocked, urgent. 'Louisa, wait!'

'No,' I throw back behind me. 'I can't… this is all too…*weird.*'

And with that I take off back up the steps, and the slope, pushing myself to go faster, even though the muscles in my legs are burning. And, as I hurl myself over the stile at the top and hurry back through the allotments, I realise that this is the second time in almost as many days that I've run away from Isaac.

# CHAPTER TEN

In the end I googled the rest of the material I needed for the article. I met with Prim, who helped with a lot of useful information and gave me a run-down of what she had planned for the town. It looked as if it would be quite a large community event by all accounts but, although the details were good to have, it didn't quite have the angle I'd been envisaging. In my mind, I'd seen the article as more of a human-interest story; about what happens in seaside towns out of season, about the people involved and their livelihoods, and how important that community is once all the holidaymakers have left. I had even imagined that I could include details of how folks could make their own version of an Ashen Yule, but there was no way to do that without going to see Isaac and that wasn't something I was prepared to do just now.

It wasn't the end of the world, but the article didn't have the personal touch I'd wanted. I'd managed to find a few recipes and mention a few other local traditions and, by putting these together with some carefully chosen stock photos, I thought I'd written a piece which fit readers' expectations of the season. I'd packaged it up with some corny but highly descriptive passages of the coast in wintertime but, in my heart of hearts, I'd known it wasn't up to my usual standard and Barbara wasted no time getting on the phone to let me know.

'Well, I'm not going to beat around the bush, Louisa, but this could have been knocked out by any of my staff writers. And that's not a criticism darling, just an acknowledgement that your writing is usually of a much higher standard, which is exactly why you've always had free rein to do whatever you want. I know I've asked for something different of you this time around, and perhaps it doesn't best suit your writing style, but—'

I cut her off before she has a chance to say anything else. None of it is a surprise, but I don't particularly want to hear it just the same. 'I know you'd hoped for more.' I sigh. 'I'm sorry, Barbara, but I don't think I'd anticipated quite how much of an upheaval this move was going to be. Or just how much of a pickle Leah and Robin had got themselves into…' It's not strictly true, but under the circumstances I think a little white lie can be forgiven. 'I haven't had as much time as I would have liked, and… well, maybe I was asking a bit too much of myself.'

'Oh, Louisa… Darling, why didn't you say? I could have found someone else to do the articles.' She pauses. 'And I don't want to say I told you so… Nor did I want to be right, but what's important is that you come back when you're ready, and not before. Now, tell me honestly…'

I let her words wash over me. Barbara's only trying to do the right thing by the magazine and I can't blame her for that. She's always been ruled by her head rather than her heart and maybe that's why she's been so successful. But, whichever way I look at it, it's not good news for me. She's playing along with being sympathetic, and I know she is, but she's a businesswoman first and foremost and my instinct tells me she's already wondering when she can cut the ties.

'… So you don't need to worry about any of this at all, but what about this chap who draws pictures in the sand? Have you got anywhere with him yet?' Her words snap me straight out of my reverie.

'Yes, I'm still working on it. In fact… I've met up with him, but I'm really not sure if this is going to run, Barbara. He's a very private person and has made it pretty clear he doesn't want any publicity. Even the beach where he draws is out of bounds to the public, he doesn't even want local people to see his work so—'

'Not a problem for you though, surely? I think you're under-estimating your skills, Louisa, dear. After all, you've tackled much more reluctant subjects before, been pretty inventive in your ways of getting the story, as I recall. And I know you, don't forget. You always get your man.'

'Yes, but this is a little different and I'm going to have to tread very carefully to get any kind of story at all. I'll keep you posted, don't worry.'

There's a pause from the other end. A much longer one than I'm used to. 'Okay, but keep in touch with me, Louisa, and if you foresee any problems for God's sake please call and let me know… Perhaps this might be the one that gets you back in the saddle, after all,' she says. 'Let's hope so.'

I end the call moments later. I'm beginning to see exactly where I stand. Nail this article or I'm history. But is that what Barbara really thinks of me? That I always get my man? As if I've hunted them down. Admittedly, some of the consumer fraud cases I've covered had been tricky to get to the bottom off. And *of course* those involved had been evasive and hadn't wanted the story to come to light; how else would they be, knowing it would expose their criminality? But it was never about bringing the perpetrators to justice, it was always about righting the wrongs for the people on the end of whichever dodgy scheme it was. Those who had lost their savings, their livelihoods. Barbara's portrayal of me says something very different indeed.

I blow out a puff of air from my cheeks, thrown by her comment, and stare at my keyboard. I need this job and there's no pretending I don't. But Isaac's story is completely different to those she was referring to, and it would be very wrong to think otherwise. Quite where that leaves me I'm not sure, but what I do know is that delivering on my promise is going to prove rather tricky.

I open a fresh document on my computer and stare at the blinking cursor, willing words to come into my head. But they're not there and instead all I can hear are raised voices floating up from below me. My heart sinks; another argument. I can't hear what's being said but it's Leah who's shouting, that much is obvious. She has a habit of slowing down her words when she's angry, enunciating every one with deliberate force. As if she's speaking to a child or can't quite believe the stupidity of what's being said to her. It's incredibly irritating; William used to do it too.

I turn my attention back to my work, looking for a punchy opening sentence to set the tone for what I want to write. I try out the words in my head, type a couple, and then rework them before readying my fingers. Just as I think I've got it, a door slams and my thoughts evaporate. Worse, I can hear footsteps coming up the stairs.

'Mum?' The plaintive call is accompanied by a none-too-subtle knock.

I swallow my frustration with a sigh and get to my feet. Leah is red in the face, pouting, and covered in white dust.

'Oh dear.'

'You have to come with me a minute,' she replies, ignoring my stare at her appearance.

'Leah, I was in the middle of something,' I say, a little irritated by the assumption that I can just drop everything. 'Can't you just give me a moment to finish what I was doing?'

Her hands are on her hips. 'It won't take long,' she flashes back, grabbing at my hand.

It probably is easier just to go with her.

She thunders down the stairs in exactly the same way as she came up and disappears into the bedroom where Robin has been busy making wardrobes. He's standing by the window, I notice, staring out at the street below, his stance weary. But my attention is almost immediately eclipsed by the gaping hole in one corner

of the ceiling, and the wreckage of plaster that has fallen to the
floor beneath it. A plume of white dust has risen and fanned out
across the room, like icing sugar dropped into a bowl. A ladder
stands to one side.

I look at Leah's face and then back to the ceiling. 'Oh…'

Robin turns at the sound of my voice but says nothing.

'Oh God, this is awful,' I add, immediately thinking for a
practical solution. 'How on earth did it happen?' I walk over
to survey the damage. 'Or more importantly, what can we do?'

Leah tuts, rather impatiently. 'I hit it accidentally with the end
of a broom handle, but never mind about that for a minute…
Look.'

She stands beside me, staring upward. I crane my neck but for
the life of me I can't work out what she expects me to see, apart
from the jagged edges of plasterwork and a dark space above.

'Hang on,' she says, fiddling with something in her hand.

For the first time I notice her phone and I wince as she shines
the torch almost directly in my face. She angles it upward and,
although the beam isn't powerful enough to fully illuminate
something so far above our heads, I can just about make out a
white shape. She waggles the phone at me.

'Take it,' she says. 'And go have a look.' Her attention is
directed towards the ladder.

'Leah, I can see what the problem is from here, I probably don't
need to look any closer.' I've never been good climbing ladders at
the best of times. It does weird things to my knees.

'No, you're looking at the hole,' she intones, her voice taking on
the same hectoring note I'd heard earlier, as if it were plainly obvious
what I was supposed to be looking at. 'Look at what's above it.'

I glance at Robin, whose lips are pursed together. He shrugs.

'Okay then,' I reply. 'But hold the bottom of the ladder.'

I take the phone and climb gingerly upward, hampered by
the lump of metal in one hand. I stop several rungs from the top

and shuffle my feet so that I'm properly balanced before shining the light upwards. There's a precarious wobble as my centre of gravity shifts, matched by an accompanying tilt in my stomach, but all at once I see what has got Leah so excited. I switch off the torch and gently lower one foot after the other until I'm back on solid ground.

Leah is waiting expectantly for my response. 'Well? Isn't it amazing?'

'Quite a find,' I agree. 'And lovely, but then it is an old house. I guess it's only natural that once you start pulling it about you're going to unearth a few things like this.' I survey the floor. 'It's made a bit of mess though, hasn't it? Is it going to be hard to repair?' I turn to Robin for comment, but he looks away.

'Oh, for crying out loud, has no one in this family got any vision at all?' moans Leah, all but glaring at me. 'I don't want to patch up the ceiling, I want to pull the whole ruddy thing down! It's the original Georgian ceiling, Mum, complete with carved cornices. And I bet the ceiling roses are still there too.' Her face has taken on a look of wild excitement. 'They're incredible.'

'But you can't…' I look back up. 'Oh, Leah…'

Robin raises his eyebrows, a movement Leah immediately spots.

'Oh right, so you're going to agree with him, are you? Brilliant.' The pout is back.

And suddenly I realise why I'm standing here.

'Leah,' I say a little more firmly. 'It's not really a question of agreeing with either one of you. I'm just speaking as I find and, lovely though the original ceiling might be, I'm more conscious of the mess it's made. That and the extra work it's given you; work you hadn't banked on, mind.'

Leah growls with frustration. 'But can't you at least see the potential it gives this room? The transformation it could reap. This bog-standard, boring, shapeless—'

'Leah, stop it,' says Robin. 'You like the room as it is now, so don't give me that. You've liked it ever since you first came in here when we viewed the place. In fact, you fell in love with all the rooms on this floor which, correct me if I'm wrong, you said are wonderful, light, airy and have huge potential. And they are still exactly that. And, more to the point, hundreds of people who've already stayed in this hotel over the years have liked this room too. How is it going to be suddenly improved by a bit of ornamental plasterwork? Which, incidentally, you have no way of knowing is intact. That corner might be okay but the rest might be in a horrendous state, and the cost of removing the ceiling, plus the extra time it will take, is not worth the risk.'

'Robin, you know as well as I do that the chances are it isn't in a mess. It was the fashion, that's all. The Georgians had these big, wonderfully lofty ceilings and then fashions changed. Everyone got boringly practical and started boarding them up to make everything modern and bland, or to save money on their heating bills.' She swivels around to face me. 'Just think what it could look like. Just think how amazing this room could look.'

I take a moment to compose my reply in my head, moderating my tone so that I speak calmly and gently. 'Leah, I can see how excited you are. And how nice it would be to pay tribute to this building's heritage. But I can also see that, at this point in your renovations, your head should probably be ruling your heart, hard though that is. Sit down, calmly, and discuss it, the pros and the cons. I think you might find the answer reveals itself.'

Leah's mouth drops open, closes again and then she turns on her heels and storms out of the room. 'Well, thank you very much,' she yells as she goes.

The air settles into an uncomfortable silence and I stand quietly, wondering what to say. I feel incredibly awkward and, if Robin's expression is anything to go by, so does he.

After a few moments he sighs. 'I know she's your daughter, Louisa, but bloody hell, she makes me so mad!' He gives me a sheepish look.

I nod in agreement. 'She's far too much like her father, I'm afraid. He was exactly the same, used to sulk for hours.'

'It makes it virtually impossible to have any kind of conversation with her at times. And, although when she calms down she's able to discuss things rationally, when she blows...' He holds up his hands in a helpless gesture. 'Plus, she has a memory like an elephant so when she's angry it all comes out; every misdemeanour I've ever supposedly been guilty of. I don't understand why she can't just draw a line under things from one day to the next. It's as if everything is cumulative, instead of starting afresh.' He huffs. 'Wipe the slate clean, Leah, for goodness' sake.'

I stare at him. 'What did you say?'

Robin looks puzzled. 'I just meant that it's infuriating when she stores everything up, there's no getting past it and—'

'No, I understand what you meant. But you said wipe the slate clean...'

He nods. 'Yes, you know...' He trails off. 'Is everything all right, Louisa?'

I shake my head, trying to dislodge the thoughts from it. 'Yes, it's just... Someone else said that to me recently and...' I frown, trying to slow down the rush of thoughts that assail me.

Robin is still gazing out across the room, unseeing. 'I don't get how you can love someone so much and yet they can make you madder than you've ever been in your life. I would walk over hot coals for Leah, but when she's like this...'

I smile, despite the situation. 'You could cheerfully throttle her.'

He nods, a pained expression on his face. 'So, what do I do now?'

I eye the door that Leah has just charged though. 'Leave her be. Let her calm down and, once she's had a chance to think about it, you'll probably find that she comes around to your way of thinking. Same way she did with the wardrobes.' I give him a sympathetic smile. 'And if she doesn't, well…' I look back up at the ceiling. '*Can* you even afford the cost of the extra work? Or the time?'

He shakes his head.

'Then you have your answer and you might just have to put your foot down. This is a massive project you've taken on, and it's put you both under an incredible amount of pressure.'

'I know…'

'And Leah's only the way she is because she's so passionate about things.'

'Yep…'

'And a perfectionist.'

'That too…' Robin throws me a rueful glance. 'I could still bloody throttle her though.' He pauses a moment, his face falling. 'We were right to buy this place. I absolutely, one hundred per cent believe that. We would never have been able to get it for such a good price if it hadn't been such a wreck, and opportunities like this don't come up very often. But…' He draws in a breath and looks at me, sadness etched across his face. 'Ever since William died…'

My heart goes out to him. 'Are things no better?'

'No, they are; they have been. Since buying this place…' He pauses. 'Louisa, it's been like having the old Leah back. You know how things were; as if she had no energy for anything, no enthusiasm. Like she was sleepwalking through life. But once we started talking about buying a hotel of our own all that started to change, and since we've been here all her old spirit has come flying back. I thought at first that it was proof. That this place was exactly what she needed; something to focus on, to throw her energy into. And I really thought she'd got over things, but now… Now the cracks are beginning to show and I still don't think she's fully over William's death. It's as if she's stuck somehow. Plus, there's been this kind of… almost manic intensity to everything she does. Which as we both know is what she does when she's trying not to think about things.'

I nod gently. 'I did wonder if you'd noticed.'

'She's like a bottle of lemonade, full of fizz, and as long as you leave the bottle alone, it's fine, it's only if you shake it up that the problems start. So, Leah was okay when she didn't really have stress anywhere else in her life, but now that she has, it's like… like it's all too much. The pressure has to be released or else every now and again—'

'She blows.'

'Exactly. She thinks I don't notice, but some days she looks like she's about to burst into tears at any moment. But then she rushes off to do something and I never quite get the chance to talk to her about it.'

I give him a sympathetic look. I'd never really considered that Robin was quite so astute as he obviously is. And he's in an impossible position.

'Just keep doing what you're doing, Robin. It's tough at the moment, but it will get easier. Maybe Leah just needs a little more time to work out how to cope with things.' I pull a face. 'I'm probably not the best person to talk to her, but I'll certainly try. And, bit by bit, as work gets completed here, she'll begin to feel a little more in control of things, I'm sure.'

'Thanks, Louisa.' He glances over at a broom propped up in one corner. 'And on that note, I'd better get this mess cleared up.'

*

Robin's words are still echoing through my head as I make some drinks down in the kitchen a few minutes later. There is a bit of a mess to be cleared up and it's not just a physical one but an emotional one too. I draw the blanket of guilt tighter around my shoulders. Leah had been distraught when news of William's death first broke. The knock on the door had come after a lovely evening together spent planning our Christmas celebrations, and Leah's animal scream of pain upon learning the news had stayed with me for a very long time. But while my tears had continued to flow, Leah's had soon dried, and she had seemed to bear William's death stoically. In the rawness of my grief I had accepted her offer to attend the inquest in my stead, and by the time I had come to my senses it had been too late. And so she had heard all the details of the accident alone, graphic ones too. Had heard the other driver giving a statement of his innocence, even though he'd been drinking. And then had to shoulder the unbelievable decision that William's death was an accident, tragic, but no more than that. The burden that had placed on her had simply been too much, and I was the one who put it there.

I take out a fresh carton of milk from the fridge and stand with it over the waste bin, wrestling the seal off, deep in thought. *Damn…*

I'd not only dropped the seal, but the plastic lid too. I peer inside the dark bin liner, at the collection of papers and wrappers right at the bottom. But it's okay, the bin hasn't much in it yet and I can see the piece of plastic just poking up. I put down the milk on the side and then, holding up the bin lid, cautiously lower my hand towards the bottom. I grab hold as I feel something of the right material brush against my fingers but, as soon as I grasp it, I realise it's not the lid I was looking for. Instead, it's a long cylindrical object.

Things may have changed over the last twenty-five years or so, but the design of these items has hardly altered, so I know exactly what I'm looking at. It's a pregnancy testing stick. And it's positive.

# CHAPTER ELEVEN

I stare down at the length of plastic in my hand, thinking perhaps I'd got it wrong; that I'd misread the information it was giving me. But of course I haven't, because now all the little signals begin to make sense. Signs I'd taken no notice of until I'd been made to look again. How Leah has seemingly gone off coffee. How a slice of tomato which she would have normally eaten and enjoyed suddenly tasted weird. And of course the mood swings, even more pronounced than usual.

I glance up towards the kitchen door, fearful I might be discovered. Worried that somehow I've done something wrong. I know I haven't, but I feel as if I'm intruding here, poking my nose into business which has nothing to do with me.

Dear God, does Robin even know?

I think back to our earlier conversation, trying to remember if there was anything he said that might give some clue, but I know there wasn't. He'd put Leah's emotional state down to unresolved grief over her father's death, not the flurry of hormones currently circulating her system. I take one more look at the stick in my hand before dropping it back into the bin, scuffling the wrappers so that it's covered over.

*Oh Leah....* My hand is over my mouth, my nose tingling with the realisation that this was Leah's intention, to hide her pregnancy away, instead of celebrating it like the joyful event it is. How must she be feeling to do something like that?

I rifle for the milk carton lid I'd dropped before washing my hands and finishing the making of our drinks. Just mine and Robin's. I looked for Leah before coming into the kitchen and I'm assuming that she's still out wherever it was she rushed to. For now, at least, I'll have to bide my time before I talk to her. Or until she comes to talk to me. I really wish she would.

By the time I get back upstairs, Robin has swept away most of the mess of plaster from the floor and is working on his wardrobes once more. But he's busy and I'm preoccupied so, beyond exchanging a few words, nothing more is said. I climb slowly to my room and, mug in hand, walk to the window.

I'd stood here when I first moved in, just a few short days ago, looking down onto rain-soaked streets, and even in that small amount of time things have become more complicated than I could ever have imagined. This move was supposed to simplify things. Sit and write, that's all I imagined I'd be doing. No worrying about debt, finally, the stress of the house sale behind me. Time to breathe, and to heal, and take the first tentative steps into a new life. But now?

I realise after a few moments that my eyes are raking the road outside for any sign that Leah has returned. But after ten more minutes, during which time I finish my tea, she still hasn't put in an appearance. I can't begin to imagine the turmoil her mind must be in. And I realise I could do with a walk too.

The beach is busy when I get there but it doesn't take long to spot Leah. She's gone to exactly the place I did when I'd wanted to think; the grouping of rocks just underneath the cliff face. Not so far that it takes an age to get there, but far enough so that she's away from the noise and bustle of the sands directly off the causeway.

I give a little wave when I see her and I'm pleased to see her face lift slightly. I'd wondered whether she'd even be in the mood for talking, let alone with me. I pick my way across the rocks and settle down beside her, shuffling until I find a flat spot that's comfortable.

'It's nice here, isn't it?' I say, staring out at the white glare of the sea. From this angle you'd hardly know it was blue at all. 'I walked here the day I arrived.'

She nods. 'People are weird,' she replies. 'They all want to sit on the same piece of beach, when for very little effort they could walk here, where there's hardly a soul.'

I shrug. 'We're all different,' I say. 'But I agree with you. I guess when you have small children it's handy being closer to the loos and the ice creams, but…' I could kick myself sometimes. *Louisa, what are you thinking?* I really hadn't meant to draw attention to the very thing I'm trying to avoid, but it seemed a natural thing to say. I study Leah's face but if she's affected by what I said it's not obvious. 'I much prefer it here, where it's quieter. It's a good place to think.'

Leah angles her face towards me. She's silent for a moment, but finally smiles. 'I even have my own rock,' she says, amused by her words. And then, 'Did Robin send you?'

I raise my eyebrows. 'No, amazingly, I came of my own volition. Although truthfully, I think Robin wanted to, but I told him to give you a little space. Plus, of course, he's very busy.' I lean into Leah's shoulder and nudge it gently.

She sighs. 'I know. It's not fair on him, is it? That he should have to shoulder most of the practical work, and now…' She trails off. 'Now, I'm not even there to do any of the things I am capable of.'

'It's a partnership, Leah. I'm sure you do your fair share. Besides, I don't feel any sense of resentment from Robin. I don't think it's about who does what. I just think he'd rather you were happy.'

'But I am happy, Mum.' She picks up a small pebble that's become lodged in a crevice between two rocks. 'It's not that, it's…'

And again I wonder if she's just about to confide in me but, although I give her a moment, she doesn't say anything further.

'Why did you buy the hotel, Leah?' I ask.

'You know why,' she says. 'We wanted somewhere that was our own, somewhere we call the shots.'

'Okay… But that wasn't quite what I meant, rather more that once everything is up and running, what do you and Robin hope to achieve from it?'

Leah thinks for a moment. She knows the answer, but she's trying to put it in a way that doesn't admit how far short of that ideal they currently are. A flash of irritation crosses her face, but then her shoulders sag.

'I sometimes wonder if we weren't just being incredibly naive,' she says. 'And that all we've done is swap one noose for another. Buying the hotel was supposed to set us free. It was supposed to give us control over our future, so that we could live the kind of life we wanted, instead of having it dictated to us. Except that now all I can see is us bound up in worries over money, arguing about stupid things and never having time to do anything that living by the sea was supposed to bring. It was supposed to be a way of life, not just a job.'

'Well, maybe you just haven't reached your destination yet,' I reply. 'Leah, I know it's tough, I can see it's tough, but you *are* on the road to all the things you hope for. But perhaps, understandably, when you're caught up in the day to day, you lose sight of the bigger picture every now and again. Try to remember what it is you're hoping to achieve and you might find that you can enjoy the whole process rather than simply waiting for the end product.'

She gives me a pointed look and it's one I know well. 'So you're saying it's my fault.'

'Leah, at what point did those words leave my lips?' I let several seconds of silence tick out. 'All I'm doing is reminding you that, even while you're stressed about all the work there is still to do, and all the money it's costing you, you can still do a little living at the same time. And you can certainly choose to enjoy the process while it's happening.'

She bows her head. And I can see she's struggling.

'It's just that…'

Something on her finger occupies her attention and she grinds to a halt. Now could be the perfect time to tell me, if she can only find the courage to confide. It would be my first grandchild. I'm trying so hard to push down the small spark of excitement that would so dearly love to burst into flame. And I understand how scared she must be feeling. I remember what it was like when I first learned that she was growing inside of me – the sheer terror that something so tiny could be entrusted to my care. Fearing that I wasn't ready, that the responsibility was too great. Despite her age, I can remember it almost as if it were yesterday.

She shakes her head and stands up. 'No, it doesn't matter.'

I'm not as quick to my feet as she is and I lurch upward, a foot slipping slightly on the rocks. 'Leah, I hope you know that you can always talk to me. About anything. I know that things haven't been easy the last year or so.' I bite my lip. There's so much I need to say. 'But, despite all of that, I will always be here if you need me… when you need me.'

A sad smile turns up the corners of her mouth. 'Thanks, Mum,' she says. 'But it's okay, honestly.' She looks out across the sand, towards the main beach. 'I should get back. Poor Robin will be wondering where I am.'

I nod and smile, watching as she picks her way over the rocks. *Oh, Leah. I've let you down so badly…*

*

I sit and wait until I'm certain that I won't be following her and then I walk slowly across the sand to the water's edge. It's late afternoon now but the day is still warm and I have nowhere to go. I don't want to return to the hotel and my work, which will only remind me of how much I've lost. Besides, Robin and Leah will probably be grateful for some time alone. I don't know how long the pregnancy testing strip has lain in the bin but it can't have been more than a day or so, otherwise the rubbish would have been thrown out. And if there is a good opportunity to tell Robin about the baby, then maybe this is it.

I set out towards Elliot's Cove, for no other reason than because I know it's there, and I take my time, slipping off my sandals and letting the edge of the waves run against my toes. The chill is comforting somehow. I haven't taken very many steps when something white glints in the sunlight, and I stoop to pick it up. It's another whelk shell, tiny and totally intact, grown into a spiral that the laws of nature have decreed to be the most perfect of shapes, that of the golden ratio. I slip it into my pocket without another thought.

By the time I get to the end of the beach, I've collected many more. Whelks, periwinkles, some limpets, and tiny halves of some others I don't know the name of, one or two of them still joined together with a minute hinge, like a butterfly. Hand thrust inside my pocket, I let them fall gently through my fingers.

I'm about to climb onto the rock when I realise that I've walked straight past the information boards, ignoring their exhortation not to venture any further. I can see the markers that Isaac painted as a guide and the sea looks to be far out to my right but... I double back. The danger has been made plain enough. I'd be foolish to risk it without checking.

And I can see straight away how easy it is to be complacent. The tide, which to me had looked to be on the way out, has actually already turned and is heading inland. At best, I will have an hour before the rocks become submerged. I draw in a deep breath, turning to look at the sea behind me; perfectly calm, sparkling under the sun. And yet in the wrong situation, deadly. My walk back along the beach is very much slower than the one out.

Spying a free bench as I make my way up through the small car park and on towards the causeway, I decide to sit with an ice cream to pass the time. If the seat is occupied by the time I get back then I can always sit on the steps lower down. I join the queue, which seems ever-present, and am just trying to choose between honeycomb fudge or honey and ginger when I feel a light touch on my arm. It's Francis. He's wearing a very apologetic smile and carrying a cup of takeaway coffee.

'I realise I'm completely hopeless, but I've been looking at you for the last couple of minutes and I just can't remember your name. Sorry.'

'It's Louisa,' I supply.

He bangs the heel of one hand against his forehead. 'Of course! I really have no excuse. Books and their authors, I have absolutely no problem with. Real people, now that's a very different story.'

'Well, I can't say I blame you. The world of fiction is often a much nicer place than the real world.'

'This is very true,' he replies, eyes flashing in amusement. 'It's so nice to meet a kindred spirit.'

He smiles and the seconds tick out between us. I'm wondering what he wants, what he's expecting me to say, when he laughs. 'I should probably tell you why I've accosted you,' he says, pausing, no doubt in response to my eyebrows shooting upward. 'Only I've got your books,' he adds. 'From the other day? You left them behind when you went to visit Elliot's Cove.'

At least a week must have passed since then, surely. It certainly feels like it. 'Oh yes, sorry, I've been a bit busy with a few things.' I'd completely forgotten about them. 'Shall I come and get them now?'

Francis eyes the line of people ahead of me. 'There's no rush.'

I step out of the queue. 'No, I'll come now. Otherwise I'll only forget and, besides, I don't want to drip ice cream all over your shop.'

'I recommend the honey and ginger,' he says. 'Or if you have a really sweet tooth, the triple chocolate.'

'Then I shall bear that in mind,' I reply, dipping my head in acknowledgement. I indicate that he should walk on ahead, smiling at his back as he turns. There's something about Francis that makes him very easy to talk to. 'So, you're a connoisseur of ice-cream flavours then,' I remark as we reach his shop.

'Occupational hazard,' he replies, opening up the door. 'That and the coffee… and the doughnuts. When Lily starts frying of a morning, the smell all along here is like a siren call. And when they're hot, just rolled in sugar and cinnamon…' He pulls a face and pats his stomach. 'I have zero willpower, I'm afraid.'

He flips the sign on the door that reads 'Back in ten minutes' and beckons me inside. The smell of warm book-paper welcomes me.

'I've got your books just under the desk here,' he says, putting down his coffee cup. 'Although, you're welcome to browse of course.'

I look over to catch another smile.

'You might not have much willpower, but you know how to sell a book or two, don't you?'

He flicks a glance towards the door. 'Just between me and you… if I wasn't so inordinately rich, I would never be able to keep this place running.'

I hold his look, trying to decide whether he's being serious or not, but a small crease tugs at the corner of his mouth. I tut and give him an amused look. 'Oh, really?'

'Okay… so not all of that sentence was one hundred per cent accurate.'

'Let me guess…'

He grins at me. 'I'm only a teeny bit rich… okay, so not rich, but twenty years in the RAF, early retirement and a damn good pension means I can just about afford not to worry about this place. Which is just as well. The seaside in summer is great for business, but outside of that… Let's put it this way, I spend more time in front of the fire reading in the wintertime than I do in here selling books.'

'I shouldn't say it, but I quite like the sound of that.' I pick up a book from a pile at my feet. 'It must be hard though, running a business here. It all looks so idyllic on the surface, but what do you do when the sun goes in and the visitors all go home?'

'Well, if you're lucky, you have the kind of set-up which means you're not totally dependent on the tourists for income. Or, you have another job which you can pick up again in the quieter months. It's feast or famine, that's for sure.'

Something about the way he says it makes me think of Isaac. And my work. There's an article here just crying out to be written, but something stops me from saying any more.

I hand him the book I'm holding. 'Then I'd better take this one as well.'

He roars with laughter. 'Christ, if I'd known that's what it takes to sell more books, I'd have put the sob story to good use long before now.' He tips his head to one side. 'You don't have to buy that, you know.'

'No, but I think I might be doing quite a bit of reading over the next few weeks. This should keep me going for a bit, and I can always come back, now I know you're here.' I fish in my bag for my purse.

'Oh… so you're not on holiday then? I just assumed when you asked for directions to Elliot's Cove.'

I hand him three pound coins. 'No. Visiting, but not on holiday as such. My daughter and son-in-law bought the Lobster Pot back in February and well, I was at a loose end too. So I'm staying with them until I get myself a bit sorted.' I'm trying to decide how much more to say. Giving Francis too many personal details feels wrong somehow, but he's only being friendly. Does it make me seem aloof if I don't explain properly? It's not like

I have anything to hide. 'I was widowed eighteen months ago,' I add. 'And fancied a change, so I sold up my house. Now, I'm just trying to decide what I want from the rest of my life. And where I want to be.'

'And in the meantime a little sea air seemed like a good idea?'

'Something like that,' I reply, grateful that he doesn't make any further comment. I hold out my hand for the books.

'Well, it's very nice to have you here, Louisa,' he says. 'For however long. And I know the Lobster Pot, I'm sure your family will be very grateful to have you around for a while. It needs a bit of work, doesn't it? I can imagine there's plenty for you to get involved with.'

'Except that I may well be more of a hindrance. It's not really my thing.'

'No? So, what do you do then?'

His words stop me in my tracks as I realise that, in the small amount of time I've been here, my lies are already waiting to trip me up. I think back, trying to recall who I've talked to and what I've said. I told the woman in the art gallery the truth, but then there's Isaac and… I think back to the photo I showed to Francis on the first day I was here, and his reply, now ringing in my ears. *Everybody knows Isaac… he's somewhat of a character.*

'I'm a writer,' I say, hoping that this is enough of a sweeping statement to get away with it. But I've forgotten I'm standing in the middle of a bookshop. And I realise a fraction of a second too late.

'What?' Francis claps a hand to his forehead. 'And you didn't think to mention it before now?' He bends forward in an elaborate bow. 'We are not worthy.'

I smile despite myself. 'I didn't say I was a good writer,' I reply.

He wrinkles his nose, eyes searching my face. 'No, but I bet you are though. So, come on, what do you write?'

I bow my head, shame flushing my cheeks, which I hope Francis takes for modesty. 'I'm a ghostwriter, actually. So I write whatever I'm paid for. Non-fiction a lot of the time, biographies, that kind of thing. Fiction occasionally.'

'Wow,' says Francis. 'You just never know, do you?' he adds. I look at him, puzzled.

'Who you're going to meet,' he says. 'Just an ordinary day and, no offence, but on the surface an ordinary person and then, wow, you find out they do something amazing like that.'

'It's not really that extraordinary.'

'It is,' insists Francis. 'God, I'm so jealous. I always wanted to do that. It's not really a coincidence that I run a bookshop.'

'So write,' I say, praying for an end to the conversation. 'You clearly have the time.'

He stares at me and for a moment I think I've offended him, but then his face splits into a grin. 'It's probably that simple, isn't it?'

My shoulders inch upward into a shrug, half a shrug. 'Note-paper and pen… that's all you really need. Well, that and a stonking good idea.'

'Not to mention a whacking great dollop of talent.' He eyes my expression. 'You're all so modest, aren't you? Isaac's just the same. Now there's a man with a story to tell.'

'Oh, how so?' It comes out rather more forcefully than I'd intended.

A cloud crosses Francis's face. 'Forget I said that. I just meant…' He smiles. 'He has a way of extracting information from you, without ever really telling you anything about himself, have you noticed? It must be that mysterious creative vibe.' He's desperately trying to steer me away from delving further. 'Not that there's anything wrong with that.' He colours suddenly. 'I got into a bit of an argument with him, actually, one day not long after he moved here. I took that photo of one of his sand drawings, the one you showed me when you first came in here, and he—'

'You took that?'

'Yes… sorry, I thought I'd said…' Francis breaks off, as if suddenly realising that he was supposed to be changing the subject. 'Anyway, he got quite cross about it. I showed it to him when he came in afterwards, I thought he might like a copy of it, but he wasn't happy, you could tell.'

'But his drawings are huge, they're meant to be noticed. Or at least you can't help it if you do.'

'That's exactly what I told him,' replies Francis. 'He was all right after that. Just mumbled something about the curse of the creative mind. I think he likes his privacy, that's all – which is fair enough, I suppose.' He pauses, looking at the books in my hand. 'Does Isaac know you're a writer? You and he would get on like a house on fire.' He stares at me, blushing again. 'Oh… Sorry… I didn't mean that you, or he…'

I hold out a hand to stop him. 'It's okay. But yes, he does know.'

Francis nods several times. It's something I also do when I'm keen to move a situation on. 'I thought he probably would.'

'I can't really remember how we got talking about it.' I smile. 'Probably the same way we did.' It's time to go. 'Anyway, thanks so much for these.' I tap the books in my hand. 'And I'll be back for more, I promise.' I get to the door before turning back. 'And remember, notepaper and pen.'

Francis raises a hand in salute. 'I will.'

I stand outside on the causeway, thinking for a moment. What an interesting conversation. Apart from the fact that Francis clearly knows Isaac better than he's letting on, he also mentioned that he has a story to tell. It's another little nugget of information for me to squirrel away. I might not want to admit it but I'm beginning to be rather intrigued by the man who paints his stories on the sand.

# CHAPTER TWELVE

The ice-cream queue is half what it was when I left it. I'm juggling books now, of course, but I can hardly go back and ask Francis to hold them for me again. They've got to come home with me sometime.

Home, now there's a thing. Such a simple, uncomplicated word, and yet the meaning and the sentiment behind it is anything but. I'm still conscious of the time, not wishing to return to the hotel too soon, and so I rejoin the end of the line, waiting patiently for a summery treat.

I choose the honey and ginger in the end, and I have to agree with Francis, it's very good. I stand for a moment, quickly licking the edges of the ice cream and, once it's a little more under control, I wander back down through the car park towards the sand. I pause as I reach the steps and then tuck myself onto the bottom one, stretching my legs out in front of me. A young family are in the process of setting themselves up for a few hours on the beach, their small child toddling across the uneven sand on chubby legs.

I could be a grandma and the sudden thought tears at my heart. In a few years' time, this could be Leah and Robin, enjoying a summer's day, together as a family. And where will I be then? In the ice-cream queue buying a treat for everyone? Or miles away, sitting in a house on my own, typing in an effort to keep the roof over my head? It wasn't how I envisaged this time in my life at all and I feel the loss of my future more keenly than ever. I turn and look in the other direction; the question of where I'll be is an impossible one to answer but it is one I'm going to have to think about, perhaps much sooner than I had thought.

After a few minutes of random people-watching, I'm suddenly aware I've been tracking the progress of a solitary figure down the beach without even realising who I was looking at. It's Isaac, his hair left loose so that it just bends on the top of his shoulders. His customary light linen clothes are rumpled, his feet are bare, and he walks with relaxed purpose, completely at ease on the soft sand.

The thought comes quietly as I watch him. He's heading in the direction of Elliot's Cove and I check my watch, recalling the tide times I'd read on the information board earlier. There may be just enough time for him to cross the rocks to the cove before the tide covers them, but it will be a one-way journey, surely, at least for several hours until the water begins to recede once more. Which means he won't be around for quite some time. And I have an open invitation, don't I? Come and use the studio any time you want, Isaac had said.

And the idea sits there, a curled temptation, beguiling and teasing. Could I? Could I really go there knowing that I'll be alone? But I've thought it now, and I can't unthink it.

I pop the end of the ice-cream cornet in my mouth, wrestling with indecision, but even as I get to my feet I know I'm going to ignore the little voice in the back of my head. The one who knows how wrong this is. I make my way purposefully across the car park. It's only a ten-minute walk to the allotments.

There are very few people around today; the same elderly man sitting in his deckchair reading a newspaper, and a much younger couple weeding in silence. They look up, smiling a welcome as I pass, but I know I'll be forgotten in a matter of moments; they're not really interested in me.

The key is exactly where it was before and, as I screw the lid back on the jar and sink it into the hole, it seems like a perfectly acceptable thing to do. It isn't until I'm standing in the middle of the studio, surrounded by everything that is Isaac, that what I'm doing ambushes me. He might have said that I was welcome to use this space, and been open about the possibility of people finding this studio, but I'm still here under false pretences. I'm still here trying to find out what I can about him without his knowledge.

I try to console myself with the thought that my intent isn't malicious, but it doesn't really work. I've been in too many situations where I *have* been poking around in someone's past, or digging through their present trying to find something incriminating, and this feels far too similar. But this is where Isaac works, a space he put together from scratch, and so if anywhere is going to give me an idea of who he is then this place will. Even if Isaac doesn't want to give me an interview for my feature, I can at least gain some more impressions of him to use in a background article. Because if I know Barbara, she's going to want *something*.

*And admit it Louisa, he intrigues you too…*

It's hot in the studio, the gauzy fabric at the windows doing little to block out the heat of the sun. I'd rather not open the door and broadcast my presence but, then again, who's going to see? The only person who would is a couple of miles away in the other direction. So I open it inward, propping it with a weighted ball of twisted rope left for exactly this purpose, and usher the breeze inside.

I've always prided myself on my journalistic nose. That ability to detect when something doesn't feel right, when it feels as if the wool is being pulled over your eyes, and, importantly, when it isn't. Because everything about this place shows me a man who cares, who lives his life exactly as he claims to. It's evident in everything – from the very existence of this studio in the first place to the way the room has been put together. Every piece of furniture has been handmade, and lovingly so. It's been crafted from the most basic of materials, much of it evidently reclaimed or repurposed, and then transformed into something of simple beauty. It tells the story of a man who likes to sit with a book in one hand and an apple in the other. Who doesn't need to surround himself with possessions and is content to live a simple and modest life.

The sound of the sea washes through the open doorway and the gulls cry overhead, wheeling about the sky with abandon. And more than anything I long to sit, to do nothing beyond allowing my thoughts to settle around me: thoughts about my future and what it holds, and also about Leah and Robin, and the new life that's growing inside my daughter. But I came here for a reason, and whether I like it or not this story is a part of my future.

I put down my books on the deckchair and turn my attention to the workbench that runs along the wall beneath the window. It's piled with things, seemingly without order, and I let my fingers trail across its surface. A group of pebbles lie to one side, all different sizes, but each worn smooth by the relentless tide. They are pink and brown and soft green and I have an urge to take one in my hand and feel its smooth, solid weight. But I leave them there and move on. There are papers too, and a pen, some pieces of plastic, and a roll of copper-coloured wire. An assortment of tools is next: pliers and wire cutters, a small hammer. But none of it tells me anything beyond what I already know, and I move to the rear of the room.

There are books here and I scan the titles, seeing the copy of *Moby Dick* that Isaac bought from Francis a few days ago. I pick it up and flip through the pages before putting it down again. There are titles on birdwatching, organic farming, forestry and woodland management. I pick up a sketchbook but examination shows the pages to be blank, and I'm about to put it back when a sheet slides from the back. A face stares back at me, soft lines drawn in charcoal, the barest outline and yet unmistakably a woman. I search for more, but this single drawing is all the book contains.

I hold it in my hand, wondering what I'm looking at. Has Isaac captured the likeness of a perfect stranger, or someone known to him? Could she be a lover, perhaps? The thought takes me by surprise. I have no right to be considering such things, and yet... There's something about the portrait, an intimacy that shouldn't be there given how little detail there is. But it is. Every line on the page speaks of familiarity. A flush of heat hits me and I replace the drawing, returning the sketchbook to its position within the line of books. Another book has been pushed behind this one, identical in shape and size, another simple black cover that would make it hard to distinguish from the first, and I pull it out, curious.

It's a diary. Of sorts. Each page is annotated with a date, or rather just the day of the week and a number. The first says simply 'Thursday the 29th' – of when I have no idea – and there are no other words on the page, just a drawing. It's a celandine, simply captured but exquisitely drawn. The next page is a Monday and shows a detail of the sky, dark clouds and a suggestion of rain, but on one edge just the faintest glimmer of a hopeful sun. There's no colour, so the sun is more an absence of shading than anything, but it's cleverly done.

The sketchbook feels nice in my hands. The cover is soft and supple, and it feels like the sort of book you should take with you wherever you go. A companion on your journey, wherever that may be. I carry it to the chair and sit down, moving my books onto the floor and sliding the cushion to one side so that my arm just rests on it. I'd forgotten how absurdly comfortable deckchairs are.

I'm only a few pages in when there is the faintest touch of something against my leg. I should be startled, but instead it only adds to the strangely soporific mood the book is exerting over me. I look down to see a tip of a black tail curl over the top of my foot as the cat walks on by. He turns and his bright golden eyes are inquisitive. He's wondering why I'm here.

I put out my hand to stroke his head, realising that it's the same cat I'd seen up on the allotments, the one Isaac had called a flirt.

But I can't recall his name. Is it his? I wonder. A full-throttle purr starts up the moment my fingers make contact with his ears, as he pushes his head against me. We'd had a cat once, when Leah was six or seven. William had brought it home one day, out of the blue, a kitten really. He'd seen a sign at the side of the road advertising them for sale and had stopped the car and gone into the farmhouse whose cat must have recently given birth. It was the only one left, he'd said, and he couldn't just leave it there, all by itself. So, he'd bought it, just like that. Leah had fallen in love with the cat, such a pretty little thing; a tortoiseshell and she'd named it Barney. William never had anything to do with him from the minute he'd brought it home, of course, but Leah and I had loved Barney, too much, as I recall. We were heartbroken when he died twelve years later, and William wouldn't have another. It's funny but I'd forgotten about that. He was the last pet I ever owned.

I scarcely feel its weight as the cat jumps nimbly onto my lap. Had he known what I was thinking? Had he sensed my moment of nostalgia, weakening any impulse I might have to push him away? His fur has been warmed by the sun and his feet leave little trails of sand across my lap as he turns, circling in that oh so familiar way before he tucks himself inward and curls, paws soft against my stomach.

I can't move now, even if I wanted to, which I don't. It's one of those curious moments when time stands still and the world shrinks down until there is only you and the immediate space that surrounds you. There is nothing else. Nothing that matters anyway. And it's been such a long time since I've felt like this that I give myself over to it, completely.

The book is still open, my thumb lying lightly as a marker between two pages, and I turn to the next, curious to see what has been captured on another day. I recognise it immediately. It's a shopfront, part of a little cottage where I imagine the owners still live. And it sits opposite the tearoom where I ate a scone on my first day's foray into this little town. Was it the same for Isaac too? Did he sit there, sipping at his drink as he contemplated the day ahead, sufficiently moved by the quaintness of the street facing him to capture its likeness on paper?

The next page is black. Its starkness jarring. And yet the more I look, the more I see that it isn't just black. It's not a colour, it's a removal, the blanking out of a day that has been scribbled over to such an extent that it has ceased to exist. There is no lightness, no variance in shade, just unremitting darkness.

I flip to the next page, a coastal scene, drawn from high on a cliff. And back again. The contrast couldn't be more dramatic, and I scan through the next few pages, looking for anything similar, but there's nothing. Just that one solitary instance of bleakness among pages that teem with life. But it's unsettling, and it takes a few minutes before I'm able to move on, a little wary of what I might find next.

It must be the absence that wakes me. The sense that something is missing. My foot jerks wildly as I come to with a start, involuntary movement caused by muscles responding whether I have full control over them yet or not. The jolt of my leg makes me realise it's the cat that's missing; the loss of the comfort he brought which had lulled me to sleep in the first place. But I see straight away that the cat hasn't left the room, he's simply removed himself from me and is sitting under the shelter of Isaac's arm in the doorway to the studio.

Their backs are to me as the two of them sit upright, side by side, staring out towards the sea. Isaac's legs dangle over the threshold and rest on the top step. And a continuous rumbling purr fills the silence.

The book in my hand feels like a hot coal, but beyond that my head is blank, my thoughts scattered. What can I possibly do to retrieve this situation? I've been caught red-handed rifling through Isaac's things, and it's the biggest abuse of his hospitality that I could make. I clear my throat a little; there must be something I can say.

At the noise, Isaac turns. I'd expected to see a scowl, or at the very least a flash of anger, yet Isaac breaks into a wide smile that is as warm as the air itself.

'I see you've discovered the one real drawback of having this place as a studio,' he says. 'I do that all the time; sit down for just a moment and then the next thing I know, two hours have gone by.' He cuffs the cat's ear gently. 'And this one can sense a vacant lap at two hundred paces.'

I tuck my legs underneath me, trying to pull myself out of a chair that seems determined to hold onto me. 'You must think I'm incredibly rude,' I stammer. 'I'm sorry, I…' I cast around me as if the words I need to find are hovering in the air. 'I really don't have an excuse.'

Isaac gets to his feet, much to the cat's dismay, and turns back to face me. 'And yet I seem to remember that I offered you the use of this place any time you wanted it,' he says. 'And I don't think I made any stipulation over what you used it *for*…' He grins. 'Although there are one or two things I'd draw the line at, obviously. That being the case, an apology isn't at all necessary. I'm only sorry that we startled you from your sleep. You looked very peaceful.'

'Did I?'

His suggestion seems surprising. I never feel at peace when I sleep. Except that, now I'm awake, there does seem to be a certain lightness to my being that wasn't there before. I glance down at my hands. I've made no move to hide what I was looking at; Isaac must have seen it.

'Yes, but…' I lift the sketchbook. 'I wasn't prying, I—' I stop suddenly. How can I say that? That's exactly what I was doing. A wave of shame washes over me. It wouldn't be so bad if Isaac was angry, if he snatched the book from my hands and forbade me from ever coming here again. I'd deserve that. But he isn't, he's being charming and generous and the contrast between his motives and mine stands out in stark relief. 'I was curious, that's all…' I finish lamely.

Isaac holds out his hand for the book. 'Again, when I issued the invite, it was in the knowledge that everything in this room is on display for whoever might be in here. If I had any deep, dark secrets, I would have hidden them away, believe me. I wouldn't want them on display where they'd be a constant reminder for me as well. People don't just hide their secrets from others, they hide them from themselves too.'

He smiles, but it's a curious thing, taking up only one side of his mouth, and it strikes me that now his words are out he's rather surprised by them, as if he never intended to say them at all. He flips idly through the pages.

'Oh God, I'd forgotten this was even in here. These are…' This time he does smile properly. 'Appalling… Oh—' He stops, and I know exactly which page he's come to. He grimaces and turns the book back around so I can see it. 'That must have been a bad day.' He frowns and is about to say something else when he shuts his mouth again. But he'll know that I'd already seen it; the black page a strident voice among all the other much softer ones.

'I didn't think they were appalling at all,' I say, finally extracting myself from the chair. Having Isaac tower over me was beginning to feel very uncomfortable. 'I thought they were beautiful, and I even recognised one or two of the places, so they can't be that bad.'

'They're from a while ago,' he says. 'I don't often draw now, in fact, I've moved on to other things.' Isaac has had enough of the sketchbook. He tosses it onto the workbench.

I nod. 'But that's a good thing, surely?' I counter. 'If your art evolves, as long as it's an organic process.'

Isaac stares at me a moment, puzzled by my words. It's not that he doesn't understand them, more that he hadn't expected me to say them. 'Of course... I forget that you're a writer,' he replies. 'So the same must be true for you too. Your work must evolve over time, just like mine. How did you start?' he asks. 'Did you always want to write?'

'Kind of,' I reply, wondering how best to explain. Journalism had always been my burning ambition. I had a notion when I was much, much younger that I would set the world alight by uncovering some huge conspiracy that would rock society. Then I grew up, I suppose.

But, of course, Isaac thinks I'm a ghostwriter. 'I was pretty good at English but never really developed a firm idea about what I wanted to do. Took my degree, same story, but I'd helped out with the student rag during my time at uni and so, when I emerged, blinking, into the harsh light of adulthood and the world of work, I got a job as a very junior reporter for a regional newspaper. In truth, I did little more than make the tea and write the obituaries, but after a while I got offered a ghostwriting job by someone I'd met while at the paper. I was under no illusions; they'd been let down at the last minute and I was available to step into the breach. No more, no less. But it became a stepping stone, as these things often do. And the rest...' I hold up my hands.

It's not the truth, but there are shades of truth within it.

'So that's why you're here.' He grins at my puzzled face. 'I don't mean here as in Eastleigh, but here as in this place, my studio. Today. You haven't got your laptop with you though, or even a pen and paper that I can see. So, I reckon you came for a bit of inspiration. I'm right, aren't I?' He tips his head to one side, weighing me up, looking for clues that his intuition has scored a hit. 'It's that little idea that's been niggling away at you for weeks, but which isn't yet straight in your head. So, you came here for a bit of peace and quiet to thrash out the details and...' He trails off. 'Fell asleep.'

I look at his crestfallen face. He so wants to be right, and it's as good a version of events as any.

'Busted,' I say, smiling.

'So did your panning reveal any gold? Are you going to come here and write your book?'

I look around the room, and then back to Isaac, the idea that he proposed floating in the space between us. I focus on the sketchbook that now lies discarded on the bench. It's the single solitary thing I've found that has revealed a glimpse into the life of this man and his work.

'Thank you,' I say. 'I'd like that.'

# CHAPTER THIRTEEN

I have thought about it in the past. As an avid reader and a writer, albeit of articles, it would be unusual if I *hadn't* thought about writing a book. But when I have, my ideas have almost always been for a non-fiction title; continuations of a particular theme that I'd dealt with in my articles, or a consumer topic that I'd really like to get my teeth into. But the thought has always been fleeting and I'd never considered it seriously. For one, I'd always been happy in what I was doing, but, more importantly, I really didn't think I had the time, the patience, or the commitment. Bottom line: I just didn't want it enough.

Yet now, even though it's a role I've sneakily put on like a fancy-dress costume, the persona of a fiction author is beginning to flirt with me. Is it something I could do? And if I did, what on earth would I write about? It's not as if I have a wellspring bubbling with ideas. But despite acknowledging it's a manufactured idea, its appeal doesn't change.

I can't explain it, even to myself, but there is something about Isaac's studio that's very soothing. As if, on entering, the weight of everything else I've been carrying in my head is simply shrugged off at the threshold. I felt unburdened, and the thought of having a space, a little sanctuary that sits just outside of reality, is very appealing. I can see myself sitting there, that's the thing. Feeling the day stretching out ahead of me, ideas flowing so fast my fingers on the keyboard can scarcely keep up with them. I don't ever feel that way about my room at the hotel. Not because I don't like it, but there's nothing there to inspire me or connect me with anything and, in comparison, it's a flat, dead space.

Which is why I'm picking my way along the allotment path this morning. Only this time I have a small rucksack on my back containing my laptop, notebook and favourite pens, a water bottle and some sandwiches, plus a banana. I want to keep it simple and I figure I don't need much else for the day. After all, the most important thing I'll need is what's inside my head. It's only when I get to the stile at the far end of the allotments that I realise there's an odd sensation in my stomach. Odd, because it's something I haven't felt for a long time, not excitement exactly, but anticipation certainly.

I know not to expect Isaac this morning, he's already told me he won't be using the studio today. He'll be out, busy with another project, but I'm still a little cautious as I descend the steps and lift the rock to check for the key. But it's still here, safe in its jam jar, so the studio must be empty. It's not exactly as it was when I left yesterday. I can see that the notebook has been returned to its home among the other books, and some more things have been added to the workbench. But the most obvious thing about the room today is that the bed has been slept in, the cover still turned down. I hadn't been expecting it, but I'm surprised by how powerfully it changes the whole room. It's now the most intimate of spaces and I'm not sure how this makes me feel.

I turn my back on it and lay my things down on the work-bench, gently relocating some of Isaac's to one side. He had made it clear before I left the day before that there was no order to any of it and that I should simply move things as I see fit, but I'm still reluctant to do so. I pull out one of the stools from under the bench and plonk myself down, realising as I do so that the bench is exactly the right height for working. I smile as I take out my laptop from my bag. It's almost as if I can hear Isaac saying, *I told you so.*

My email programme is still running as I open the lid, the message from Barbara staring at me. It arrived just as I was preparing to leave the hotel and I could have delayed my departure to answer it quite easily – why would another five minutes have mattered? But something made me snap the lid closed and ignore it. And now I have no internet, I couldn't respond even if I wanted to. Every time I get one of her emails I have an image in my mind of Barbara ticking me off a list. That may be unjustified but I can't help it. Somewhere over the last year or so our correspondence has changed, or at least that's how it feels to me. It no longer feels like two friends chatting, but instead the familiarity and sympathetic tone feels forced; I can picture the smile dropping from her face the moment she presses send or hangs up the phone.

The message simply reads *Hi lovely, how's it all going?* But it isn't the open-ended question it appears to be. Instead, it's a request for information. A report of exactly where I am with the story I've told her I'm writing, and how long before she can expect to receive it. It's a very pointed reminder of why I'm sitting here. Writing a book isn't a quick-fix answer to the problem of what happens if Barbara 'lets me go'. In fact, it might not be any kind of a fix at all, but it does at least have a glimmer about it. And just now, a glimmer is all I have. Aside from Isaac's story of course.

My eyes are drawn to the sea below, a line of silver against the sky. Once the sun moves westward as the day wears on the water will change in colour from silver through palest blue and azure to the deep mauve-violet of evening and, if clouds hide the silvering moon, the deepest black of night. Just like the page in Isaac's sketchbook.

I close down my email programme and reopen the document I've been working on, the one that tells Isaac's story. It's just a collection of notes really; observations, things I might ask him should the occasion arise. From what the assistant at the art gallery said, Isaac hasn't lived in Eastleigh that long, so I wonder whether he drew those same sand pictures where he lived before. If there was a beach, of course. But it explains why people aren't aware of what he does; that and the fact that Isaac doesn't want to tell them.

I sit back, thinking. My left hand is idly playing with a pebble I picked up from the bench, my fingers turning the smooth stone over and over. I hadn't even realised I was doing it, but now the movement catches all my attention. It's not the stone itself, but more that all the while I've been thinking about Isaac, I'd been holding one of the objects he collected from the beach, finding some sort of comfort from it. And I'm suddenly very aware of where I'm sitting. In his studio, taking full advantage of his kindness and hospitality, lapping up the chance to work somewhere so quiet and peaceful. A rush of heat hits my face and I push the notebook away from me. I can't think about this here; collecting together notes on a story he knows nothing about. What kind of monster does this make me?

I swallow and sit myself straighter on the stool, clearing my throat and giving a small cough, drawing a line under my thoughts. *A line in the sand…* My laptop screen has gone dark and I wake it, quickly starting a new document and writing those same words as a heading. And it's there that my thought processes end, but it's a start, something to work with at least.

Many years ago I thought about writing a book. I'd even gone so far as to make a few notes about it and, although I can scarcely remember what it was to be about, there's something about that title that has struck a chord. It takes me several minutes to find it; a file I'd tucked away in an obscure folder, loath to get rid of, and a little flicker of excitement dances in the pit of my stomach as I click to open it. Except that when I read what's written there, I'm so disappointed I could cry.

The page is filled with random sentences that without any context mean absolutely nothing to me. At the time I presumably hadn't felt the need to add in any more detail because the ideas had been fresh in my head and I hadn't expected it to be so long before I looked at them again. But now, years later, these words are not enough to jog my memory.

A loud creak from behind me interrupts my thoughts, but it's only when another sounds a second later that I realise what they mean. Someone is coming down the wooden steps to the studio, and it can only be one person. Moments later Isaac hoves into view.

He looks dreadful. His hair is loose, but whereas before it looked clean and sleek, this morning it hangs in clumps, clearly not yet brushed. His normally healthy complexion appears sallow, his eyes sunken beneath puffy skin which is pale and drawn. And he seems to be walking awkwardly too. He raises a hand in greeting as he enters the studio but his smile is thin, barely there.

'Morning,' he says. 'I hoped to find you'd taken me up on my offer, but don't worry, I'm not stopping long. I won't disturb you.' He moves to the bed and immediately straightens the cover, plumping the pillows ineffectually. It's an instant reminder that it's me who is invading his space, and not the other way around.

'Nothing to disturb,' I reply, lightly. 'I haven't really got going yet. Still struggling for inspiration.'

A flash of pain crosses his face as he stands upright. 'This place usually works its magic. Just give it time.' He looks back at the bed. 'I had a bit of a late one last night, and by the time I realised just how late it was, I couldn't face going home. Staying here was fine except that I wasn't exactly prepared.' He pushes a hand up through his hair. 'My apologies.'

I don't know what to say. He certainly doesn't need to apologise to me. 'Didn't you sleep well?' I ask. 'You look as if you've hurt your back.'

Isaac's eyes flash to mine and for a second I see a glimmer of panic. He doesn't want to talk to me about this. But then he gives a tight smile.

'Age,' he replies. 'And an old war wound... Not literally of course, I'm not that old, just...' He breaks off. 'So anyway, I popped out first thing for a spot of breakfast and a very large mug of coffee and now I'm just about ready to face the day.' He shrugs his bag from his back. 'And I brought these for you.' He flips the bag around and opens it up, pulling out two packages wrapped in brown paper. 'Green beans and tomatoes, I'm not sure if you like them.'

'Oh...' I have no idea what to say. It's such a kind thought. And one I really don't deserve.

'Yes, I love them, thank you. I can't remember the last time I had beans...' I grind to a halt, thinking. 'Probably this time last year actually.' It would have been last summer; I used to buy them from my local farm shop. But I've left that far behind me now.

I feel the warmth of his hand against mine for a moment as I take them from him, wondering where to put them. I settle for the bench in the end, squishing them into the space beside my laptop. When I turn back around Isaac has fished a hairband from somewhere and is doing his best to tie back his hair.

'I'll let you get on,' he says. 'I just need to pick up a couple of things first.'

Again, it's almost as if he feels that he's the one who is invading my space.

'You're not interrupting me, Isaac, so don't feel you need to go. I haven't been here long myself and there's only one problem with deciding to write a book, which is that I have absolutely no idea what to write about. Some vague impressions, that's all.'

He doesn't quite meet my eye. 'Sometimes that's all you need. An idea of where something wants to go can be enough to build on. And on that note, I had better get going.'

He fishes out a key from his pocket and unlocks the cupboard at the rear of the room. His body blocks most of the view, but not before I have an impression of paper, lots of sheets crumpled and crammed inside threatening to spill into the room. He takes something down from a shelf and closes the door. It's a bag containing grey powder.

'I'll probably be out for most of the day,' he says, checking his watch. 'But stay here for as little or as long as you want. Just put the key back when you're done.'

There's something about his action that catches my attention. 'Are you going to Elliot's Cove?' I ask.

He nods. 'Just need to catch the tide. Why, did you want to come?'

I shouldn't, not really, but those questions I have about Isaac aren't going to answer themselves. 'I'm just wondering if some fresh air might be a good idea,' I reply. 'I'm going around in circles a little here. But I don't want to be in your way, whatever you're doing.'

'It's a big beach,' he says. 'I'm sure there's room for both of us.' His hand passes across the top of his head, smoothing his hair. 'Although…' He gives me another smile. 'I'm feeling distinctly under par this morning and was thinking a day's solitude might be best for everyone concerned. But on second thoughts, perhaps that isn't such a good idea, after all. I'm not drawing another sand circle today, but I am doing something else you could lend a hand with. If you wanted to, that is. It isn't particularly strenuous, more painstaking repetition – which might be another word for boring.' He squints up at me through his lashes.

'Well, now I'm intrigued,' I say. 'Will we be coming back here? Or shall I bring my things with me?'

'Bring them, just in case.' He breaks into a sudden smile. 'You never know, you might get bitten by the bug…'

I give him a quizzical look, but he just taps the side of his nose. 'Come on then, look sharp or we'll get caught on the rocks.'

We're mostly silent on the way. The path back up to the allotments is steep in places and Isaac sets a fast pace. It's all I can do to keep up with him, let alone hold a conversation. After that, there doesn't seem much more to say as we navigate our way down the road into the town. But that's okay, it's not an altogether uncomfortable silence. More anticipatory...

Once we reach the beach, however, the reason for it becomes clear. Isaac visibly relaxes and I realise how at home he is here. Even though there are plenty of people around, I can sense his breathing become deeper and his stride become looser and slower. It's as if the very air has a calming effect on him. Already he looks better; more alive, with a rosier colour to his cheeks. We've hardly gone any distance at all before he stoops to pick something up. It's a small pearly-white shell. He turns it in his fingers for a moment before walking on.

'Are you still collecting these?' I ask, eyes on the sand.

He grins. 'Yep.'

There's such amusement in his voice that I stop and look across at him.

'What?'

'Nothing... just that collecting shells is an ongoing project,' he replies. 'I need quite a few.'

'Are you going to tell me what for?'

'I might do, in a bit.' He pushes his hands into the small of his back and sighs. 'Can we walk?' he says. 'I'm better if I keep moving.'

I nod and fall into step beside him.

We've covered nearly half the distance to the rocks before he speaks again.

'So, what are the vague impressions you have of your book?' he asks. 'Are we talking plotlines or more the general tone?'

'A little of both,' I say, knowing I'm evading the question. I don't really want to talk about something I know little about, Isaac is bound to notice. 'Did you know that Francis wants to write a book?' I add. Classic diversionary tactic; follow a question with one of your own.

'Francis has been wanting to write a book ever since I've known him,' replies Isaac, a smile twitching up the corners of his mouth.

'That sounds like it might have been a long time,' I comment.

'No, less than a year actually.'

'Oh, I thought… I don't know why really, but I got the impression that you'd lived here for years. You seem to know the place so well. And people know you too; everyone does.'

'Along the beachfront, perhaps. But I'm a near constant presence so that's hardly surprising. But no, I moved here after my marriage broke down actually. Some things needed to change, and I was one of them.'

Isaac isn't looking at me, and I'm surprised by his candour. Surprised and a little embarrassed. Would I ever have the courage to admit something like that to myself, let alone to a virtual stranger?

'I'm better on my own,' he adds, bending to pick up another shell. No wince this time, I notice. 'But who knows just how long Francis has been harbouring his secret desire. Years probably.'

'Starting to write is the hardest thing,' I say. 'Knowing that there are tens of thousands of words ahead of you and every page is blank. It's daunting, even when you've been writing for years.'

Isaac considers my response. 'I think part of the problem is that Francis is already living the dream. Not many people achieve it, but he has his life exactly where he wants it and he thinks that writing will change all that. He's scared. But once he loses the fear, he'll be able to make a start; he'll realise that change doesn't have to be bad, in fact, I'd argue that it's always a good thing, then he'll understand why he wants to write. And what he'll gain from doing so.'

*Change is always a good thing…* It's a good job Isaac is focused on the beach ahead and not on me as my footsteps slow to a halt. He turns to see why I'm suddenly no longer beside him.

'Are you okay?' he asks.

I frown slightly, squinting into the sun as I look at him. 'Yes, but I was just thinking about what you said about change. And I don't think I can agree that it's always a good thing, not when many a time it arrives unbidden. Unannounced and unwelcome.'

Isaac's smile is warm. 'I know,' he says simply. 'She's a fickle thing. Like fortune; changes with the wind. And even when you think she's good, she can turn on you and sour in the blink of an eye. But... Even though change brings good and bad with it, if you consider that your life is a journey and that you can't learn anything new from a static situation, then change of any sort has its merits.' He raises his eyebrows a little, softening what might otherwise be pompous, and smiles a touch sheepishly. 'Although I admit, it doesn't always feel that way.'

He waits while I catch him up but, although I smile, I don't say another word until we finally reach the rocks. I can't. I wouldn't know where to begin.

Isaac still hasn't said anything about what we're going to do and, even as we clamber down onto Elliot's beach to walk along the sand, my questions remain unanswered. But there's a definite lightness to his step.

Once we reach the tideline, he takes his bag from his back and, opening it, removes another bag, made of soft cloth tied with a drawstring. I can already guess what it contains and, sure enough, it makes a rewarding crunching noise as he pulls on the strings. I hold out my hand automatically and relinquish the handful of shells that I've collected as we walked. Isaac digs deep into his pocket, emptying it out to do the same. Then he picks up his backpack with a grin.

'If you could just stay here a moment,' he says. 'I won't be long.'

I eye the huge expanse of beach which, apart from a couple of walkers, is empty. 'Why? Where are you going? Isaac, you haven't even told me what it is you want my help with.'

'All will be revealed,' he replies. 'Quite literally. But if you want the full *tah-dah* experience, I should turn and face the other way if I were you.' He points to the far side of the beach. 'That way you won't even see where I'm going.'

From the expression on his face I can see that this is exactly what Isaac wants me to do, and for some reason it's important to him that I comply. No more than three minutes can have passed before I hear him again, his approach signalled by the soft sludgy noise his feet make in the sand. But I almost wish he had taken longer. It feels so good to be standing here, in the wild open space, letting the wind take my hair where it will.

His enquiry, when it comes, is gentle. 'Are you ready?' he asks.

He leads the way back over to the rock face, but this time much further inland than the little alcove where he stores the rakes he uses to draw with. In fact, the sand here is much deeper, and tufted with marram grass. He pauses as we reach a small outcrop of the cliff face.

'You're not claustrophobic, are you?' he asks.

'No… but if you're going to make me squeeze into some teeny-tiny hole and crawl into the bowels of the earth then you can think again. I get hot just thinking about it.'

'No, there's plenty of space, just no windows.' He grins.

It's suddenly become very obvious that I'm about to be led inside a cave, and I can't help but wonder if this isn't the most stupid thing I've ever done. I barely know Isaac.

He skirts the outcrop and, straight away, I see a darker space; a hole in the rock, like a doorway. It's a little taller than I am, and only as wide; anyone larger would struggle to pass. But, just as I realise that the cave would be completely hidden from the vast majority of the beach, I also become aware that there's a soft glow coming from inside.

I give Isaac a quizzical look but he just nods and smiles, walking on further. I have no choice but to follow him, my curiosity getting the better of my sensibility.

The flickering glow brightens a little and, once I'm inside and my eyes have adjusted to the gloom, I can see a short passage in front of me, only about five foot in length. It smells of salt, a cold tang in the air that feels centuries old. The passage turns to one side and, as I reach the end, I'm suddenly aware of a sense of space opening around me. A cavern stretches dome-like above my head, extending outward on all sides, and I see immediately where the light is coming from.

On the floor are six hurricane lamps, their golden glow dancing and reflecting off…

I peer closer, move forward, my mouth open in wonder.

On one side, patterns swirl and coalesce across the cave wall, gleaming milky white in places and darker in others from the million tiny shells that stare back at me.

One hand goes to my mouth and the other reaches out to touch, oh so gently, the surface closest to me. But it's real, I'm not dreaming.

And I've never seen anything quite so incredible.

A shell grotto.

# CHAPTER FOURTEEN

I'm still trying to process what I'm looking at when I spy something else lying on the floor. Just to the side of a hurricane lamp is a tray onto which handfuls of shells have been scattered. Beside that is a cloth tote bag, bulging at the bottom, and I know that inside are what could be thousands more shells. And it's suddenly very clear what Isaac has been doing.

'You made this?' I ask, looking around me in wonder. 'It's incredible, I can't believe it's here.'

'No. Not me. But that was my first thought too,' replies Isaac. 'I couldn't conceive that it was here, or understand why it had been done in the first place. I just knew it was the most wonderful thing I'd ever seen, and knowing that no one else knew about it made it all the more special.'

I'm confused. 'So you found it? Is that what you're saying?'

Isaac nods. 'A little over six months ago. At about the same time I started the sand drawings. As you know, I store the tools in another cave, much smaller than this, but it made me suspect that if there was one cave here, then there could be several. I have no idea what made me think of doing it, but one day I just decided to start looking.' He pauses and slides me a sideways glance. 'Humour me, but I like to think that maybe it was Elliot's guiding hand.'

My eyes have been following a particularly intricate pattern which extends up one wall and right across the ceiling, but I stop to stare at him. *Guiding hand…*

'Or you got lucky,' I suggest. 'But you're saying this is Elliot's cave. How on earth do you know that?'

'I don't. But it seems the most logical explanation. Once I'd got over the shock of finding it, I examined the way the thing had been put together. I'm not an expert but I don't think this grotto has been here all that long. Decorating with shells was popular in Victorian times, but if that were the case then surely people would know this was here. It would be a tourist attraction, or preserved or... something. Not abandoned and forgotten. No, I don't think anyone knew about this in the first place, only the person who made it, and I think that person was Elliot. He's the only one who had any real connection with this beach and, by all accounts, he was quite a quirky individual. I think you'd need to be to even contemplate starting something like this. As for why he did it, that's possibly easier to answer.'

'Go on...'

'Have you ever been for a walk and collected something to bring home? I don't know, a shiny conker, a cluster of acorns, a feather?'

'Yes, all the time.' I smile at the memory. 'My husband could never understand it. He used to say it was only for people who like to hoard stuff and clutter their houses with junk and—' I break off, surprised by my sudden reference to William. 'Why though, what's that got to do with anything?'

'Well, like you, it's something I've always done too. Lots of people do it. But did you ever stop to think why?'

I meet his smile. 'Go on then, tell me.'

'Because these things are a reminder. On the ground, in a wood, or on the beach or street, these treasures belong to everyone, and you have the memory of them, you feel the pleasure of having seen them, but only for a moment. Take them home, however, and they become yours alone, for as long as you want them. They're a small pleasure that you can experience day after day and, in the sometimes harsh reality of our everyday lives, they provide solace and the memory of what beautiful is.'

Isaac's eyes stay on mine for just a second or two longer than is comfortable and I look away, ambushed by the memory of William's pink linen shirt; the one I'd kept, that hadn't been washed. It was soft and smelled of his cologne, mingled with everything that was him. It was the only way I could bring him back, if just for a few seconds. But the scent has all but gone now, and I wish with all my heart that I had a more tangible reminder of him.

I turn a slow circle, looking around me but also buying time until I can speak again. 'It's a nice way to think of it,' I say, turning back. 'And I guess it does make sense for Elliot to have wanted to keep this place secret. But you don't know that was his reason.'

'No, I don't,' replies Isaac. 'But it's the reason why I'm finishing it.'

Even in the dim light I can see the pain etched across his face. The dark shadow in his eyes.

'Sometimes, when you have nothing, you have to look for the smallest things to give you hope. One tiny thing, but it's a start. It lets you know that such a thing still exists. And if you put all those same tiny things together then, bit by bit, the empty void you started with becomes filled.' His voice is soft and yet it reverberates around the space so that his words seem to linger in the air for much longer than usual.

'Something out of nothing…' I murmur.

A friend said that to me once, in the bleakest months following William's death. And I had thought it such a stupid thing to say. But perhaps she was right… She told me that no one else can fill a void for you, and if they do then you may find it filled with entirely the wrong things, things you might not want there at all. The only way is to own it and fill it yourself.

I look at the detail on the wall, each shell hardly any bigger than a thumbnail. On their own they could be overlooked, perhaps even crushed underfoot, but together they have achieved something far bigger and far more beautiful than one shell could ever do by itself. Each one is a tiny drop of hope for the future. A permanent reminder that such things exist and endure, long into the future. If only you recognise their potential.

Isaac is looking at the ground, perhaps regretting bringing me here at all. Or that he shared something so personal, something that requires him to place a huge trust in me. I move to stand in front of the nearest wall and lay my fingers lightly on the shells, tracing a pearlescent swirl.

'So how do we do this?' I ask.

It's actually incredibly simple. The bag of grey powder Isaac brought with him turns out to be cement and, seeing as there are ready quantities of both sand and water on the beach, it doesn't take long to produce mortar, the recipe for which Isaac has perfected by trial and error. Beyond that, all that's required is a pointing tool to lay the mortar against the rock wall a small section at a time. The shells are then simply pressed into it. There are no rules, says Isaac, just let the pattern, shape and colours flow as you see fit.

He shows me where Elliot finished and where he began, and it's virtually impossible to distinguish one from the other. The only difference is a slight lightening of the mortar in the areas that Isaac has worked. But it's an incredibly slow process. Elliot had completed nearly one side of the circular room and a little way up onto the ceiling, but it's impossible to say how long it took him. Where Isaac picked up has increased the finished area by a couple of metres or so, but that has taken him months – not working every day, but usually a couple of days at a time. And in between has been the constant search for more shells. Collecting them has become a way of life. Even so, it's like a jigsaw puzzle that someone else has started; almost impossible to resist the urge to find another piece, and Isaac's excitement is infectious, just like it was on the day he drew the sand picture. Once he's shown me how to apply the mortar and to what depth to press the shells to make sure they stick firm, I'm off and running like a thing possessed.

It's only after we've been working for several hours that the feeling creeps over me. Portent; it's the only word I can think of to describe it. That sense that something is about to happen, or has happened, but I haven't yet worked out what. But I know where it grew from.

To start with I'd been concentrating so hard on getting everything right that I hadn't really been thinking about anything much, too gripped by the task itself. But, as it became more familiar, the opportunity I had to think about other things expanded. And the more I think, the more I acknowledge that, aside from Isaac, there isn't anyone else who knows about this cave and the awe it contains. Apart from the degree of trust this places on me, it also bestows huge privilege and it's a heady brew to consume.

And then something else hits me: because I'm standing here, a tray of shells in my hand, carefully selecting and pressing each into the mortar, and I *can* see transformation before my eyes. I *can* see a void being filled, the creation of something from nothing, and there's no getting away from that fact. So now I'm also thinking about Elliot, who as far as we know was the person who started this. And I want to know why. This man, about who little was known, lived a solitary but no less extraordinary life, and I suddenly realise that I want to tell his story.

My sharp intake of breath at this thought is loud enough to cause Isaac to look up, an expression of concern crossing his face.

'Are you okay?'

I almost laugh out loud. A surge of hope has bloomed inside me and it's in such contrast to the way I have been feeling of late that I almost don't recognise it. It seems such an alien emotion.

'Yes, I'm fine. I just had a thought, that's all.'

Isaac raises his eyebrows. 'Blimey, shall I inform the nation's press?' He grins at me. 'Sorry…'

But I smile back, sharing the enjoyment of his teasing comment. 'It's just that I've been thinking about Elliot or, more specifically, thinking about what made him start creating this grotto when it seemed unlikely that anyone was ever going to see it. And it's just struck me that his story would make a perfect plot for my book. I mean, it wouldn't be his story, it couldn't be, because we don't know exactly what that is, but it could be one interpretation of his life and how he came to live it the way he did. But sympathetic, almost a tribute to the memory of him.'

Isaac is silent for a moment, and at first I think he hates the idea, but then a slow smile turns up the corners of his mouth. 'I think that's brilliant,' he says, nodding as he warms to the theme. 'Yes… yes, definitely. It seems so fitting in a way, that he shouldn't be forgotten. And that the very thing which sparked the story would be something he had left behind as his legacy.'

Even in the dim light I can see his eyes are sparkling and it makes me rather uncomfortable. I'd started this day thinking of how I might find out more about Isaac, but by stealthy means, not through honesty, and his generosity of spirit is in such stark contrast that a wave of shame washes over me. But I can't let Isaac's words go.

'You know, when we were talking earlier about why Elliot might have decided to create this grotto, you spoke about how it could have been to provide solace, as a moment of beauty in an otherwise harsh world…' I falter slightly when I see a guarded expression cross Isaac's face. 'You said that, although you couldn't be sure that was *Elliot's* motivation, it was certainly yours. What did you mean?'

As soon as the words leave my mouth, I want to snatch them back. It's as if the light that Isaac carries is visibly draining out of him.

'The world *is* harsh, Louisa,' he says. 'Or hadn't you noticed?'

His reply hangs in the air between us, thick with the salty tang of the sea. Or perhaps it's the threat of guilt-laden tears.

'It's none of my business,' I stammer. 'I'm sorry, I should never have asked.'

But Isaac is quick to make amends. 'No, *I'm* sorry, that was uncalled for.' He holds his hands up helplessly as he looks around the space. 'This place… It's very special, anyone can see that. But if I hadn't wanted you to comment on what I said, then I should never have said it in the first place. I thought maybe you would understand.'

'I do understand. Why wouldn't I?' I close my eyes briefly as I feel the conversation slipping ever further away from me. *Why are you being so defensive, Louisa?*

Isaac hangs his head. 'No reason. I shouldn't have said anything, anything at all. Just forget it.' He looks away, sighing, but then he checks himself. 'I just thought… Stupid, I suppose, but I thought bringing you here, having you see this would help. You wear such an air of sadness about you, Louisa.'

I stare at him. Do I? Even now I want to argue, except that, deep down, I know that he's right. I can see it sometimes when I catch sight of myself in a mirror, unexpectedly, and I hardly recognise the woman who looks back at me.

Isaac holds out a hand, not for me to take, but as if to steady something. 'You'd have every right to, but Louisa, please don't run off on me again. You're a writer and words are your thing, how you express yourself, but for me… I don't always explain myself very well, but I just know how special this place is for me, and I shared it with you only because I thought it might bring you some of the things it's brought me. I'm sorry if I've offended you.'

He holds my look for a moment, a beseeching expression on his face.

I can only smile in reply. 'Actually, that was very eloquent,' I say. 'And I know you've put huge faith in me by bringing me here when you didn't have to. So, apart from anything else, you have my word that I won't go blabbing about it to anyone. You're right, it is a very special place, I'd have to be made of stone not to feel it.' I touch a finger to a particularly pretty shell, a delicate pearly pink. 'And, on the basis that, quite unexpectedly, today has been a lovelier one than I've had in a long while, plus the fact that I just might have found the most perfect inspiration for my novel, how about we draw a line underneath things and carry on? What do you say?'

'That I'd be an even bigger fool not to,' he replies, softly, taking a slow breath in. 'So, come on then, tell me what you're thinking for your book. Would you tell the story from Elliot's point of view? Or would he be a mysterious stranger who comes to someone's rescue?'

And so, as it turns out, I'm doubly grateful to Elliot, not only for this amazing space but for also getting us safely past a very awkward spot. And once the conversation starts, it doesn't stop for at least another hour until we break for a bite to eat. I share my sandwiches while Isaac unpacks some slices of quiche and a flask of tea. We carry on afterwards, but in the end it's the light that determines the end of the day.

I hadn't really noticed the cave was getting progressively dimmer until I become aware of the light flickering. The candles in the storm lanterns have burned down and we reluctantly concede that it's time to pack up.

'Besides, I try to make it a rule to work only for the duration of one candle at a time,' says Isaac. 'There's something about doing this that gets inside you, but I don't think it's healthy to keep at it for too long. It can be a bit disorientating, as I've found to my cost,' he explains. 'Plus, look…' He nudges the cloth bag full of shells with his foot, its volume considerably reduced.

'You always think there's enough to finish the whole cave, but sadly…' He breaks off to indicate the area we've been working on. 'We've used hundreds of shells today as it is. Time to restock before we have another go.' He checks his watch. 'And it's time to leave in any case.'

I stand back to admire our handiwork. Up close, it's hard to see the individual patterns and nuances of colour but, from further away, it's all revealed in its glory. And it truly is glorious. It's also very hard to see where we originally started this morning, but, guessing correctly what I'm searching for, Isaac taps a milky spiral of shells to my right.

'Before I start afresh, I always fix in my head the place where I last finished. Otherwise it's almost impossible to tell. And measurably seeing what's been achieved really helps, otherwise it doesn't look like you've made any headway at all. Even when you can see it, it's a pitifully small area considering the length of time it takes.'

'Perhaps,' I say. 'But then progress isn't always measured in linear form.'

Isaac's smile is warm. 'Yes,' he replies. 'I think you're right.'

He takes my arm as we leave the cave, just for a second, to slow my passage. I don't think he meant to, it's instinctive.

'Wait a moment,' he advises. 'Just let your eyes acclimatise for a minute. It's very bright here on the beach and the shock of emerging out into bright sunshine and a large expanse of space can be pretty powerful.'

I wobble, even as I recognise the truth in his words, my hand flailing for stability as a wave of dizziness passes over me. I find it in his fingers, in the palm of his hand which lies open beneath mine, resting softly against it. For just a minute. And then I laugh as I pull it away, wiping my finger underneath my eye, which waters from the sudden exposure to the light. I peer at my hands, feeling the gritty deposits on my skin.

Isaac laughs too. 'Yes, that's another thing; you never realise quite how filthy you get either. Come on, I'll walk you back to the rocks.'

I turn back to him. 'Oh, are you not coming?'

There's an odd expression on his face. Not sadness exactly, more… But I can't put my finger on it. 'No. Early evening is lovely here. The tide is just about to turn again, but I think I might wait for the next one.'

*

I don't remember much of the walk back to the hotel. My head is a confused jumble of thoughts: disappointment that I'm walking back alone, shame that I could ever have seen today as an opportunity to prise information from Isaac for my own ends, but mostly the recognition of what today has brought me. And I'm not entirely sure how to deal with any of those things.

I'm almost at the hotel now and I fumble in my bag for the keys to the back door. My hand touches my notebook and I remember the words I'd written there, and why. But my perspective has shifted so far that they now seem meaningless, my idea that I could write about Isaac ridiculous. I need to speak to Barbara. And soon.

It's cool inside the kitchen and I'm glad of it after the heat of the beach. I'm longing for some calm and quiet to unscramble the turmoil of thoughts in my head. I close the door softly behind me and lean against it for a moment, before crossing to the sink and filling a glass with water, drinking almost immediately.

I've almost finished when the door from the inner hallway explodes open and Leah strides through, letting it bang shut behind her. Seconds later Robin follows suit.

'For God's sake, Leah, will you just stand still and talk to me,' he shouts. 'You can't run away from this one, so don't you bloody dare!'

His mouth hangs open as they both catch sight of me. Leah stares at me, stricken, while Robin throws his hands up and then bangs his fist down hard against the edge of the table in the centre of the room. He seems more enraged than ever.

'And I bet you bloody know as well, don't you?' he sneers. 'Of course you do... Mother and daughter, plotting and planning between them.'

I look between the two of them, hand hovering against my chest. 'I'm sorry, Robin, I don't know what you're talking about. What on earth is it I'm planning?'

I look sharply at Leah who reaches out towards me just a fraction too late as Robin takes a step closer.

'Oh, don't come the innocent, Louisa. Of course you bloody know about the abortion.'

# CHAPTER FIFTEEN

His words travel through the room like a pressure wave, robbing me of my very breath. I couldn't have spoken if I'd tried. Now there's nothing but a void between us, as if the very air has been removed, leaving a vacuum that wants to suck everything else inside.

I look at Leah, an agonising, searching look that I fling at her, begging for some sign that Robin has got it wrong. But she dodges it, staring instead at Robin, red-faced and furious. Is she angry at him because he disagrees with her? Or because he's let the cat out of the bag by telling me? I can't be certain but, when he looks at me, I can see that he's already made up his mind which side I'm on.

A sob from Leah breaks the silence, a pitiful, heartbreaking sound that makes me want to scoop her up as I did when she was a small child, telling her that everything was going to be okay. Except that I can't, because I can't make those kinds of promises now we're adults.

'Leah?' I just want her to say something. Anything. But she doesn't. 'Oh God, please tell me you haven't…'

She turns her head away, her lips trembling, but before she can speak Robin growls, a low guttural noise of sheer frustration.

'Oh… So, you obviously knew about the baby then.' His eyes flash between us, first one way and then the other. 'When did she tell you? A month ago? Two weeks? Or when you moved in? And for chrissakes, why am *I* the last one to know? I'm the bloody father and yet I seem to have no say in this, no say in anything.

You're all the same, you women; like a secret sect, all huddling together, sharing your secrets, keeping the menfolk—'

'Robin!' My voice is sharper than I had imagined. 'Whatever else is going on here, I can assure you that whatever I know about the pregnancy, it didn't come from Leah.' I drop my head. 'I only found the pregnancy test yesterday, purely by accident, but I'm her mother, Robin, and I could see as soon as I arrived that something wasn't quite right. In fact, so did you, if you think about it, but you just attributed it to something else.'

Leah is watching me like a hawk, her jaw clenched in anger. I soften my expression, speaking to her. 'And when you've had a child, you know the signs. So your going off coffee, finding that certain foods tasted weird; that's just how it was for me when I was pregnant with you.'

'Stop it,' yells Leah. 'I don't want to hear how it was for you. All your sweet tales of my childhood and a perfect pregnancy to boot. I am not you. And this is my life, not yours.'

The force of her words, her rejection of me as a mother, burrows inside, piercing the most tender parts of my heart. I have to dig very deep to keep my voice calm.

'Leah, no one is disputing that. And when have I ever told you how to live your life? I've never done so before and I'm certainly not about to start now. But you can't keep things like this to yourself, you know that. Please… However upset you are, however you're feeling, you need to talk about it.' I inhale a deep breath. 'Please, Leah, talk to us. Come and sit down.'

She wavers for just a moment, and I can see she's torn. Not knowing whether to run or stay but, inadvertently, I've found myself caught in the middle of their 'discussion' and, from where she's standing, it's two against one. And those are never good odds. Her whole body is trembling.

'Leah, at least tell me what we're dealing with here, sweetheart. Please, I want to help you.' I pause, thinking carefully about what words to use. I can't bring myself to say some of them. 'Are you even... Are you still pregnant?'

'Yes, I am,' fires back Leah, her voice no less calm than before. 'More's the pity. I should have just taken care of it on my own, and no one would be any the wiser.'

Robin visibly crumples beside me and my heart goes out to him. 'Leah, you don't mean that... Love, think about what you're saying, please...'

I risk a glance at him, and his eyes are full of tears. I should go, I shouldn't be here, caught in the middle of their marriage, but I can't, not with things as they are.

'Leah, a baby isn't just something that you can take a decision on by yourself, however much you might want to, or even think you have a right to. If your circumstances were different, then perhaps, but you're in a committed and loving relationship. You need to make this decision together.'

'But we're never going to agree, Mum. Robin wants this baby and I don't, and no amount of talking *calmly* is going to change that.'

It isn't so much what she says but the way she says it that brings forth a surge of anger. The snide way she says *calmly* as if this is at the root of all their problems.

'So why don't you want it then?' I counter. 'You know, for most people, having a baby is cause for celebration. What's so different for you?'

She rolls her eyes and gives me the look that she perfected so well in her teens. 'For God's sake, Mum, look around you. I should have thought it was obvious.' She throws her hands up in the air. 'We're up to our necks in things here. We've got so much work still to do, work I can't do if I'm the size of a house. And we need to get finished here as soon as possible. Every day we're not open is a day when more money drains out of our bank account. We can't possibly afford to have a child now, not on top of everything else, and that's apart from the absolute chaos a baby would bring. Suppose we did manage to get this place ready by some miracle. How can we run a new business with a baby in tow? I can't physically look after it and run this place at the same time. It's just not possible. And that's without the sleepless nights, for us and, more importantly, our guests, listening to a baby wailing at all hours.'

'Leah,' I say quietly. 'You might not be able to look after a baby all the time, but I could. Think about it. You wouldn't be the first mother who needed childcare, and it could be so easy here. You wouldn't need to put the baby in a nursery miles away from you and you wouldn't be doing this on your own either. We'd all be here, helping.'

'Mum, you don't even live here.'

My breath catches in my throat, astonished that she could say such a thing. My voice is stiff. 'Well, thank you for that reminder. And as you're very well aware, my intention has always been to find a place of my own as soon as work picks up again and I'm a bit more settled. I do apologise if I'm in the way, but, regardless, I am here for now. And while I admit I haven't yet given much thought to where I am going to live, I have at least considered that it should be somewhere reasonably close to you. Given the current situation that would seem to make more sense than ever, but if that isn't what you want, perhaps you need to make that clear, so we all know where we stand.'

'Louisa, she didn't mean it like that,' pleads Robin, and I can see that he at least is open to the possibility of my helping out. Perhaps even grateful for it.

'All I'm saying is that I know how incredibly scary the thought of having a child is, but much more so if you think you're going to be doing it on your own. Please don't think like that, Leah, it doesn't have to be that way.'

She has the grace to look a little sheepish, but it still doesn't alter her defensive stance, or the slightly defiant jut of her chin.

But this has always been her way. And, despite how angry she makes me, I also know that underneath the sometimes hard exterior, she can be very soft indeed. It isn't that she doesn't care, but rather it's a self-defence mechanism, a shield that she puts up to stop herself from getting hurt. It's just as I feared.

'Nobody's saying that it would be easy,' says Robin, gently. 'But the best things in life often demand the best of you too. And I know you, Leah, you'd be an amazing mum.'

I don't know whether the two of them have discussed having children before, but I'm guessing that they must have. And while it may not have been a recent topic of conversation, I can see that now, faced with the reality of a baby, there's nothing Robin would like more. There is a vulnerability about him that's almost painful to witness.

Leah pauses while she digests what Robin has said, her expression relaxing a little. I know she will have thought endlessly about what kind of a mother she'd be, inevitably looking to me for comparison, and I feel my own inadequacies keenly.

'Give yourself time, Leah,' I add. 'Time to get used to the idea. Time to work out the practicalities and—'

'Time to get close to it.' She glares at me. 'I haven't got time, Mum. I might have, one day, but not right now. Not when we've worked so hard for all of this. No, it was a mistake and that's all there is to it.'

Robin lets out a gasp. 'Jesus, Leah… How can something born out of love be a mistake? You should listen to yourself sometimes.'

She flinches at his words, tears threatening now. Because this isn't just about the baby, it's about her and Robin, their life together.

'I don't mean us. Us having a baby, that's not a mistake, Robin, I don't mean that. But just now… I can't do this…' She breaks off, unable to continue.

'But everything else is fixable, Leah. I know it doesn't seem that way, but it is. And we've always said that we wanted this move

to be about finding a way of life that was different from what
we had before. Our own business, but also something that is an
extension of the way we live our lives. And this could be such a
wonderful place to raise a family.'

'I know…' The tears are flowing now. 'But what if I can't…
what if I can't love it, Robin?'

'Oh, sweetheart… you would.' His arms are outstretched as
he walks towards her, looking to enfold her in his arms. 'What
on earth makes you think that you wouldn't?'

She lets herself be comforted, but there's still tension in her
arms and, even though her head is resting against Robin's shoulder,
she flicks a glance up at me, one I wasn't meant to see. And it
makes me very nervous.

'I'm scared I don't know how, because every time I… Every
time I tried to…'

Robin pulls back to gaze at her, to stroke her hair away from
her face. 'Love, that's not making any sense.' He looks to me, a
helpless expression on his face. 'Every time what?'

And again I see it, the tiny flicker of a glance in my direction;
not even that, the merest movement of her eye. But it's there.

'Every time I tried to love, I got turned away.'

I swallow. 'Leah…?'

She buries her head in Robin's chest, turning it the other way
as her sobs come in earnest, shaking her slender frame. He looks
at me again, over the top of her head, thinking about her words,
sensing her pulling away; not from him, but from me.

'Shh, now, it's okay,' he murmurs, frowning. 'Come on,
sweetheart, tell me, I don't know what you mean. Got turned
away from who, love?'

And with a violent twist Leah snaps back towards me, her
tear-stained face pale and blotchy.

'Turned away from Dad,' she cries. 'He virtually ignored me
as a child, and I did everything I could to be the way he wanted

me to be. But you and Dad were too busy having the grand love affair to notice when your child needed anything. You put him above me every time, Mum, have you any idea how that felt? How I *still* feel, thinking that it was my fault he was that way with me, because no one could ever say a bad word against him. They couldn't then, and they certainly can't now he's dead.'

I take a step backwards as if I've been struck. 'Well now you're just being silly,' I retort.

'No, Mum. No, I'm not. He loved that you put him on a pedestal and that was bad enough when he was alive, but now that he's dead, God, it's even worse. He's not a bloody saint! But he was still my dad and I still loved him even though there were times when I thought I hated him. I even thought I was glad he was dead, because then at least I'd get you back, but how could I possibly say any of this when there was never room for anyone else's grief but yours? You would never understand. He even took *you* away from me.'

'And what are *you* doing now if you take away this baby, Leah? Just how many people have to die?' I clamp my hand over my mouth the moment I've said it. But it's too late. Leah's eyes widen in shock and the colour drains from her face. She gives Robin one last pleading look and then pushes herself away from him, rushing from the room.

'Leah, wait!' I look at Robin helplessly, but she's already gone.

The seconds tick by, but the room is far from silent. It still echoes with the sound of the words flung across it.

Robin stands, arms hanging empty by his side, as if he no longer knows what to do with them now that Leah has gone.

'She didn't mean it,' he says. 'Any more than you did… it's just…' He trails off, knowing that whatever he says won't make anything better. But it should be me comforting him, not the other way around.

'I'm so sorry,' I say. 'This isn't even a discussion I should have been a part of, but I couldn't just ignore what was going on.'

'I know, you couldn't have…'

'Except… now this isn't even about the baby and that's not right.' I give him a tentative smile. 'What are you going to do?'

He inhales deeply, looking towards the ceiling, and I know it's to stop tears from spilling down his face. I almost wish he would cry though and let out all that he's feeling. I'm suddenly very conscious of the fact that Robin never has the opportunity to do just that. I touch a hand to his arm.

'Hope,' he says simply, looking at me with eyes that are still watery despite his efforts. 'I'm going to hope that Leah is just emotionally overwrought at the moment and that, once she's had some time to reflect, she'll want to keep our baby. That's all I *can* do.'

I nod sadly. 'Yes, I think it probably is. That, and be as you always are, Robin; Leah's rock. It might seem as if she's pushing you away, but she has need of you now more than ever. And you'll come to the right decision, I know you will, together.'

'But you'd like to be a grandma?' he asks, his voice tentative, almost shy.

'Oh, Robin, I'd like nothing more, but what *I* think isn't especially relevant, or helpful at the moment. It's probably selfish too. My life has been so concerned with endings rather than beginnings of late; maybe I'm just latching onto something that speaks of a future. And what Leah says about timing is right; you *do* have an awful lot on your plate at the moment. But one thing I do know is that if you wait for it, there will never be a right time to have a baby. There will always be something that crops up, and the years pass by so quickly.'

His head is bobbing up and down and I'm aware I'm not telling him anything he doesn't already know.

'But hope is always good, Robin, never lose sight of it.'

His lips purse together as he studies my face. 'I hadn't realised she'd been feeling that way though, about you and William, I mean.'

'No,' I whisper. 'Me neither. I knew there was something, we both did but…' I draw in a deep breath. 'That's something for Leah and me to sort out. And it certainly shouldn't be something that affects how you feel about being parents. Finding out she's pregnant has been a huge shock for Leah, not to mention the very pronounced effect it's had on her emotions. Perhaps it's heightened how she feels, but even so.' I swallow. 'Again, I'm sorry, Robin. I really had no idea that things were so bad.'

'It wasn't a nice thing to hear though.'

'No.'

I suddenly have a longing for some space of my own, to sort out my jumble of thoughts. But there are greater things at issue here than how I feel. I drag the brightest smile I can find onto my face.

'Don't you go worrying about that, though,' I say. 'That's my job, and you don't need to have *me* on your mind along with everything else.' I look at my watch. I don't really care what time it is, but it will give us both the excuse we need to escape. 'It's getting late, Robin, and it's been a very hot, sticky and tiring day. I might go and have a bath, if you don't mind. And I'm sure you would much rather be somewhere else. So, go on, scoot.' I wave him away.

He's relieved to be let off the hook, and I can't say I blame him. He has an awful lot resting on his young shoulders.

Even my stuffy, airless room feels like a sanctuary this evening and, as I dump my bag onto the bed, I'm reminded that a home is where you choose to make it. And it doesn't have to be filled with everything you've ever wanted either; if it feels like home inside, then it will be.

It's something I'm going to have to think about, sooner rather than later, because I haven't really given it much consideration since I've been here. I told myself I needed to settle first, to find my working feet again and, only then, could I look for somewhere to live. Except that my financial situation is virtually unchanged from when I arrived. More importantly, however, whether I'd noticed or not – and deep down I think I probably had – this little town *has* begun to feel like home over the last few days. While I might not have actively made a decision, it now feels like the most logical thing in the world to want to settle here. And that brings me straight back around again to Leah, and her pregnancy.

Did I know that this was how Leah felt? About me? About William? Or am I just pretending I didn't and fooling myself all over again? Because I can remember something William once said to me. Something I'd done my best to block out, to thrust to the farthest reaches of my mind so I wouldn't have to think about it. And funnily enough it had been seeing Isaac's cat yesterday that reminded me of it – how William had behaved once he realised the effect that Barney would have on our household. Once he realised just how much Leah and I would love the cat. He'd been jealous. There can be no other real explanation for it.

I can't even remember the incident that had provoked William's remark now, but he had taken umbrage at something that had occurred, and the resultant disagreement had been one of those that should never have amounted to anything much, but nonetheless had rapidly developed into a full-blown argument. As he'd stalked from the kitchen in a huff, his parting shot had been that I loved the bloody cat more than I loved him. And the reason why it had stuck in my head on that particular occasion was because he had once said exactly the same thing about Leah, when she was seven months old.

She'd been suffering from croup and, as any parent of a child who's had it will tell you, it's the scariest thing to see your child struggling to breathe, with each bout of coughing leaving them limp and exhausted. It had been after several days of round-the-clock care, with my anxiety levels going through the roof, that William had said the words I'd tried so hard to forget. You love that child more than you love me, he'd said. *You love that child more than you love me…*

And so, what had I done? Had I lived the rest of our lives proving to William that he had been wrong?

I'm so distracted by my thoughts that I scarcely hear the timid knock at the door. Over an hour has passed and I'm still sitting on the edge of the bed, one hand fiddling with the strap on my bag.

It's Leah, her face still marked by her earlier tears and incongruously carrying a plate full of sausage, chips and beans.

'None of us has had any tea,' she says. 'We only just realised.' Her face is a mixture of sadness, shame and a tentative query all rolled into one.

'Oh, Leah…' I take the plate from her and move it to the small chest of drawers against the wall, and then I pull her wordlessly into a hug. She clings to me like a small child.

'Mum, I don't know what to do,' she stammers, muffled against my chest. 'I've hurt Robin so much.'

I pull gently away to look at her. 'Which, surprisingly, he understands,' I reply. 'That's not to say he isn't hurt, but you don't give him nearly enough credit for how much he understands, or how well he knows you.'

'I know.' Her lip trembles again, and she swipes a hand under her eyes.

'And fortunately for you, Robin is also the type of person who loves unconditionally, and maybe that's something that you and I are not so good at.'

She holds my look. 'I'm sorry, Mum.'

I pull her back into my arms. 'Oh, Leah, I'm sorry too.'

We stay like this for several more moments. There is still much to say, but tonight, perhaps, not the best time to say it. It's all still too fresh, too raw, and the embers of our argument are not yet cold. A little air is all it would take to stoke the glowing embers into a flame.

I stroke her hair, her face so familiar, so similar to mine. 'It's been a long day,' I say. 'And much as you and I need to talk, I think what's more important is that you and Robin share what's left of this evening together. Downtime has been very thin on the ground for you both of late. Go for a walk, watch a film, anything, but just be together with nothing else on the agenda. And then maybe tomorrow you and I can have a chat?'

She nods, biting her lip.

'And we'll work it out, Leah, I promise.'

'I'm so lucky to have Robin. I don't know what I'd do without him.'

'You are,' I agree. 'But he's very lucky to have you too.'

Her eyes fill with tears again. 'It's just when I think about what my life would be without him in it, I… I couldn't bear it—'

I still her words. 'Shh now, you still have Robin, sweetheart, very much so.'

'I know. I just meant that I don't think I ever really understood how you felt losing Dad. Or didn't try to understand… I'm so sorry, Mum.'

I smile sadly. 'Sometimes we don't ever realise what we've lost until it's gone. But neither do we understand what we could stand to gain, if only we could recognise it. I don't think I ever really grasped that, but perhaps I'm beginning to.' I pull her close and kiss her forehead. 'Go on now, sweetheart, and thank Robin for dinner for me.'

She sniffs and nods repeatedly, pulling herself together.

'I will, and… night, Mum.'

'Night, love.'

I close the door softly behind her, leaning my forehead against the cool surface for a moment. I think I really am beginning to understand what I've lost, and I don't mean William.

I eat my tea with an appetite that surprises me and then have that long soothing bath after all. The day is still warm but, afterwards, turning down the bed, the sheet feels cool when I place my hand against it. I climb in and lie still, knowing I'll be unlikely to sleep, but feeling strangely at peace. And then I use the time I'm awake to run through all the memories I have of my life with William.

Had it really ever been what I'd thought it was?

# CHAPTER SIXTEEN

I feel oddly like I'm floating when I come to. The room is light and a check on the clock beside the bed shows it to be nearly half past eight. The last time I looked it had just gone five, so I must have fallen asleep. But my body feels light as a feather, almost as if I'm not really here at all.

I wash and dress quickly, heading downstairs to the kitchen for a much-needed mug of coffee. I can hear the murmur of voices as I approach and I pause a moment, reluctant to intrude. But as I slow, I realise their tone is perfectly normal.

'Mum!' Leah starts as I enter the room, scooting from her stool and crossing the room.

She stands in front of me, hesitant and a little wary, much how I'm feeling myself. I don't even know if I should hug her or not. But then she reaches forward and pulls me into a tight embrace. I squeeze her back. It's brief, but it's a start.

'I've just made a pot of coffee,' she says. 'Would you like one?'

Robin swivels around from his position by the cooker. 'Morning, Louisa. Come and sit down and I'll get you some breakfast. What would you like? I've done the works this morning.'

'Oh…' I hadn't given food a second thought. I take a seat at the table. 'Just toast would be fine, thanks.'

Robin gives me a pointed look. 'Really?' he says. 'At least have some bacon with it, or sausage? An egg?'

A rush of saliva fills my mouth at the sudden thought of something I haven't had in years. 'Could I have bacon and egg?' I ask. 'A toasted sandwich?'

He smiles in approval. 'Coming right up.'

Leah returns seconds later with a mug of coffee, plus the pot. 'In case one's not enough,' she says.

I look at her carefully. Gone is the taut skin around her eyes that was present the night before, the dried salt from her tears washed away, but she still looks pale and fragile.

'Aren't you having one?' I ask, as she takes a seat beside me.

She motions a gagging reflex.

'But you've had something, though?'

She nods and there's an accompanying smile. 'Robin's been looking after me,' she says, her eyes flicking down at the last minute.

I wrap my hands around the mug to test the heat and risk a sip anyway. 'How are you feeling?' I ask.

'Sick… but better.' She smiles a little shyly.

'Then I've been thinking. Would some fresh air do you good?'

Leah glances across at Robin but he's busy beside the oven, his back to us. 'Yes, that's what we both said – that I should get out today, take the day off from working here. Robin says he's quite happy pottering along by himself.'

He turns, a plate in his hand. 'Actually, what I said was that I didn't want her to set foot in this place today and that's she's banned.' He looks at me. 'The day is yours, go and do what you will, both of you.'

Leah nibbles at the edge of her lip. 'Would that be all right, Mum?' she asks. 'We don't have to, if you've got work to do.'

I take my breakfast from Robin with a grateful smile. The smell is amazing. 'No, nothing that can't wait. I think I shall take a day off too. Now, what would you like to do?'

Leah looks down at the table, rubbing at a mark with one finger. 'You're going to think I'm silly…'

'Why?'

'Because we could go anywhere, do anything, but actually what I want to do is just be like everyone else. I want to sit on the beach, and read magazines, eat ice cream, have a picnic and doze in the afternoon sun. Does that sound horrendously boring?'

I shake my head. 'Not at all. I have a book that I've been meaning to make a start on, and I know the perfect place. Not too far away and it comes with guaranteed peace and quiet too. But first…'

I pick up one half of my sandwich and sink my teeth into it, eyes closing in pleasure at the different tastes and textures.

'God, that's good,' I manage in between mouthfuls.

*

By the time we've collected everything we'll need for our day on the beach, there's rather more than I first bargained for but, I figure, once we're there, we'll have the whole day before we have to do it again on the return journey.

It isn't surprising that Leah has never been to Elliot's Cove before. She and Robin have scarcely had a day off since they arrived at the Lobster Pot and the plethora of warning signs at the far end of the local beach are sufficient to put off most people. As it is Leah stops dead at the one that says 'Extreme Danger to Life'. Her hand is on my arm, pulling me back.

'Mum, this really isn't a good idea. Look, if we retrace our steps a little, we can easily sit here instead. What's so special about Elliot's Cove anyway?'

'Well, when we get there, you can tell me,' I reply. 'Leah, it's honestly fine and—' I break off abruptly. I'd been about to say Isaac's name. About to tell her that he was the one who had shown me this place, that he was… My thoughts come to a sudden halt.

What is Isaac, exactly? What would I say? I fan myself as if I'm hot from carrying my belongings. 'I met someone recently, kind of a guide, who explained exactly what the problems are and how to avoid them. As long as you abide by the tide tables it's perfectly safe. And I have them saved in my phone and written down on a slip of paper too for extra security.'

Leah eyes me a little suspiciously, but then she gives a cheerful smile. 'As long as you're sure…' She hitches the bag she's carrying a little higher on her shoulder. 'And it had better be worth it!'

I start to wonder myself as we navigate the rocks, hampered by our belongings, but the moment we reach the top and the bay comes into view, her gasp of surprise is audible. We take our time clambering down the other side before stepping onto the beach, where Leah turns a slow circle, drinking in everything she sees.

'Blimey, I can see why Elliot wanted to keep this to himself,' she says. 'It's absolutely stunning.'

'Isn't it? Although I don't think Elliot was particularly selfish. He may have been a bit of an odd character, but he was more of a self-appointed guardian, I believe; he used to keep a lookout for people coming here and help them if they got stranded.'

'So, the stories aren't true then?'

I stare at her in surprise. It never even occurred to me that there could be other versions of Elliot's story than the one Isaac put to me. 'What stories?'

'That Elliot used to scare people away,' she replies. 'That he hated anyone coming near the place and chased them away if he caught them. He was a drunk too; that's how he died. Got pissed as a newt one day and slipped on the rocks, cracking his head open.'

'Oh…' I stare down the length of beach in front of us. That can't be true, can it? 'Well, he's not around now, whatever the rumours, so we can just have the lovely day we always planned.'

We carry on in silence for a moment, but I can't get Leah's words out of my head for some reason. It suddenly seems very important that I set the record straight somehow, that my version of Elliot's story be the one that folks believe. I lead us towards the cliffs at the rear of the beach.

'Let's sit here,' I suggest. 'That way we're sheltered from the wind as well.'

It's a relief to divest ourselves of our belongings, especially the camp chairs, which aren't heavy, but bulky and awkward. Minutes later we've set up camp and Leah sinks into a chair as if it's all her legs can do to keep supporting her. I'd already made up my mind that I wouldn't be the one to broach any difficult subjects today, but instead let Leah get to them when, and if, she chooses to. Besides, I've brought a notebook with me and I'm keen to start drafting some ideas.

Leah leans her head against the back of the chair and closes her eyes immediately. She's probably exhausted, and I remember just how fatigued early pregnancy can make you. I seem to recall joking that I could sleep on a washing line when I was carrying her. And so, without even having to think about anything else, the minutes begin to slide past.

The moment I pick up my pen the thoughts start flowing and I scribble them down quickly for fear of them disappearing. Somehow, Leah's earlier comments about Elliot have made him feel almost tangible. As if at any moment he might stroll across the beach and introduce himself. Then he'd simply sit for a while and tell me his story and we'd become narrator and scribe. I have no way of knowing if my thoughts are right, but they're coming from somewhere I don't want to question.

'Did you mean it, about finding somewhere to live around here?'

Leah's voice is soft, and she'd been so quiet, so still, I thought she'd fallen asleep. Her eyes are still closed though.

'I think so,' I reply. 'At first I just saw being here as a stopgap, a means to an end. And that's not because I didn't want to be here,'

I add quickly, 'but more because of a strong sense of transience. I don't know what's changed that feeling, but, over the last few days, I've felt less like a visitor. In fact, the thought of leaving has lessened to the point that it's almost disappeared.' I think for a moment, choosing my words carefully. 'What made you and Robin choose this place in the end?' I ask. 'You looked at so many hotels.'

Leah opens her eyes and slides me a curious look. 'I actually have no idea,' she replies. 'Most unlike me, you know how pragmatic I usually am. I don't do anything based on gut feeling or intuition, but with the Lobster Pot it was different.'

'I remember you saying at the time how much of a long shot it was.'

'On paper it didn't really stack up. The trading figures were dreadful and, though we knew the area was popular, we'd always envisaged buying something out in the country, with space around, certainly not crammed into a street right in the middle of town. But when we came here, I don't know what it was, but Robin felt exactly the same. Neither of us said anything for ages in the car on the way home though. I was pretty sure Robin was going to say that our fears were justified, and it was a waste of time coming here. I was surprised by just how disappointed that made me feel.'

'And Robin felt the same?'

Yes.' She smiles. 'He didn't want to say anything, because he thought I'd hated it. But once we did start talking, it became one of those weird conversations where neither of you really says anything and yet you both know exactly what the other means. And that was it. It might be the biggest mistake we've ever made but…'

'It felt right.'

'It did. It still does.'

I nod, smiling. As someone whose heart has always ruled her head, this makes perfect sense to me, but I know how alien it must feel to Leah.

'I think that's why finding out I'm pregnant has come as such a shock,' she says. 'Because it didn't feel like it was meant to be, not in the way that everything else has.'

'I can understand that,' I reply. 'You've always been so unlike your dad and I in that regard. We always flew by the seat of our pants, whereas you preferred to plan things out in detail, even as a small child. Although moving here felt right, maybe it's thrown you out of your comfort zone more than you realised. And unexpectedly finding out you're having a baby very definitely falls into the pant-flying category. Your natural instinct is to counter that kind of feeling, perhaps that's all it is. But do a little more of it and it becomes second nature,' I say lightly.

She doesn't reply, but purses her lips, thinking. I wonder if she's realised that both her hands are clasped over her belly.

'It's Dad's birthday next week, isn't it?'

'Yes, on Thursday.' Present tense, I notice.

'Do you think he'd be pleased? About the baby, I mean.'

I inhale a deep breath. 'Yes, if he were still alive, I think he'd be happy. But I also think that once the baby arrived, he'd find it quite difficult. It would worry me that what he actually felt about the matter compared with the impression he gave could seem like two very different things.'

I can see my response surprises her.

'Go on,' she says carefully.

'We all have our faults, Leah, and your dad's was that he often took flying by the seat of his pants to the extreme. So much so that he was always looking for the next thing, the next excitement. Restless, I suppose you'd call it. Anyway, it could often feel like he didn't care about something, like he'd left it behind and was no longer interested in it. It wasn't true, but it often came across that way.' A balmy breeze blows my hair across my eyes and I tuck it back behind my ears so I can see her better. 'I know you felt it… and I did too.'

She looks at me, startled, her mouth slightly parted.

'I've often wondered if that's why I'm the way I am,' I continue. 'No, that's not quite right. It's not the way I am, but it's the way I behaved, simply so that I could keep up with him. You had to, you see, because unless you were there with him, in the moment of whatever it was he was up to, then it felt like you faded into nothing. He loved me being his bright spark; I was like oxygen to his flame. He always wanted to burn bright, but if the spark wasn't there then he simply smouldered, and he hated that.'

I stop to swallow, my thoughts gathering in a tight ball in my throat.

'I loved your father, very, very much. I still do. And you know how hard his death hit me. But I think I've only just realised it was because suddenly the bright shining light that I was so used to being bathed in was gone. And in the shadow, everything felt so cold and dark. I didn't think I would ever find the light again.'

A slow tear makes its way down Leah's cheek as she reaches out her hand towards me. 'Oh Mum… Why did I never understand that?'

I give her a sad smile. 'Perhaps because *I* didn't… or wouldn't. Things could have been very different for you if I'd taken the time to realise it myself – I could have brought you with me to stand under his light together. There was plenty of room for both of us. But I didn't, and now it's too late.'

'No,' replies Leah. 'You mustn't blame yourself, Mum, it wasn't your fault. What you said about Dad is true; I *did* feel like he didn't care a lot of the time, yet I could never understand it, because he could also be the most generous, loving father anyone could ever wish for. But, even then, I always felt like it was on his terms and not mine. And I was jealous of you, Mum. I think I've only just realised that.' She drops her head and closes her eyes for a moment. 'Worse, a part of me was glad when he died…'

'Leah, I—'

She holds out her hand. One that trembles under the weight of her emotion. 'No, let me finish. I felt relieved that I wouldn't have to try so hard, that I wouldn't have to live my life trying to make him notice me, that I could have you all to myself… And I've struggled so much with that, because how could I possibly tell you how I felt? Not when I could see how hard his death hit you. But it was selfish. I was only thinking about myself and—'

'Leah, if anyone has been selfish, it's me. As if I was the only one who could possibly be affected by his death. And the debt just made it worse, because it made me into a martyr. Poor, poor Louisa, literally…' I offer her a small smile. 'I think I've milked that one for all it was worth. But the very worst thing I did was to make you go to the inquest, to put all of that added pressure onto your shoulders, when it should have been on mine. I should have realised how hard that would be for you. To hear all the graphic details of William's death, to bear the coroner's decision…'

'Mum, you didn't make me go, I offered, remember?'

'Only because you could see that I would never have coped with it. You're so much stronger than I am, Leah, you always have been.'

She's quiet for a moment, thinking about my words. Thinking about those days probably, reliving them one more time. She looks up and stares across the beach. And then to my surprise she shakes her head.

'You know, I've only ever thought about my childhood in terms of what I didn't have,' says Leah softly, 'not in terms of what I did have. Maybe you and he gave me more than I thought. Maybe I'm more like you than both of us realise.'

I give her a puzzled look.

'I think I just chose to be the opposite way to you and Dad because I didn't believe I could be like you. Out of sheer bloody-mindedness perhaps, I don't know. But being pedantic and controlling, dotting every "i" and crossing every "t" made me feel more in control of things, and I did it so much it just became who I am.' She stares down at her lap, a look of wonder dawning on her face. 'Until we came here and something changed, because I found a little bit of spontaneity, after all. So maybe I do have it in me.' Her hand is still lying across her taut stomach. 'I've been fighting it every step of the way, and I don't really know why,' she adds, an amazed expression on her face. 'I really don't.' But then her face falls. 'Except it isn't that easy, is it? Because I have the weight of a whole lifetime behind me. I can't change how I feel in just one day…'

'No one says you need to, Leah. And neither is it solely your responsibility. I have a lot of readjusting to do; in the way I think about your father, about our life together, but, most importantly, in my relationship with you. I have a lot of time to make up and I'm truly sorry that I'm only seeing this now.'

'I'm sorry too, Mum. I shouldn't have said the things I did last night. I'm as much to blame.'

And there it is again. That word. The one we all love to use, pointing the finger… 'You know, Leah, I don't think anyone's to blame. It's just the way it is, that's all. And perhaps we should try to accept, rather than to blame. People are difficult, complicated, wonderful, beautiful things, and we must celebrate every moment we have with them, the good and the bad. Because it's a part of who they are.'

And, as I say it, I realise I can hear Isaac's words in my head. You don't have to mourn something because it's gone, instead you can choose to celebrate that it was here at all… The good, mingled with the bad. All of it.

She nods. 'So, what do we do now?'

I smile. 'That's a tough one, but for now perhaps it's enough to think that we've made a start. We have a foundation on which we can build, and time can do the rest.'

Leah is quiet for a moment and I can see she's thinking about all that's been said. 'I think you're right,' she says, a slight tremor in her voice. 'But I don't have all the time in the world, do I?'

And it's now I realise that Leah is right too, because we aren't talking about hypothetical situations and what might happen in an ideal world; reality is far from that. And whatever happened in the past *has* brought us very firmly to the present day. And how Leah feels about her pregnancy.

'It's all a bit of a mess, isn't it?' she whispers.

'Oh Leah… I know it feels that way, but sometimes life *is* messy. But wouldn't it be boring if it were pristine the whole time? You have a big decision ahead of you, but if you want your future to change, then bring what you've learned from the past and use it to make every decision work towards the way you want things to be, not the way things were. Life is always going to be about the choices we make, but you won't go far wrong if you make them hopeful, instead of hopeless.'

# CHAPTER SEVENTEEN

Even though it's early, Isaac is already at the studio by the time I arrive there the next morning. I sat up writing late into the night yesterday and today I'm filled with more optimism than I've felt in a long time.

After talking for a while on the beach yesterday, Leah and I spent the rest of our time there just reading, or in my case writing, and relaxing. We paddled a little before making our way back to the town beach, where we had an ice cream and some doughnuts before heading up into the maze of streets. We had a leisurely late lunch at a hotel whose owners Leah knows and then after that we ventured into a few shops including the art gallery I'd first visited where she picked up one of Isaac's sculptures, completely unbidden, entranced by it. I can't wait to tell him.

By the time we got back to the Lobster Pot it was early evening and, leaving Leah to catch up with Robin, I snuck off for a nap. I was exhausted, but the kind of tiredness that feels as if it's been earned and, although I'd intended to have an early night, the thoughts began to flow again as soon as I sat down at my desk after dinner. By the time I'd finished I felt as though what I'd done was beginning to look book-shaped.

This morning I'm going to make a start on the first chapter and, as I walk up the hill to the allotments, I realise that aside from feeling a nervous excitement, I'm actually looking forward to the day. Things aren't completely settled with Leah, but they're better than they've been for a long while, and whatever decision she and Robin take about the baby, perhaps now she can look at it with a slightly different viewpoint. But whatever their decision is, I must accept it. They're both going to need a lot of support, one way or the other.

The door to the studio is open, as are the windows, gauzy curtains blowing in the strong breeze. But I'm glad of it today, the temperature is already climbing fast.

'Hello…' My enquiry is tentative, even though I'm pretty sure that Isaac will have heard me arriving.

But the cheerful greeting I'm expecting doesn't come. In fact, there's no response at all.

I stick my head around the door, clearing my throat as I do so. 'Morning, Isaac.'

He's sitting at the workbench, seemingly transfixed by what looks like a piece of glass in his hand.

'Is it okay if I come in?' I'm wondering if he's lost in some creative vision. I get like that sometimes when I'm writing, although not that bad. But his face when he finally turns to me looks awful, as if he's in pain; dark with shadows that have nothing to do with the light in the room.

He puts the glass down and swallows. 'Louisa, sorry, yes come in, please do.' He grimaces. 'I was miles away…'

I smile. 'Anywhere nice?'

I was aiming for levity but suddenly I'm smiling at a rigid mask, Isaac's features frozen at my words. I'm reminded of the saying that eyes are like the windows of the soul. And the quick glimpse I get of Isaac's before he recovers himself look bleak as a winter sky.

He shakes his head. 'Sorry,' he says again. 'Staring into middle distance is somewhat of an occupational hazard, don't you find?' He grins unexpectedly. 'We like to claim it's our creativity and that we're thinking, when really we're just dog-tired and daydreaming.' He gets to his feet. 'I brought an enormous flask of coffee with me this morning, would you like one?'

'Thank you, that would be lovely.' I'm still standing virtually in the doorway, now somewhat awkwardly. I'm so used to Isaac being cheerful and jocular that it's rather a shock to find him withdrawn and clearly troubled. But the even bigger shock is realising how disappointed this makes me feel.

'So, how's it going?' he asks. 'Have you thought some more about what you're going to write?'

'I'm about to start, actually. I've got my plot worked out and I'm just going to dive right in.' Even as I say it, I can feel excitement bubbling up.

Isaac's eyes widen. 'Really? But that's brilliant, Louisa. I'm so pleased.' He shoots a glance at the floor. 'In fact, that's the best news I've had in a while. See, I told you Elliot was special, didn't I?'

'You did… And I should thank you.' I'm relieved to see him looking much more like his old self. 'In fact…' But I trail off, realising I was about to tell him I couldn't have done it without him. 'I'm just pleased to be able to tell his story, or one version of it at least.' My cheeks are growing hot and I finally move into the room, crossing to put my bag down on the workbench.

'Are you sure I won't disturb you?' I ask.

'Why, what are you planning?' counters Isaac.

I look at him, confused. 'Just writing, that's all. I have my laptop and—'

'So, no wild dancing, singing loudly at the top of your voice, or turning cartwheels across the floor…' He raises his eyebrows at my expression. 'Then you won't be disturbing me.' He pours rich-smelling coffee into a mug. 'And just in case you were wondering, my cartwheeling days are long behind me.' He hands the cup to me with a grin. 'I shall be tinkering. I can't guarantee silence, but it's not a particularly loud process.'

'Perfect,' I say, holding the rim of the mug to my lips and inhaling the fragrant brew. 'Are you working on something new?'

'Probably,' he replies. 'I had an idea, and I've been trying to gather together some raw materials that I can use, but I'm never really sure it's going to work or not until I sit down and try.'

'Right, well, we'd best crack on then, I guess.'

He slips back onto his stool and picks up a length of something from the bench. 'Look at this.'

I put down my mug and take the object from him; it's about twenty centimetres long by about half as wide and, although crusted with dirt, looks to be shiny underneath. Some sort of metal. I rub at the green-tinged surface.

'What is it?' I ask.

'I have no idea,' he replies. 'But I found it on the beach, would you believe. Maybe it came from a boat or… I don't know, but I think it's copper.'

'Is it?' I rub a little more. 'God, I think you might be right. But that's amazing, it could be really beautiful. What are you going to make from it?'

He takes it back. 'I'm not sure yet, I'm going to clean it up first and see, but I was thinking… a boat of some sort. Possibly a sky boat.'

'A sky boat?'

'Yes, they're—'

'I know what they are. The ancient Egyptians believed that the sun god used such a vessel to traverse the sky during the day.'

'And the underworld at night. They thought such a boat might also carry someone who had died to their final resting place…'

My eyes flick to his and his gaze is calm and clear. Had I not already been sitting down it would have taken the legs out from under me. I take out my laptop from my bag, opening it up to try to buy some time.

'And if not a sky boat, then perhaps just a hanging sculpture of some kind. Maybe somewhere you could keep those small treasures you collect on a walk.' He smirks a little. 'Good excuse for hoarding, I reckon. What do you think?'

I swallow, blushing. 'I think those are lovely ideas.'

And they are, but they also seem… odd. I'm not quite sure what's going on, but Isaac's in a very strange mood this morning. And his mention of the sky boat has brought something else to mind; something I thought of only yesterday when I was talking with Leah. And it could be just the thing to cheer Isaac up a little. Besides, I don't have to go into huge detail…

'Actually, I was thinking,' I begin. 'I wondered if you might be able to do something for me…?'

'Go on…'

'I wondered if you might draw a sand picture for me. It's for a birthday next week, of someone very special to me. Someone I lost recently. I know it's a big ask, but…' I wrap my hands tighter around the mug and take a sip of coffee. 'I'd help obviously, I wouldn't leave you to do it by yourself and—'

'No.' His abrupt response is harsh as well as unexpected. He clears his throat. 'Sorry, Louisa, but no, I don't do them, not for anyone.'

'But—'

'Don't, please.' He holds up his hand. 'Because I'm not going to change my mind, and you're just going to make this worse if you carry on.'

I frown, a flicker of irritation crossing my face. What on earth is that supposed to mean? 'Make it worse? Make what worse? I only asked—'

'I really don't want to argue about this, Louisa. Please, just respect what I've said. I know it isn't the answer you wanted but those drawings are not for anyone else. Apart from the fact that the minute I do something like that, I'll have a queue of people asking me to draw their marriage proposals and say happy birthday to their aunt Hilda, I don't want to do it.'

Judging by the look on his face, he obviously isn't going to change his mind. I'm disappointed, but also a little bewildered that what I'd hoped Isaac would see as good news, a compliment even, hasn't been received at all well.

'Okay, I'm sorry. I hadn't realised you felt so strongly about it.'

He stares at me for a moment, mouth opening and closing as he thinks of and discards things to say. He heaves a sigh and looks away for just a second, and I swear he almost rolls his eyes.

'And yet I told you those drawings were just for me. So what didn't you realise? Didn't I make it obvious enough? Besides which, it's a free beach, no one's stopping you from doing it yourself. What do you need me for?'

I'm flustered now. 'I don't know, Isaac. Sorry, I just thought that perhaps it was something you might like to do. You let me draw with you before and—'

'Because I thought it would help you!'

'Help me with what? I…'

His gaze drops to the floor and I can see his jaw is clenched. Whatever it is that has put Isaac in such an odd mood this morning, he's barely managing to keep it contained.

'Look, I'm sorry, okay, I should never have asked. Something's obviously upset you this morning and—'

Isaac whirls around and picks up the piece of glass he was holding when I first came in. He thrusts it out towards me. 'What do you see?' he demands.

I take it from him. It's a piece about the size of a coaster, from the bottom of a bottle perhaps, its edges worn perfectly smooth by the tide. It's pale green, almost translucent, and slightly left of centre something has struck the glass, causing a small dent. Myriad cracks fan out from it almost like a starburst, or the facets of a diamond.

I look up. 'It's very pretty,' I offer, handing it back.

'It is?' His voice is flat and cold. 'Well, pretty is not what I see. I see a windscreen, hit by a piece of debris, cracking it so that it appears as if a gun has been fired clean through it. Crazed ripples fire out into all directions, cleaving the glass, cleaving a massive crack through the middle of someone's life... It's one of the things I think I shall always see, for ever and ever...'

His eyes are blazing now and a chill begins to flicker around the base of my spine.

'What are you talking about, Isaac?' But I'm not sure I want to know the answer.

'I saw you yesterday,' he says, seemingly changing the subject. 'You and your daughter. You were walking back along the beach, towards the town.'

I shake my head. I'm not sure what that's got to do with anything. 'Yes, we'd been to Elliot's Cove actually, we—'

'I should have recognised the resemblance, straight away. You're very alike.' He narrows his eyes. 'Perhaps I did...' He looks up at me as if light has suddenly dawned.

'Isaac, I'm sorry, I'm not sure—'

'What do you know about me?' he interrupts.

A ripple of guilt stirs my stomach. Has he seen my thoughts? The ones I've kept hidden from him. The ones Barbara put there. Does he know what my intention has been all along?

*No, it hasn't,* I remind myself. *I was never going to write...* And as soon as I think it, I realise how true this is. I can't write an article about Isaac and I'm going to have to tell Barbara, sooner rather than later. But my thoughts crash to a halt as I stare at the piece of glass, still in Isaac's hand. He isn't talking about the article... And the guilt is replaced by fear.

But Isaac doesn't look threatening, or even angry. Instead he looks close to tears.

'Oh, Louisa...' He rakes a hand through his hair. 'Why did you have to come here and ask me to draw a picture for your husband's birthday? I wanted to talk to you. I—'

'Okay, Isaac, just forget it. I can see it was really bad timing on my part…' I tail off as his words force their way into my brain, my mind far too slow to take in the meaning. And then it hits me. 'I never said the drawing would be for my husband.'

'Did you need to? For chrissakes, Louisa, how could it be for anyone else? How many other people have you lost?' He draws quote marks around his last word, and it sends anger firing through me.

'How dare you! How dare you make fun of me!'

His head drops and I see his shoulders begin to quake. The silence is thick, like fog rolling in off the sea. Eventually his head lifts and he swallows, his eyes red.

'Louisa… My name *is* Isaac, I haven't lied to you. But my full name is Rowan Isaac Farmer…'

He doesn't even need the last name, the first is enough. It's a name I will never forget. I take a step backward as if seared by invisible flames.

'*You!*' The word explodes from my lips. I'm trying to reconcile what I knew of this man before to the one standing in front of me now. Gone is the dark suit, the short grey hair, the designer stubble, but…

'Louisa, I can explain, I…'

But he can't explain, he can never explain.

This is the man who so carelessly held up the jar containing everything I loved, turned it upside down and shook it until all the pieces fell out and smashed to the floor. He may not look like the photos I've seen of him, but neither does he look like the picture I still have of him in my mind most nights, the reckless driver of the car that killed my husband, his face contorted into a grinning mask of evil. The two images – Isaac – and this other man – couldn't be more different, but somewhere between the two of them lies the truth.

'You should have told me!'

'Louisa, I didn't know, I swear, I—'

'You let me talk about all sorts of things…' My voice sounds tinny, incredulous. 'You offered to help me with my article on Christmas customs, let me draw a sand picture with you. Let me come here… the shell grotto… Jesus, what were you doing? It's… it's sick—'

'No, I didn't know! Not until yesterday when I saw her, your daughter… Louisa, I had no idea who you were, I promise. I would never have… Jesus…' He breaks off, swallowing hard. 'I'm not trying to deceive you, you have to believe me, I've told you the first opportunity I've had, but what can I say? Sorry doesn't quite seem to cut it.' He throws the piece of glass carelessly back on the workbench.

His eyes are searching my face and it's all I can do not to look away.

'At least let me try to explain,' he says.

'Explain?' I stare at him, incredulous. 'Jesus, Isaac, there's nothing to explain. And you really think apologising is going to make it better? As if I'd just accept it and say, "Oh, okay then, no hard feelings"! You were drink driving. You lost control of your car and you killed my husband. That's all I need to know.'

His eyes are dark with anger. 'Is it? Did I?' His questions hang in the space between us and he leaves them there as the seconds tick past. One. Two. *What the hell does he mean by that?* Three…

'See? You're not interested, are you? You don't even want to know the truth. And I admit I had one drink, just one, but you're not even interested in why, or what happened next. It's like you think I did it on purpose. Like I just decided when I got up that morning to ruin someone's life. Well it ruined mine too, did you ever stop to think about that? No, of course not,' he says bitterly. 'Do you think there isn't a day goes by when I don't think about what happened? And how I wish it were different. But wishing doesn't change things, Louisa. If it did, we'd all be happy as Larry.

I haven't let one drop of alcohol pass my lips since that day, and yet I see other people around me all the time, knocking back the booze; at parties, Christmas, at birthday celebrations, members of my own family, and I know that some of those people get in their cars and drive. And I'm not saying it's right, but nothing happens to *them*, Louisa. So, what was it about me that singled me out? What had I done that was so wrong I needed to be punished? Because when it came down to it, it was a question of my word against another man's, a man who was no longer able to give his side of the story. So mine was judged on the basis of one drink, because there was nothing else they could find to argue against. Except that *I* know what happened, Louisa. And I have to live with that every day.'

'And I don't?'

'No, you do… We've both been issued with a life sentence. And yes, it's changed our lives, but at least I'm trying to learn from those changes. To grow, and become the person I always thought I had the potential to be. But what about you? You're not trying to move on at all. You're stuck, Louisa. Stuck in a life full of self-pity, looking constantly for someone to blame. And it doesn't even make you feel better, does it?'

The anger is ebbing out of him now and being replaced by something that makes me more furious than ever.

'You don't even know me,' I hiss. 'So don't you dare pity me. What gives you the right to sit in judgement of me, when I've done nothing wrong?'

He shakes his head sadly. 'Because you refuse to see what's in front of you, that's why. Open your eyes, Louisa.' He tips his head at me. 'Let me ask you another question then. Just who is it you're angry at? Is it your husband, whose moment of recklessness has left you on your own? Is it yourself for even thinking of the possibility of life without him, when surely miring yourself in grief is the only way to prove you loved him? Or is it me, for having the audacity to try to help, to make you think about things you really don't want to…'

I open my mouth to reply, but he holds up a hand. 'I've tried to help you, Louisa, or haven't you noticed? And do you want to know why? Because I could see how much pain you were in. No other reason. I simply saw another human being going through some things I recognised and thought that if I shared my experiences, maybe it might help you to feel differently. Well, if that's a crime, then I'm guilty as charged. But that's all. That's it.'

I can't speak. Tears are prickling my eyes as I wordlessly open and close my mouth.

'Yeah, the truth hurts, doesn't it? But you know, the quicker you accept it, both the good and the bad, the quicker you can start to turn things around.'

'And you know that for a fact, do you?' I sneer. 'Well let me tell you, Isaac, you don't, not at all. I don't need your "help".'

'I know that being a martyr to your grief and desolation isn't going to make it all better. I know it won't bring William back, and that all you're doing in the process is fucking up your own life. He died, Louisa, and it changed your life. But it didn't end it. Don't try to honour his memory by turning yourself into something he would probably hate and despise.'

I snap down the lid of my laptop and bundle it into my bag. My cheeks are flaming and I know I'm either inches away from bursting into tears or letting fly with my anger. And I really don't want to do either.

'I don't have to stand here and listen to this.'

'No, you're absolutely right, you don't. Do what you always do, Louisa.'

I swing back round. 'And what the hell is that supposed to mean?'

'Just go…' His voice is softer now, almost resigned… weary? 'Run away and carry on believing what you want to.'

I stare at him, eyes burning into his, wishing I could shake him or… I snatch up my bag, catching the edge of my mug as I do so. A flood of coffee runs in a dark stain across the workbench, but I ignore it, pushing myself past him.

'Jesus, I thought I liked you, but I don't know how I could have been so stupid. It's not me who's in the wrong here, it's you, and I don't know what on earth has got into you this morning but—'

'Exactly my point. You *don't* know… And therein lies the nub of this whole matter.' He gives a sad smile.

'Well, I bloody well know one thing. You've shown your true colours very clearly indeed.'

He holds my gaze for just a second before he looks away. 'Then I'm glad. I wish you well, Louisa.'

# CHAPTER EIGHTEEN

I'm out of breath by the time I get back to the hotel. My anger lent fuel to my passage and it burned undiminished the entire way, my legs pounding the pavement just as hard as my heart pounded against my chest, desperate to be set free. I sometimes wish it were, and the relentless pain could end.

I've thought endlessly about what I would do, what I would say, if I were ever faced with William's killer, but on none of those occasions had it ever been like it was. A situation that I walked into blindly, sneaking up on me unannounced. And what hurts the most is not that I've found the person responsible for William's death, but that the person turned out to be Isaac. It really hurts. And I don't know how to handle that.

And what would have happened if Isaac hadn't seen me with Leah yesterday? Would our friendship have grown? Continued growing? Unaware of the trap that was lying in wait for us, ready to spring its steel jaws shut at any time. Surely it's better that it happened now, before anything... I stop myself from thinking any further.

Up in my room I pace the floor. Then sit on the bed. Go into the bathroom and wash my hands. But none of it helps. I'm more shocked than anything. And astonished, because the day I thought I was going to have has turned out to be anything but. I was looking forward to seeing Isaac this morning. I'd even pictured myself chatting to him easily on all manner of subjects, maybe even about Leah… or William. That maybe we'd reached a place where I might start to open up a little about my past, and to think about my future.

I shake my head and growl with frustration at my stupidity. And it's worse now because not only did Isaac split my world apart, but he's derided my sorrow too. My thoughts trail off as I sit down heavily on the bed, but the next second I'm up on my feet again, pacing the room.

There's a latent ball of hurt and anger inside of me that I want to hurl at something, smashing it to smithereens. I want to tear something apart, to rip, to strike out… But there's nowhere for my rage to go and it burns inside of me, my anger only increasing with my impotence.

My bag is still lying on the bed where I practically threw it, and I yank my laptop from it, dumping it on the desk and wrenching open the lid. I stare at it, moving forward to hover my fingers over the keys before walking away again, restless with indecision. I turn back as it connects with the hotel Wi-Fi, and a chime sounds, signalling the arrival of new emails. Seconds later a blue oblong slides onto the bottom right-hand corner of the screen, where it hovers for a few seconds before sliding away again. But it was long enough to read the first line of the message.

*Hi, my lovely, how's it all going? Listen sweetheart, I don't want to hassle you, but have you remembered that copy deadline is still the 20th…*

My phone is in my hand before I've even finished reading her email. And in typical Barbara fashion, she answers seconds later.

'Louisa, darling, it's so lovely to hear from you. But I do hope you're ringing with good news.' There's an upward inflection on the end of her sentence that's going to make it very hard to do otherwise.

'Not exactly… Barbara, I've just seen your email and ordinarily you know I would get a story to you by the deadline, but this thing with Isaac, it's—'

'Isaac?'

'The sand artist… it's a lot more complicated than I first thought and, I'm sorry, Barbara, but—'

'How complicated?'

I pause and take a breath. 'I can't write the article, Barbara, I'm sorry. Circumstances have changed and… I'll see if I can send you something else. I'm sure I can, I had an idea the other day and—'

'Louisa…?' She waits until she knows she has my attention. 'Louisa, I don't want another article, I wanted this one. It fits so perfectly with everything else we have and, besides, I'd rather set my heart on it.' She lets her words dangle between us and when I don't reply draws in an audible breath. 'Oh Louisa, are you really going to disappoint me? You are, aren't you?' There's another pause. 'At least tell me why…'

It doesn't take long. There's not a huge amount to say beyond stating the facts. Barbara will know how I feel.

'Darling… I don't know what to say… And you had no idea it was him?'

'None. There's no reason why I should. I've never seen him in person, remember, he simply recognised Leah from the inquest. Besides, from the odd photos I have seen of him in the past, he looks very different now.'

'But that's appalling… No, of course, you can't write it, that's—' She breaks off and to my amazement gives a low chuckle. 'Oh, I'm sorry, Louisa, but think about it for a moment. How delicious would it be? To tell his story, in your words. All those things you never got the chance to say…'

I stare at my phone. 'No. Barbara, I can't write about it, it's… This is my life we're talking about here. Apart from anything else there's Leah to consider and… God, she doesn't even know yet.'

'Yes, but don't you see, you'd be doing it for her too? This would be the perfect closure for both of you, it's exactly what you need. One last hurrah to draw a line underneath it all; you get on with your life and he gets on with his. But, you, you will have had the final say. The chance to put your side of the story, the chance to say why the inquest was such a farce. I'd need to think about it… but I'm sure there's a way we could tell it without mentioning names. Make it really personal to you, without laying ourselves open to a libel case.'

I'm so shocked I can hardly speak. 'Barbara, no. This *is* personal to me. I don't want to have to think about it any more than I already am.'

For a moment the silence is so profound I think I've lost the connection, but then Barbara's voice comes back on the line, quiet and measured.

'I do understand how you feel Louisa, of course I do. But while Isaac and his story is very personal to you, it's also a matter of public record. I may not know his full name but I can find it, very easily, and I can certainly write a story about how he ran away to the seaside to start a new life… Because, let's be clear about this, Louisa, that's exactly what he has done.

'But I don't want to do that – out of regard for you, darling, but also because I'm not the one who should be telling his story. I wouldn't do it justice, not like you could. Think about it… Think about it as the conversation you always wanted to have but never got the chance. Think about it as a means of righting the wrong that was done to you. Think about it as your future. You, and only you, are the one who can do this justice, who can use it to relaunch your career. You need this story, Louisa.'

I end the call moments later. I think Barbara's made it perfectly clear where I stand. I'm also well aware that her email this morning was a shot across the bows, and quite possibly my last chance. I *had* forgotten about the date. When I'd discussed writing the article with her, I'd somehow thought I would just send it in whenever, but I should have known that Barbara would only ever cut me so much slack and no more. She'd given me all the time she could, but once I'd got back in contact with her the clock had started ticking again and my days were, literally, numbered. And now I have the potential to give her a gem of a story too. If I want to keep my job, and my only source of income, I have no choice.

I place my phone slowly back down on the desk and close the lid of my laptop. Barbara is not my only concern right now. There's Leah too.

I drift down the stairs and head towards the pungent aroma coming from the hallway on the second floor. It's reminiscent of something and, as I walk towards it, I realise what it is: polish. It's just how my old school hall used to smell all those years ago with its old-fashioned parquet flooring. And now the scent is distinctly comforting.

The reason for it is immediately apparent as I stick my head around one of the bedroom doors. Leah and Robin are both on their hands and knees in front of one of the wardrobes that Robin built and are liberally applying wax to it. They're so engrossed in their task they don't even realise I'm there until I'm almost beside them.

'That's incredible…'

Robin looks up and grins. 'Yeah… not too shabby if I do say so myself.' He stands up, grimacing as he does so and arches his back. 'Getting old,' he says, smiling.

I'm pleased to see he looks a little happier this morning. Yesterday his face was abnormally pale and his freckles stood out, almost as if in relief, but today he looks far more relaxed, even a little pink.

'That looks like it's a lot of hard work,' I remark, my eyes scanning the rich and beautiful tones of the wood.

'Worth it though,' replies Leah. 'Aren't they beautiful?'

I nod. 'When Robin was just making the carcass, I couldn't really visualise how it would look when it was finished. I thought it would look…'

'Rough?' he suggests.

'A little embarrassing to admit, but yes, I did actually… But now I can see what a transformation has taken place. They look fabulous and, curiously, as if they've always been here,' I add. 'That's a compliment by the way.'

Robin grins. 'Almost as if they're part of the furniture, eh?' He rubs at the area where he's just applied the polish, encouraging it to sink into the wood. 'A few more applications of this, and then the top coat and it will look even better. And, importantly, last for years.'

'You have a lot of skills,' I say. 'That I'm not sure I ever gave you credit for. You both do. And I think this place is going to be amazing.'

Leah beams up at me. 'So do I.' She gets to her feet, smiling. 'It's going to be brilliant.'

I falter as I look at her face, at Robin's, happier than I've seen them in days. And it sends a flicker of anger around my system, that I'm going to have to ruin their day, and that the reach of Isaac's responsibility, his ruin, extends even to this.

I look around, wondering if we ought to go somewhere else. Standing here doesn't seem quite the right place to tell them something so appalling.

'Mum…?' Leah gives me a wary look and my throat begins to close.

'Sweetheart…'

Robin takes a step forward. 'Louisa, is everything okay?'

My lip begins to tremble. This is all still so raw.

'I met someone recently, I think I told you. He's an artist who Barbara wanted me to find. She'd seen some work of his and… well, we got talking, but…' I trail off again, my hand covering my mouth for a moment. 'Leah, I'm so sorry, but I've just found out something about him that… There's no easy way to tell you this. His name's Isaac, although that's not the name we know him by, and—'

Leah's eyes shoot downward and the speed of her reaction sets the hairs rising on the back of my neck.

'Leah…?'

The seconds of silence tick by.

Her face is quite pale when she finally lifts her gaze to meet mine.

'Yes, I know he's here,' she says. And her words drop into the room like an unexploded bomb.

'What?'

'I know he's here, Mum. Rowan Farmer. Isaac's his middle name.'

'I don't give a stuff what his name is,' I retort, my voice several degrees louder. 'For God's sake, Leah, you knew this man was here and you didn't think to tell me! You let me come here, knowing that I might see him one day?' I can't say any more.

She doesn't comment because we both know I didn't have any other choice.

Her eyes gaze into mine for a moment. 'Mum, I'm sorry, I didn't know what to do. I *don't* know what to do. I never thought for a minute that you would meet him, or even know who he was if you did. And I was going to tell you, but then…' She stops, and I know what she was going to say. Rather a lot seems to have happened since I arrived.

She licks her lips. 'I bumped into him about two weeks after we first arrived. And do you know *how* I bumped into him? Because he came to my rescue, that's how, during a storm. I got caught in it unloading things from the car and he just happened to be walking past. I mean, the heavens opened and the rain came down in a torrent, but he came to my aid, taking things from me to save them from falling. And by the time he'd helped me carry everything inside he was dripping wet too, but when he saw I was okay he simply said goodbye and carried on his way. So what was I supposed to do? Run after him and accuse him of killing my dad when he'd just presented himself as a Good Samaritan? He obviously didn't recognise me, my hair was plastered over my face and, well, neither of us was really looking at the other and… I almost didn't recognise *him*. He's lost a lot of weight, and his hair certainly wasn't white before.'

'But you knew it was him?'

'Yes,' she replies quietly.

'It was you he recognised,' I say. 'He saw us together yesterday.'

She nods. 'I couldn't tell you at the time, not over the phone, not something like that, and besides… When I realised who he was I could hardly speak, Mum, I was just intent of getting in out of the rain for one, but afterwards… afterwards I went into a complete meltdown. Ask Robin if you don't believe me.' She pauses to throw him a glance.

'But the thing is, Mum, once I'd calmed down, even though I was shocked, and hurt and upset, I realised that he has just as much right to be here as I do, as any of us do. He exists, Mum. And you can't simply remove the man from the world because of how he makes you feel. You can't change what happened, and… Isaac seems like an okay bloke, you know, and Dad's death was an *accident*, Mum.' She bites her lip. It's something she always does when she doesn't want to tell me something. 'And you didn't see him. You didn't see how he was at the inquest. How broken he was…'

I stare at her incredulously. 'What, you believe *him* now, is that it?'

'Mum, I didn't say that. But you weren't there and…'

Tears fill her eyes and I know she's only telling the truth, finally, now that she can.

'Oh Leah…' And suddenly I see the breadth of the burden that I placed on her. The truths that she's had to hide from me, to shoulder alone. Truths I would never have believed at the time.

So what do I believe now?

Robin slides his hand into Leah's. 'I know how much of a shock this must have been for you, Louisa, but Leah's right. William's accident was a horrific and tragic thing to have happened, but it was still an accident. And Isaac isn't going to hurt you unless you let him. Maybe it's time to just live your life and let him live his.'

I stare at his face, and then that of my daughter. 'And tell me, just how am I supposed to do that? When at any minute I could bump into him, a constant reminder of all that I've lost. I'm *trying* to move on, Leah. You still should have told me, instead of letting me come here unaware of what I was walking into.'

'But what choice did you have, Mum? What choice did I have? We wanted you here with us and now, more than ever, that's what's important. If I had to take that decision again, I'd probably still do the same thing. It was right then. It's still right now.'

'But how can I stay, knowing that he's here too?'

A single tear rolls down her cheek. 'I don't know, Mum, only you can decide that.'

# CHAPTER NINETEEN

My room is hot as I close the door behind me and lean my head against it for a moment. Leah's words are still ringing in my ears and I can see the sense in them, but I'm fighting them hard. How can any of this be right?

I sink down on the bed, staring across the room to the window where I had looked down at the street below when I first arrived. Tired, emotionally overwrought, but happy to be here, and filled with hope that I might finally be able to put the past behind me and move on. And then I'd met Isaac.

I narrow my eyes, catching at the words that have wormed their way into my head. It's Leah's voice: *It was right then. It's still right now…* I shake my head. No, those weren't the words I wanted, but they're similar… And then I have them, not Leah's words, but Barbara's… *Think about it as a means of righting a wrong. Think about it as your future…*

And suddenly I know exactly what I have to do.

I pull my chair slowly away from the desk and sit down, settling myself with a series of precise movements that I know from experience are a means of slowing down the process of beginning to write. It gives my brain the few extra seconds it needs to start composing the first sentence. And by the time my programme loads giving me a blank page for my words, I have it. And the next. And the one after that.

I work for the next two and a half hours, thoughts ripping out of me, neither pausing to drink nor eat. The process of writing has become one with my body, so much a part of me that it almost feels like breathing; natural, sustainable and virtually involuntary. At the end of that time I have a total of two thousand and eight hundred words and I stare at them, utterly exhilarated by the experience. But, more importantly, sated. I have set the record straight.

I sit back, moving my fingers on the touchpad to open my emails. Several more have arrived since Barbara's but I ignore them, clicking instead to reread my editor's full message. I think for a moment before clicking on the reply button.

> *Hi Barbara, I've been mulling over what you said, and when you read the attached, I don't think you'll be disappointed. I don't want to say too much now but get back to me once you've had a look.*
>
> *L xx*

I quickly attach the file and press send without another moment's thought.

My hands lift off the keyboard. Then I sit back. And stand up. And stare at the now ordinary screen in front of me. The cursor winks back at me, and for a second or two it beats in time with my heart. But then mine overtakes it and we disconnect.

And what's done is done.

I step back into the room and look around me, a little surprised to find that everything looks familiar and unchanged. That what seemed momentous has had no physical effect on my surroundings.

I pull open my bedroom door and peer out onto the small landing before propping it open and listening. Straight away I can hear sounds of industry coming from the floor below me, and I breathe a sigh of relief. More than anything I don't want to be alone just now.

If Barbara still works the way she used to, it won't be long before she gets back to me. I don't know how she does it, but there isn't a thing that anyone says, does or writes that she misses. Eternally plugged into her emails, phone and social media, she processes huge amounts of information every day and her decision-making skills are legendary, especially towards deadline day.

The room where I'd left Leah and Robin is now empty, the wardrobe gleaming under its coats of polish. But there are noises coming from further down the hallway and I follow them to another of the bedrooms. Leah is pulling out a clump of something from the front of her hair when I find her, trying to untangle it without resorting to yanking it out. The whole floor is covered in similar strips of sticky wallpaper which she's in the process of removing from the walls.

'Here,' I say, crossing the room. 'Let me.'

She smiles and stands patiently while I remove the lump of goo from her hair, her eyes roving my face the whole while. Once removed, I drop it to the floor with all of the others.

'It's already a vast improvement,' I say, pointing behind her. 'That is truly awful, isn't it?' With its paper removed, the surface of the wall beneath is pale and mottled, and in stark contrast to the disgusting ice-cream-pink flock wallpaper which still clads the rest of the room.

She shakes her hand to dislodge another strip of paper from it. 'And yet the height of fashion at one time,' she replies. 'But it's vile stuff and takes an absolute age to remove. There's more than one layer too.'

'It will be worth it though,' I comment. 'Despite the hard work.'

She still has a quizzical look on her face and I smile reassuringly. 'I thought I might give you a hand,' I say. 'And in answer to your question, I'm fine. Not absolutely fine, obviously, but as good as I'm going get right now. I've been writing, actually, it's very cathartic, but now I've finished, I don't want to hear another word about Isaac. I just need to keep busy, if that's okay? How are *you* feeling anyway? Hopefully a little better after taking a much-needed break yesterday.'

She takes my cue and smiles brightly even if she does still look tired. The signs of early pregnancy are easy to spot if you know what you're looking for: blotchy skin and limp hair. She hasn't yet reached the stage where she'll begin to bloom.

'I do, but…' She grinds to a halt, as if wondering whether now is the right moment to talk about her own issues when I've clearly indicated that I want to gloss over mine. I nod in encouragement. 'One minute I feel nothing but relief, that it's all going to be okay, and then the next I'm struck by abject terror that makes me wonder how I could even contemplate having a baby at all. I'm sorry, Mum, I know that's probably not what you want to hear but it's all I have at the moment.' She wrinkles her nose.

'I think it's absolutely okay not to know how you feel yet. And perfectly normal as it happens.' I give her a warm smile. 'We make a right pair, don't we?'

It's not really a joke, but my light-hearted comment gets us both past a tricky moment.

Smiling, Leah gestures around the room. 'Did you really mean it about giving me a hand? This stuff is absolutely revolting, it takes an age to remove, but it's got to come off. A couple of the rooms have pretty large cracks on the walls that have literally been papered over, several times. Our surveyors had a look at them and they're nothing serious, but it's better to attend to them now rather than have them cause problems in the future. Robin's always told me that decoration is nine-tenths preparation and he's right. Although it's time-consuming, it's a risk we can't afford to take.'

I eye the debris covering the floor. 'I might regret saying this, but I'm free all afternoon. Admittedly, I haven't stripped wallpaper off too many walls before, but simple observation makes it clear that it'll be considerably quicker and easier with two people.'

A look of gratitude floods Leah's face. 'Oh, would you? I seem to have been doing this for days and it's mind-numbingly boring. Even having someone to talk to will make it better. Get changed first though,' she adds, 'or your clothes will get ruined. There's so much glue on all these layers of paper that anything which touches you, sticks, and once it's dry it doesn't come off. You can borrow some of my work clothes if you like.'

None of my stuff is particularly new, or fancy, but with no money coming in for a while it's going to need to last me, so I readily agree. 'I need to pop back upstairs for a few minutes anyway. I have an email I need to send.'

I head down to the kitchen to make everyone a drink first, and by the time I get back to my room with Leah's spare clothes, I've only been gone about twenty minutes. But there's already a reply from Barbara. I had a feeling there would be.

*Darling!*

*Oh, Louisa… It's so lovely to have you back, I can't tell you how much I've missed your work, and oh my goodness, lovely, you've done it again!! Every time I need something pulling out of the bag, you're the woman that makes the magic happen.*

*I can't say I'm not surprised but goodness, this article has every-thing and oh… tears, darling, there were tears as well! It's honestly one of the best things you've ever written and so hard-hitting. You've absolutely nailed the tone and the content, and I know that readers are going to love it. And while it's very personal to you, you've written it with them in mind and that's absolutely why you're so good, our readership is, after all, the reason we do what we do.*

*I've no hesitation in publishing it. I might need to make the odd tweak here and there, but they will be few and far between,*

*trust me. So, listen carefully to me, my darling, because we are*
*very much back in business. Send whatever new ideas you have!*

*Barbara x*

I read it through one more time before letting my thoughts go
for a moment. Not that it's necessary, I've been thinking about
this for so long now that I know my mind is already made up.
Committing to my decision though, that's another thing entirely.
But what reasons do I have not to? If I think about it logically,
then now is probably the perfect time… But it's still a big step.

I sit down, laying my fingers gently on the mouse, and before
I give myself the opportunity to think any further, click reply. It's
time to leave my past behind. Time to end this once and for all.

I run through the words I want to write in my head, feeling
the heft of them, and then my fingers begin to fly.

*Hi Barbara,*

*I'm so happy you like it! Believe me, that article came from some-*
*where very deep… But in writing it I've also realised something*
*else – that it's time to draw a line under the past and move on.*

*I've been giving things a great deal of thought over the last*
*couple of weeks and this is going to be my last article for you,*
*Barbara. And while I realise I might be fooling myself that you*
*would want to, please don't try to change my mind.*

*I really didn't expect to be writing this, but now that I am,*
*I realise how much I want it. As for what I'm going to do next,*
*well, Leah and Robin need my help here, but I'm also planning*
*some other projects about which I'm very excited. It's all very*
*early days but that's okay, I have to start somewhere.*

*You've always been one of my biggest fans, Barbara, and your*
*support and friendship throughout my career has meant a very*

*great deal to me. So, I hope you know how difficult a decision this has been, but it is one to which I've given a very great deal of thought. I hope also that we can keep in touch, and if you ever fancy a very reasonably priced break by the sea, I know just the place!*

*It's been a hard few weeks, but if I've learned anything it's that when change arrives it's always better to welcome it in. And I fully intend to do so.*

*Much love, Louisa x*

And then I hit the send button and slowly close the lid of my laptop. I'm done here.

# CHAPTER TWENTY

I'm not used to physical work and I'm more tired than I can remember being in a long while, but even as I step out of the shower and begin to towel myself dry, my mind burbles with thoughts. I should probably dry my hair and go to bed but there's a sentence running through my head and if I don't write it down now, I'll forget it.

Trouble is, if I open my laptop, I'm bound to see a message from Barbara and I don't want to read it just now. I'm pleased she was so complimentary about my article, but her email still rankles. Despite her praise and enthusiasm to see me returned in all my former glory, it's a hollow sentiment. She'd already made her position perfectly clear and I'm under no illusion what would have happened if she hadn't liked the piece, or if I hadn't turned in one at all. Well, she has her article now and I've used it to draw a much-needed line in the sand. I don't know what I'm going to do now I've cut my ties with her, but Barbara doesn't belong in my new life. She had to go.

I minimise my emails with the barest of glances and then open a document, committing the words in my head to type before I lose them altogether. But, before I've even finished the sentence, the next has already arrived, and just over thirty breathless minutes later I have my first thousand words. It's not a chapter, it's not even a complete scene, but my novel has a beginning and I sit back and grin at it.

I wonder how close I'll get to the truth. The fact that Isaac assumed Elliot to be the shell grotto's architect doesn't make it true.

Elliot may not have even known it was there, let alone sculpted its magnificence. It's the most likely scenario, but no one can ever be certain, because the only man who knows that particular truth is no longer around to speak it. *Just like William...*

The thought draws me to a halt for a second, but then I let it play out, reaching its natural conclusion. I can never know what happened on the evening of William's accident, not from his point of view anyway. I've only ever seen it replayed through another's eyes. I try to push the thought away but Leah's earlier words come back to me: *it's a risk we can't afford to take...* She was talking about their work at the hotel of course, but her words are an echo, one that takes me straight back in time to the night of the accident.

Because those were the exact same words that William said to me on the last evening I saw him. There'd been a last-minute hiccup for that damn new project of his; the one he'd spent every minute trying to get off the ground, going that little bit further because he loved the adrenaline rush it gave him. I had walked down the path with him to his car, the cold air biting at me as I'd asked him one last time if he really needed to go out. And knowing that he would, had kissed him and told him not to worry, to take care and that everything would be all right. *It's a risk I can't afford to take*, he'd replied, moments before he'd driven off. Except that, perhaps he hadn't taken care. It was one of the things that had always worried me about William. That he was always in a rush, trying to do too many things at once, fiddling with the radio, fussing with the heater... *Keep your eyes on the road*, I'd said on more than one occasion.

And the truth is right there. He *had* been rushing, he *had* taken the risk despite the weather.

And I've known that all along...

I stare back at my laptop, at the keyboard, at the winking cursor, an invitation to start writing again. I can still hear Leah's voice, reminding me that I'd never seen Isaac at the inquest. I'd never seen how broken he was. And it's staring me in the face – how my articles have only ever shown one side of the story, the side I'd chosen to tell. It doesn't matter *why* I was writing them perhaps so much as *how* I was writing them – and just like art, perspective can change a thing's appearance dramatically. And that *is* the nub of the matter. Just as Isaac said it was.

I sit back, feeling a flush of shame hit my face, because despite all the other things Isaac said, there's also something else nudging me, asking me to take another look at it. Perhaps something that he didn't outright refer to, but that was there all along, sitting behind his words.

*You don't know*, Isaac had said, but it was in reply to my comment. But what? I screw my eyes up, trying to remember. It was just before I left, and I've run most of our conversation backwards and forwards in my head for the best part of the day but this, this was his parting shot.

I'd snatched up my bag… and knocked over my coffee, seen it run in a dark river across the workbench. Then I'd pushed my way past him and…

The memory comes back to me.

*I don't know what on earth has got into you this morning*, I'd said, and Isaac had replied, *Exactly my point, you* don't *know…* Not that I didn't know what had happened on the evening of the accident, but that I didn't know what had happened to him *that* morning… this morning.

But something had.

So now I'm searching through my other memories to see if there's anything else that will give me a clue to what had changed his behaviour from the easy-going and well-tempered man I'd got to know. He'd recognised Leah, of course, and discovered who I was, but there's something else… A reason why he was running. A reason why he moved to Eastleigh in the first place. In search of change, in search of a new life, because something in his old one had become unbearable…

But the only thing I can think of is the blackened page of his sketchbook that I had found in his studio; a diary of sorts in which one of the days had been obliterated. Not a day that was just slightly darker in subject matter than the rest, but one which had been comprehensively reduced to nothingness. But I have no way of knowing how long ago Isaac used that notebook or when the day in question had fallen. And all the other pages on either side had seemed fine, so what was it about that one particular day that marked it out from all the rest?

I think about my life, both before and after William's death, and the times, especially before he died, when something awful had happened. But I'm struggling to think of any. I'm sure there must have been some, but now the benefit of hindsight has taught me that everything is relative – that a day you thought was awful pales into insignificance beside the day when your husband is killed. Even the succession of dark days that came afterward were never quite as bad as that one. In which case, if my life were the pages in a notebook, how many would I have blacked out? Just the one.

So what could have happened in Isaac's life that would stand out from all the rest? And I guess the answer to that is the same as for anyone else. An accident… the breakdown of a relationship maybe… a death… But it also leaves me wondering what's so special about today that triggered such a dramatic downturn in Isaac's mood, one that he himself acknowledged. An anniversary of some sort?

I'm already reaching into the desk drawer as I think these thoughts, pulling out the blue folder tucked right beneath everything else. It's a folder that I don't look in any more, I've learned not to. But at one time I thought it made me feel better, and I would often sift through the articles it contains, feeling anger burn through me, or sorrow pour tears from my eyes. The articles aren't numerous. What for me was an enduring reality became a story that the press soon lost interest in. But the few clippings that are here detail the accident and the resultant inquiry, even though they never covered the verdict. And I know what they say almost off by heart, but was there something I'd missed? Something I'd dismissed as trivial when held up against the enormity of what had happened?

And of course, I see it as soon as I start looking.

It's a detail I'd read over and over, part of a statement from a witness, supporting Isaac's story of events preceding the accident. But even though I'd read it, it had little or no impact. In my head I was certain I knew what had happened – Isaac was guilty and I didn't need to read any statements that said otherwise. In fact, when I had read them, I had done so in scorn. But what I hadn't taken regard of was who had been giving the statement, or more importantly what this might mean.

A quick Google search gives me all the information I need.

I check my watch; it's gone half eight, but the summer evening will be light for quite some while to come. If I hurry, I might just be in time. I dress quickly and hasten downstairs, slipping unseen out of the back door of the hotel and into the car park. Moments later I'm pulling out into the street, turning left to head away from the town.

The roads are still quite busy with people; holidaymakers taking their time over dinner or heading out to one of the pubs to enjoy a drink in the warm evening air. Even the local dogs are being walked for one last trip out of the day. The ebb and flow of daily life. For most folks at least.

I park in exactly the same spot as before and hurry across the tufty grass beside the road until I'm standing on the cliff edge looking down onto Elliot's Cove. I sink to my knees. It seems only a few hours ago since I had last sat here, weeping at the sight of one of Isaac's drawings, disappearing before my eyes, and seeing only ruin.

The beach below me is empty but for one lone figure, and I don't need to see any more clearly to know that it's Isaac, sat cross-legged on the beach as he watches the tide take his drawing. Almost all of it is gone, save for one corner, but I can see that it must have been just as large and intricate as all his others – a mandala – and if the part I can see is indicative of the rest, then it's a shape I've seen before. The design is created from a series of overlapping circles within a strict geometric pattern. It's been used throughout history, on many different materials – as tiles in ancient buildings, to patterns on quilts – but it's universally known as the Flower of Life.

It would have taken incredible skill to recreate it on the beach, and on such a large scale. The physical endurance needed alone would be huge; it must have taken hours. But then I guess when what you're doing is for someone special, the measure of effort is simply a measure of love and knows no bounds.

And now I see it as Isaac does, a thing of beauty; not disappearing with the tide, but instead transmuted into something else. Each tiny grain of sand, picked up and put down, is the same as each atom within her body passing from one realm to the next. He isn't so much saying goodbye, as acknowledging that she still exists, in a place he cannot go to, and simply rearranged into a form he can no longer see. But she is still beautiful.

Elena. His daughter.

I sit and watch for a few moments more, aware that tears are streaming down my cheeks, but I let them fall, unchecked. For all that has gone. And for all that will never be. And then I get to my feet and, in the greying light, drive slowly back to the hotel, thoughts chasing around and around in my head.

Dear God, what have I done?

*

The next morning dawns with a harsh, stark light that hurts my eyes. My head pounds and my neck is stiff from a night spent tossing and turning or lying, tense and miserable.

During the night, I'd explored every avenue for finding out what happened to Elena that doesn't involve talking to Isaac, but there isn't one. Even Francis, who is possibly closer to Isaac than most, probably doesn't know, and finding out from someone else is simple cowardice on my part.

The bare facts I know. Isaac's daughter had given evidence at the inquest. She had been with him in the car when the accident happened and her statements would have been key in helping the coroner reach his verdict. But at some point just over a year ago, Elena had died, alone, from natural causes. And, stricken with grief, Isaac had moved to Eastleigh to try to make some sense out of her death and, importantly, find a way to live his life. But these bare facts don't tell me anything about what actually happened, they don't tell Isaac's story at all, and I'm very aware just how much I want to hear it.

Which brings me back to my article… How could I have been so stupid? So cruel? I didn't know about Isaac's daughter when I wrote it, but that's no excuse. Once it's published Isaac will know exactly how I feel, and so will everyone else. I should try to talk to him, try to explain, but it's not going to be that easy.

I turn the covers aside and pad stiffly across the room to my laptop. I had studiously ignored it last night, but this morning I need to see the response from Barbara. Whether her chief emotion is anger, or whether there might be a way I can negotiate pulling my piece altogether. It's my only hope.

And there's no reply at all.

I scan my emails, in case I'd missed it, in case it had been hidden as part of an earlier conversation. I even check my junk mail folder. But the fact is that she hasn't responded at all. I let the weight of that sink in for a few moments. But it doesn't surprise me, however much I don't want to admit it. And with that one single action, or rather lack of action, I see how dispensable I really am, how I'm only ever 'brilliant' and a 'star' and all the other things that Barbara has called me over time just so long as I'm playing the game. What does surprise me is the instant realisation that I no longer want to.

It's still early but I'm hopeful that Leah will already be up. There's something I want to say to her.

She's in the kitchen when I find her, a plate of buttery toast on the table which she appears to be eating with relish. She smiles as I enter.

'Morning, Mum. Are you okay?' she asks. 'Not feeling the effects of yesterday too much I hope?'

Her comment throws me for a moment until I realise that she's referring to the wallpaper stripping. So much seems to have happened since then that it feels as if it was days ago.

'A bit stiff,' I reply, without elaborating. 'But you look better.'

She nods. 'I don't actually feel sick this morning, which is heavenly. I'd forgotten just how good hot toast dripping in butter really is.'

I eye her food appreciatively. 'I might just join you,' I reply. 'But first I need a huge mug of coffee. Would you like—?'

But I don't even get my question out.

Leah pulls a face and groans. 'No thanks,' she says. 'I can't believe I ever liked that stuff, it's revolting.' But she grins. 'I wonder if I'll ever get to like it again.'

'With me it was olives, except the other way around. I couldn't stand them before I was pregnant. But then, when I was expecting you, we went out for a meal with some friends one evening and there was a small bowl of them on the table in the restaurant. Without thinking, I popped one in my mouth like it was the most natural thing for me to do. And I remember feeling such surprise at how gorgeous they were. And, as you know, to this day, I still love them.'

A soft smile crosses my face as I switch on the kettle. I daren't hope to imagine what her comment might mean. I join her a few minutes later with my coffee and toast.

'Leah... can I ask you something?'

She looks up, faintly alarmed.

'It's just that I've made a decision about something that might be considered a little rash, and I need to run it past you. It has implications, you see, for things here.'

She nods.

'And I would like you to answer truthfully,' I add, smiling in reassurance as her eyebrows rise.

'Mum, just tell me what it is.' She rolls her eyes, but it's a teasing, affectionate reaction.

'Well, you know how my plan was always to get my job up and running again, so I could support myself first before even thinking about buying a place somewhere? Well, I've just jacked in my job with Barbara. I won't be working for her any more.'

'But, Mum, you're a freelance writer,' she says carefully. 'You've never actually worked for Barbara.'

'No, but we both know the reality of it has been that I do. It's been a very long time since I submitted elsewhere and that's because of the arrangement we had. It suited us both for all sorts of reasons, but I've decided it's not what I want any more.'

'Go on...'

'I've just submitted an article to her, but I've also told her that it's the last I'm going to write for the magazine. I hadn't even realised, but I've been coming to some conclusions over the last few days and her lack of a reply has only confirmed what I've known for a while. I just hadn't wanted to admit it to myself. It's time, finally, to do that.'

Leah had left a crust of bread on her plate but now she takes a cautious bite of it. Her eyes are watchful.

'I think it suited me to write my articles for Barbara. I knew that she would publish them, but I also knew that they gave me the opportunity to live the kind of life I have – going where the story was, chasing down the bad guys, righting wrongs…'

I pause to inhale a deep breath. 'What I was actually doing was ensuring I was the kind of person your dad wanted me to be; the independent go-getter, the trailblazer, anything but be a wife living the kind of staid, domesticated life he would have hated. And I thought I hated it too, but I'd also dismissed it as a valid way for anyone to live. And I know better now. I'm not saying it's how I want to live exactly, but there's a happy balance and that's one thing I never appreciated. Things have always been black and white for me, Leah, even the articles I wrote… especially the articles I wrote. I never took into account all the nuanced colours of things, the ambiguities of light and shade, and in doing so my judgements have been… misplaced.'

Leah's chewing slows. She swallows. 'What are you saying, Mum?'

'I think I'm trying to say that I'm sorry. For always putting what I believed was right, first. Above you, above everything.'

'Oh Mum…' Leah's hand reaches out across the table and takes mine. Her fingers are soft and warm. 'It was never that bad. And you've done some amazing stuff and should be rightfully proud of it. Don't be so hard on yourself.'

I give her a soft smile. 'But I also need to admit when I've got it wrong. And to learn from my mistakes. I want things to be different, which is why I've told Barbara I'm quitting. It's one of the things that needs to go if I'm ever to change.'

Leah looks at me, a puzzled expression on her face. 'So, what are you going to do?'

I know what I need to do, but I can't talk to Leah about the article, not yet. 'I want to write a book,' I say. 'I *am* writing a book. And it's going to be thoughtful, and balanced, and nuanced, and… beautiful, if I can make it so.'

My fingers get another little squeeze. 'I think it will be,' Leah says. 'I know it will be.' Her expression is gentle, in fact her whole face looks much softer than I've seen it in a long while. Perhaps it's just that we've both realised our vulnerability is what it takes to allow us to be more open, and that can only be a good thing.

'But there's one potential problem,' I add.

To my surprise Leah shakes her head immediately. 'No, there isn't, Mum. You can stay here for as long as you like.'

# CHAPTER TWENTY-ONE

I ambush Francis in the queue beside the coffee stall as he waits for his early morning dose of caffeine. It's not even nine o'clock yet, and the other stallholders and shopkeepers along the causeway are busy setting out their wares for the day.

'Morning, Francis, I don't suppose you've seen Isaac this morning, have you?'

'Mmm, about ten minutes ago, fifteen maybe…' He takes a step forward as the queue shortens. 'And looking a damn sight better than he did yesterday. I don't know what the problem was but—'

'Do you know where he was going?'

'Erm, no, at least…' He stops, taken aback by the urgency in my voice. 'Is everything okay?'

I aim for breezy this time. 'Yes, fine. I said I'd meet up with him this morning, that's all, and I'm later than I thought. I wasn't sure where he'd be.'

A flicker of doubt shows in Francis's eyes, and I realise how stupid that sounds. 'It wasn't a definite arrangement,' I add, smiling.

'Ah, I see. Well, he went towards the town, so the allotment, maybe, I don't know.'

I start to back away. 'Great, I'll try there. Thanks, Francis.'

He gives a wave as if to call me back. 'You were right, by the way,' he says.

I frown. 'Sorry?'

'You were right,' he repeats. 'About the writing. I'm like a thing possessed.'

His face is animated with excitement, but it falls when he realises I haven't a clue what he's talking about. My last conversation with him feels as if it was weeks ago. But I have to say something.

'Of course! Sorry, Francis, I'm miles away this morning. How's it all going?' It's as vague a response as I can make it.

'I've filled half a notebook already. And it's amazing how I'd been kidding myself that I don't have the time to write, when even just scribbling a little bit in between customers really adds up. They seem to like it too; everyone asks what I'm writing.'

I smile warmly as my memory suddenly connects with my brain. 'It feels nice, doesn't it? When people ask what you're doing and you say, oh, I'm writing a book.'

His face lights up. 'Course, I'm not a proper writer yet but, well…'

I'm anxious to get away but I don't want to let him down. 'Francis, if you're writing, then you're a writer, it's as simple as that. But I'm so happy to hear it's all going well. Just keep going. And you wait and see, now you've been bitten by the bug there'll be no stopping you.'

'It really does feel like that.' He smiles up at the stallholder. 'Hi, Janine, just my usual please.'

I touch his arm, taking the break in conversation as my opportunity to leave. 'Listen, Francis, I'd better get going, but I'll pop in soon, I promise. I can't wait to hear all about it.'

'Maybe we could even… Could I pick your brains a little?'

'Yes, sure. No problem.' I beam a smile at him as I take a few steps backwards. 'Bye then.'

He gives a little wave, distracted as he's handed his cup of coffee, and I turn quickly, my own hand still in the air.

I practically run up the hill to the allotments.

I'm hot and bothered by the time I get there, grateful that the day is overcast. A few spots of rain are already blowing in the wind and as I walk through the gate the view of the sea that normally opens up in front of me is almost entirely gone. A veil of mist hangs over the join where the sky meets the ocean and, above it, shades of grey clouds hang, unmoving.

I make my way up to the far end of the plots just in time to see Isaac's figure turn onto the path, moving away from me. He's pushing a wheelbarrow.

And all at once I'm stuck, because I have no idea what I'm going to say. I hang back, bizarrely now hoping that he doesn't see me at all and wondering if I can turn and leave without being noticed. However, the moment he reaches his own allotment, he'll spin around, and I'll be in full view. I steel myself. *You came here to say something, Louisa, and you can't back out now.*

I'm frantically trying to compose my greeting when Samson decides to take matters into his own paws. The cat trots towards me like I'm his long-lost owner and, despite the circumstances, I can't help but smile. Cats are such contrary creatures; I can almost guarantee that on any other day Samson would ignore me. Isaac follows his movements with his eyes, wondering where the cat is off to in such a hurry. He turns, straightens, and suddenly there's just the two of us, maybe fifteen feet apart, staring at one another. And for a moment it's as if nothing else exists.

Isaac is the first to recover. He lowers the wheelbarrow to the ground.

'I have to say I wasn't expecting to see you this morning.'

His voice isn't angry, or harsh, or abrasive in any way, and yet the memory of the way it sounded the day before hovers in front of me, like an invitation. But I push it aside. If I take up its offer then we won't achieve anything, and everything I came here to say will be lost. I can feel my fingernails digging into the palms of my clenched hands.

'No, I...' I take a deep breath. 'I came here to apologise. I didn't listen and...' There's so much to say and I don't even know where to begin. 'I didn't listen. To anything.'

He doesn't reply immediately, and it's all I can do to keep from running away. Just like he accused me of in fact. But then he pushes a hand through his hair and with a visible breath he walks towards me.

'Then may I offer one of my own,' he says. 'I said some things which, while they may have reflected what I was feeling, weren't said in the way they should have been. And I'm sorry.' There's a ghost of a smile on his lips. 'The most inadequate word in the world.'

Samson is still winding himself around my legs and I drop to a crouch to rub my hand across his head. A second later he arches his tail in the air and walks away. 'Well, that told me, didn't it?'

Suddenly Isaac's face brightens. 'Shall we start again? Morning, Louisa.'

'Morning...' It's better, but I still don't know where to begin. If only we could start everything over, not just the day. 'Could we...?' I break off, glancing down at the wheelbarrow. 'Sorry, are you busy?'

'Yep, but I can take a break for a moment.' He eyes the sky. 'Today might not be a good day for deliveries anyway. And I've done the ones I need to. The others are optional, shall we say.'

'Or I could help you?' But I realise as soon as I say it that it's a silly idea. We both know this isn't what I came here to do. 'Actually, would you mind if we went somewhere... to talk? I feel there are some things I should explain.' A flicker of nerves stirs my stomach.

'We could go to the studio?' He smiles again. 'There's a bit more room than in the shed.'

By unspoken agreement he turns to move off and I fall into step with him, a couple of paces behind. By the time we get to the stile at the end of the allotments it's raining steadily.

'We should pick up the pace a little,' he says, pointing ahead and, as he does so, I realise that the line of mist I had seen on the horizon isn't mist at all but a wall of rain. The wind is blowing it in off the sea.

My hair whips across my face as I climb the stile, stumbling a little as I drop down the other side. It's making it hard to see and I tuck it resolutely behind my ears, where it stays for no more than a second before being whisked away again. A slew of raindrops hits my cheek.

We're half-jogging down the grassy bank, reaching the wooden steps above the studio just as the squall moves directly overhead, dousing us in fat raindrops. I almost slip on the topmost step, but Isaac's hand thrusts out towards me and I grip it gratefully, righting myself. I hold it all the way to the bottom.

It's a relief to be inside as we tumble through the door, the rain battering against it as Isaac shuts out the weather. I hadn't expected the studio to be open, but the reason becomes clear as I wipe the wet from my face. The bed has been slept in, blankets heaped beside it as if kicked off in the night, and paper litters the floor. A mug stands on the sanded floorboards and my eyes flick guiltily to the workbench where I'd spilled my coffee the day before. It's been wiped away, but a dark stain still lingers where I'd made my mark.

It's calm in here out of the elements, like the hush after a violent argument, but the air seems heavy. Perhaps it's just the weight of Isaac's sorrow, almost visible in the room. It's there in the tangle of bedclothes, the angry twists of paper, and the slightly sour smell that even the blast of sea air can't dispel.

Isaac fishes for something in a cupboard and he turns, handing me a towel in his outstretched hand. He takes another for himself, tousling his hair, which is plastered to his head. Much like mine, I suspect. And now, with it pushed back from his face, I can see his sadness exposed. The dark circles sunk beneath his eyes and the hollow look from within.

'Thank you,' I say, holding the towel against my face. It smells faintly of lavender.

I finish drying my face and hair and am wondering what to do next when Isaac takes the towel from me, folding it with his and placing them on the workbench. I can see the circle of glass he'd showed me the day before, the one with the cracks running through it, and heat begins to gather on my face.

'I should…' I pause, wondering yet again how to begin. There are so many things I need to say.

'Louisa…' Isaac turns and leans against the bench, crossing his feet at the ankles. 'Let me, first. My temper got the better of me yesterday and I reacted badly to your suggestion. It wasn't how I wanted our conversation to be. It should have been…' His eyes search my face, his full of anguish. 'I wanted to pick a good time to tell you, or rather a better time. I know there was never going to be a good time, but yesterday was… it just—'

But I put out my hand to stop him. 'No,' I interrupt. 'I didn't listen, to anything you said. Nor did I appreciate how difficult it was for you either. I was defensive, jumped to conclusions, and determined to think the worst. I never even stopped to think how awful it must have been for you to tell me who you are.'

The words *and what you did* hover unspoken in the air between us.

Isaac drops his head. And suddenly I have to know. I can't say the things I need to unless I understand it all.

'Tell me about Elena,' I say, quietly.

For a moment I think he hasn't heard me. Or isn't going to answer at all. But then he looks up. And it's as if all the air in the room stops moving. Even the furious pummelling of rain on the roof stills.

'How do you know?' he asks eventually, borne on the back of a sigh.

'I saw your drawing last night,' I reply. 'From up on the cliff. The Flower of Life…' I see his eyes widen. 'Although I worked it out before then. There was something about yesterday that marked it out as a day different from all the rest.'

'It was her birthday.'

My eyes close in silent agony. And so it had been my comment, my stupid, thoughtless request that he draw a picture for William that had reminded him so painfully of his own loss.

'I'm so sorry,' I say.

'She would have been twenty-five.'

The same age as Leah.

'She'd just won a National Sculpture Award. She was quite, quite, brilliant. Her work shone through everything, she…' He trails off. 'She was just about to host her first solo exhibition.'

His face is barren as his eyes lock with mine. 'She didn't deserve to die, Louisa. She had a whole life ahead of her in which to be brilliant, and she would have been. She already was.'

There's no way I could have known any of this when I'd asked Isaac to draw a picture for me, but there's no excuse. I'd never listened to what he'd been saying. Really saying. The words that lay behind the ones that made it out of his mouth. The way he spoke about grief, about loss and beauty. With hindsight it's obvious, but I wish with all my heart I could take back what I'd said to him yesterday. But it's as Isaac said, if wishes came true, we'd all be as happy as Larry.

'We used to come here for holidays when Elena was a child,' he continues. 'Every day, on the beach, we could never keep her away from the place. It's where she discovered how to draw, how much she loved it; like the sand was one vast canvas just for her. She would draw huge patterns…'

And now it all makes perfect sense. This is the one place where Isaac still feels close to his daughter, where he can honour her memory and learn to heal his life. His drawings are his way of talking to her.

'When did she die?' I whisper.

'Just over a year ago. A short while before I moved here. Although in reality she died the night of the accident, just the same as William did. I killed them both.'

His words burrow into my skin.

'She had a seizure a couple of months after that night. She'd been working hard and the consultant said it was probably just stress from the accident and her workload. She was so committed to her art and she often worked late into the night, hours and hours every day in pursuit of perfection. They said they would do tests, to make sure that it wasn't epilepsy, but they never got to finish them. She had another seizure, alone in her studio, and died. It doesn't normally happen that way. Sudden unexplained death in epilepsy, they call it, rare and there's no way of predicting it either. She was just unlucky. But it had nothing to do with luck; it was the accident that triggered the seizures. The doctors told me they couldn't be certain, but there's a link. And what other reason would there be? She was young, and healthy, it shouldn't have happened.'

I'd had no idea. All of this had been going on in Isaac's life during the weeks surrounding the accident and the inquiry and we none of us knew. We saw a guilty man and that had been all that mattered. And it's all I've seen since.

'But you mustn't blame yourself, Isaac. From the sounds of it there was nothing anyone could have done.'

A tight smile tugs at the corners of his mouth for a second. 'Yes, that's what everyone says. The truth of it though is that the blow to the head she received at the time of the accident is most likely what caused the seizures. And if she hadn't been in the car with me... or I hadn't had a drink—'

'Or William hadn't been driving the same route at the same time... There are far too many variables to ever really know the truth of it, Isaac. And you can't know that what happened to Elena was as a result of the accident...' I let my sentence trail off, with just enough ambiguity to let Isaac know how I'm feeling.

And then his eyes meet mine. 'So, do you want to know what happened, Louisa?'

'Isaac, I've seen the testimony. I—'

'From my point of view. Not what was said in court.'

A flicker of challenge glints in his eye.

'Because I did have a drink that day, Louisa, you and I both know that. Except that I'm not what you think I am; an irresponsible drunkard who cares little for the law or other people. I had *one* drink, a glass of champagne to toast my daughter's success. My wife and I were at home and I wasn't expecting to go anywhere that evening, but when Elena's car was stolen, from right outside our house, we called the police and I offered to drive her home. It turned out to be quite a night, didn't it?'

'Isaac, you couldn't have known, you—'

'I should have got her a taxi home. That's what I should have done. But I didn't, and there isn't a day goes by when I don't wish I had. But I swear to you, Louisa, that William just came out of nowhere, he…' Isaac drops his head, pressing a finger across his eyebrow as if in pain.

'What?' I say.

But he doesn't answer. Instead he walks over to the bed and starts to straighten the rumpled covers, picking up a blanket from the floor and wrapping it over his arm.

'William what, Isaac? What were you going to say?'

'It doesn't matter,' he replies, quietly. 'It won't change anything. And if I tell you, it will only be for the wrong reason; to make me feel better. And I think I've done enough damage. You know, Louisa, perhaps it's best if we just agree to leave this be. I can't see what good it will do to keep going over it.'

*No, except that I haven't yet said what I came here to.*

'So, can I ask you a different question then?' I say. 'Why did you tell me at all? You didn't have to. You could have just left things as they were, gradually drawn away from me. I'd have been none the wiser.'

The rain is lessening now, the patter of raindrops slowing.

'Because I still feel guilty, Louisa. Because I thought I owed you an explanation if nothing else, and… I don't know, perhaps I thought that sharing my experiences of dealing with my own grief might help you too. But in reality that was probably just another way for me to make myself feel better.' He dumps the blanket back on the bed and stoops to pick up a piece of paper. 'Although I'm not sure anything will ever really do that. Because however much we talk about it, however much we argue who was to blame, no one will ever know for sure who caused the accident. It's an impossible answer to an impossible question.'

'Then perhaps the answer is to simply accept it,' I say. 'Instead of trying to figure out who was to blame, however unintention-ally—' I hold up my hand to prevent him from speaking for a moment. It's important that I get this out. 'Because either way, the result is the same. William and Elena still died. We both lost someone, Isaac, and no amount of apportioning blame is ever going to change that.'

He stares down at the piece of paper in his hands. I can't see it clearly, but it looks to be a sketch.

'And where does that leave us?' he asks.

I stare at him for a moment, confused. 'Us…?'

His eyes bore into mine. 'Yes, us, Louisa. You and me. The fact that we've met, that we're both standing here. Us.'

But I have no answer for him. And in that split second, I realise the full extent of what I've done.

And what I stand to lose.

How can I possibly tell Isaac about the article now?

As my agonisingly slow brain makes this discovery, I see the answer that he takes from my silence. The hurt is writ large upon his face.

I have to tell him the truth now, whatever the cost. Even though I fear the price will be too great. I swallow.

'I've written an article, Isaac. I'm not a ghostwriter, I never have been. I'm a journalist and I write for a magazine; for a column that exposes injustices, fraudulent companies, that sort of thing.'

His head comes up slowly and I can hardly bear to look at him.

'When William died, he left me with nothing. He wasn't the world's most organised man and, unbeknown to me, he'd let the life insurance policy lapse. William was somehow always of the belief that death was for other people, and he was too busy living to worry about things like that. We had a stupidly large and grand house and, without his salary coming in, debt began to pile up on me at either side. I struggled on for months, but in the end I had to sell the house, bank what little was left and move in with my daughter so that at least I had a roof over my head. I had no other real choice. And, naively, I thought that I could just pick up my old job again, despite the fact that I hadn't written anything for months. But things had moved on in the time I'd been away, and my editor had nothing for me but a series of articles for the Homes and Gardens section. That and one other thing…'

I can see the light beginning to dawn in his eyes.

'She'd come across a photo of one of your sand drawings. I've no idea where she got it from, but she sent it to me thinking it might make for a great article. She knew it was taken around here and her message was clear: find the artist and find the story. So that's what I set out to do. And I know I should have told you, been upfront from the start, but I needed this story, Isaac, and I could see how private a person you were. I didn't think you would give me an interview if I asked you outright and so…' I trail off, ashamed. 'I thought I could get to know you first and then…'

'You found out who I really was and…' A look of abject disgust crosses his face. 'You saw an opportunity for vengeance, is that it?'

I flinch at the harshness of the word he's chosen. But I can't blame him; it's my lack of honesty that has led us here.

'No, not vengeance. Isaac, but I honestly believed it was a story that people needed to hear. A wrong that I could right, and—'

'Get out.'

'Isaac, please, I haven't finished yet… It's not what you think, I didn't—'

'Louisa, don't insult me even more.'

'I'm not. I came here to apologise, to let you know that—'

But Isaac holds up the flat of his palm. 'I don't think we have anything else to say to one another, do you? Now get out of my studio, Louisa. Just leave me alone.'

He's made his position very clear. And whether that's right or wrong, he isn't going to listen to me now, and I can't say I blame him. This mess is my responsibility and mine alone.

So I turn and walk back out into the summer rain.

# CHAPTER TWENTY-TWO

I'm soaked by the time I return to the hotel, my hair hanging in strings and clothes wet through, but I don't care. At least the rain on my face will hide my tears.

How have I only just realised the way I was feeling about Isaac? Something else in the long list of things I've been deluding myself about, instead of being honest. And it took my own emotion, mirrored on another's face, before I could even acknowledge that I felt the same.

And writing that article… that isn't something you do to someone you care about. It's going to cause unimaginable pain and it's all I can think about now. I just have to hope that I have time to pull it, although I'm already pretty certain I'll be out of luck. Barbara runs a tight ship and her deadlines are as late as she can make them. Too late and you're out, submit on time and you're in. All her staff and writers know the score.

But my room is still the place I head to as soon as I enter the Lobster Pot, and within minutes I'm perched on the bed, opening my laptop. If I'm lucky there may be something from Barbara anyway. It's a false hope though, and dashed as soon as I open my emails. I check on my phone, again, but there's nothing there either. It's another reminder that I no longer feature in Barbara's life.

My call connects but, as I listen to the tone ringing out, I already know it's going straight to answerphone. I don't think I've ever had to wait longer than three rings before. I try her landline at the office too but it's the same situation there and I'm just about to hang up when the phone is answered, a rather breathless voice almost shouting hello at me.

'Oh, hi... I was after Barbara, who's this?'

'Sadie. She's not here, sorry.'

My heart sinks. Sadie is Barbara's assistant, but she would never answer Barbara's personal line unless she had to. 'It's Louisa, Sadie. Hi, how are you doing?'

'Oh, *hi*... Loved your new piece by the way. Barbara showed it to me before she left. How *are* you?'

'I'm fine, but sorry, Sadie, I haven't got time to chat just now, I need to get hold of Barbara really urgently. Do you know when she'll be back?'

There's an ominous silence from the other end of the phone.

'Oh... I thought you knew. It's the last week in July, Louisa.'

*The week that Barbara goes away every year... how could I have forgotten?*

Shit... shit, shit...

I try to think quickly, my heartbeat quickening with every passing second.

'So, who's manning the desk these days when Barbara's away, is it still Michael?'

'Yes, but...' Her voice is wary. 'What did you want, Louisa?'

Everyone knows that Michael may be Barbara's second-in-command, but in name only. He won't take any decisions in her absence. Not if he knows what's good for him.

'It's a long story, but I need to pull my article, Sadie. It's really important, you know I wouldn't ask otherwise.'

I can picture her running her long blonde hair through her fingers and twirling the ends. It's something she always does when she's thinking.

'Louisa, it's already gone. You know what she's like; it was set before she left yesterday. We didn't even need to use anything from the reserve list this month. She was really pleased with it all.'

'But you do have things in reserve?'

'I'm sorry, I can't—'

'But this is really urgent, Sadie. Can't you contact her, please, just this once?'

Her silence is all the answer I need. It's the only week in the year that Barbara goes underground. And no one disturbs her holiday. Ever.

'Okay, Sadie, thanks. I'm sorry, I know I shouldn't have asked.'

'Louisa, I'd do it if I could, you know that, but… Is everything okay?'

'Yes, it's fine, thanks, not to worry.'

There's a pause for a moment and then, 'So, when are we going to see you again? It's been so long. And now that you're back on board, you have to come into the office to see everyone.'

But I'm not back on board, doesn't she know? And I realise that it's an irrelevant question; the office and Sadie and Barbara and my whole life before suddenly seems a million years away.

'I'll have to have a think, Sadie, I'm a bit busy just now, and London isn't on my doorstep any more.' In fact, the thought of stepping foot in the city now just fills me with horror.

I make my excuses and finish the call, staring at my phone as I hang up. What on earth am I going to do now?

And the answer is that there's very little I can do. What's done is done, and I have to accept whatever lies ahead of me now. But that still doesn't stop me wondering how Isaac is. Is he still in the studio, standing among the screwed-up bits of paper and messy bedclothes, his anger cooled? Or does it still burn bright, his long legs carrying him down to the beach, to stride out his pain?

Who could have foreseen what the last eighteen months have brought? And, in many ways, it's been far worse for Isaac. He was probably just beginning to get his life back together again and would have been so proud, celebrating his daughter's success, and then it had been cruelly snatched away from him. As if he hadn't already been punished enough.

My blow came much earlier of course, and it hasn't been easy. Not just losing William, but also the strain of living under so much debt which obliterated everything else and left me feeling shackled, all my choices taken away from me. I'd lost our house too, where we'd built our home, and the life I'd carved out for myself in the village where we lived. But I know now that I had plenty of choices. Instead, I'd let my grief and the pall of gloom I'd pulled over myself become the biggest barrier to anything changing in my life. And I'd made no effort to change either. Or rather to live in spite of the changes in my life, not giving up because of them.

I'm still lost in thoughts of Isaac's daughter when a soft tap at the door interrupts them. It's Leah, wearing a bright smile.

'Oh dear…' Her hand goes to her mouth at the sight of me, partly in surprise, but partly because she's trying hard not to smile. I haven't got changed yet and goodness only knows what I must look like.

'Yes, the rain rather caught me by surprise.'

She does grin then. 'No offence, Mum, but you look like a drowned rat.' But then her face falls slightly. 'Is everything okay?'

I manufacture a shiver. 'Yes, fine love, just got a bit chilled, that's all. I thought I'd make it back before the heavens opened but… obviously not.' I smile as brightly as I can. There will be a time to tell her about Isaac, about the article, but it's not now.

'Well, have a shower and warm yourself up. I'll go and put the kettle on so you can have a hot drink when you come down. Although the sun will probably be shining by then, it tends to do that here.' She pauses a moment. 'Actually, I was wondering if you could come down for a minute, anyway. Only I wasn't sure if you'd be writing or…' She glances over my shoulder. 'Or if you were busy.'

'Not especially,' I remark. 'Is everything all right?'

Her face brightens once more. 'Yes, fine. I just wondered if you'd come and help us, that's all. We want to pick out the wallpapers and soft furnishings and I'd love if you could help us decide.'

'Oh…' I'm so surprised I can't help myself. 'Yes… yes, I'd love to.' I glance at my watch. 'Can you just give me a few minutes to sort myself out and I'll come down.'

Leah smiles. 'There's no rush, Mum. Robin has only just got back with all the samples. Come whenever.' She studies my face for a moment. 'Are you sure you're okay? You look… I don't know, a bit… scattered?'

It's on the tip of my tongue to tell her. But this isn't just about me; William might have been my husband, but he was her father. Leah lost someone too. Besides, she'll find out soon enough once the article is published.

I find my smile again. 'My head's a bit stuffed full of ideas, that's all it is,' I reply. 'Now that I've started writing, it's like I've loosened the floodgates. That's why I went for a walk, actually, to see if I could clear a few of them out, or sort them into order, at least. Trouble is, I think all I've ended up doing is coming up with even more.'

'But that's a good thing, isn't it?' she says, frowning gently.

'Probably,' I accept. 'It just fried my brain a little bit.'

She nods. 'Okay, let me go and make that drink and then we're in the dining room when you're ready. The break might be just the thing you need to clear the muddle in your head.'

Would that it was that easy. 'I'm sure you're right,' I say. 'I expect it's just what I need. And very exciting. Give me ten minutes, I won't be long.'

And this time my smile is genuine. It *is* exciting but, more than that, it's the start of my new future, sharing my life with Leah, and her family. And right now that's exactly what I need.

I push my other thoughts to the back of my head. There's no place for them just now.

Leah was right. By the time I get back downstairs the rain has stopped and the sun is trying its hardest to make a reappearance. The dining room has always been a beautifully light room, but stripped of its dingy wallpaper and dowdy carpets it's a bright, bare shell just waiting to be transformed.

Piled high onto the table in the centre of the room are numerous pattern sample books, both for fabric and wallpaper. There must be twenty or so altogether, and Leah's and Robin's heads are already bent over one, almost touching.

'Blimey, how are you ever going to choose between that lot?' I remark, entering the room.

Robin grins. 'I admit, I wasn't expecting there to be quite so many books. But they were very insistent that I take them all. I think business might be a little slack at the moment.'

Leah pulls a face. 'I guess most people leave refurbishments to the quieter months, don't they? The winter, not the height of the summer season. Only mad idiots like us.'

'Nah… we're just ahead of the curve. Isn't that right, Louisa?'

I nod, returning his smile. Robin, ever the optimist.

'So then, tell me what you're looking for,' I say, joining them at the table. '*Where* are we looking for?'

'All of it,' replies Leah, rolling her eyes. 'This room, the lounge, conservatory, the bedrooms, hallway… You name it, we need to decorate it.'

My eyes widen. 'And you want to choose all that today?'

'Well, maybe not today, but in the next few days certainly.' She darts Robin a glance. 'We want to really crack on with things as much as we can, but there's a lot to decide and we could really use your advice.'

'*My* advice?'

She nods rapidly. 'Yes… It's knowing where to start, and what look we're trying to achieve that we're finding difficult. And you've done it before; got that really "together" look that's actually really carefully coordinated, but which seems effortless at the same time. Almost as if it happened by accident and not design.'

'Have I…?' I say faintly, not altogether sure what she's referring to.

'Yes, our house, Mum. It always looked so beautiful, and yet… I don't know, I could never quite put my finger on why it did.'

She's looking directly at me as she says it and, somewhere very deep within, a small warm feeling begins to grow.

'So, we want to know how you see this place, Louisa,' says Robin. 'I think we've got a bit lost over the last few weeks.' His smile is a mixture of so many things – apology, embarrassment – but all of it wrapped up in the warmth of sincerity. I return it just as warmly.

'Blimey, no pressure then.' I look around me. 'I guess it depends on several key things. Whether you want a modern, more minimalist look? Or something more in keeping with the style of the building. What colour palette you like and what you want your guests to feel while they're here.'

'What they want to feel?' echoes Robin.

I nod. 'Yes, you know, whether they should feel pampered, in the height of luxury, or relaxed and comfortable, peaceful even…'

Robin looks a little panic-stricken, but Leah just smiles dreamily. 'Oh, peaceful,' she says. 'Definitely. But also, things shouldn't be so smart and pristine that it looks like a show home and they wouldn't be able to relax. It's going to be a family hotel, after all.' A slightly nervous look comes over her face. 'That's right, isn't it, Robin?'

He takes his wife's hand. 'I think that sounds perfect,' he says.

There's a question just begging to be asked but I push it back down. I don't want to direct the conversation. The information will come, when the time is right.

'Okay… so what colours were you thinking of?'

'I like them all,' says Robin. 'Sorry… that doesn't help. Except purple.'

'What would you choose, Mum? Say for in here, for example.'

I think for a moment, narrowing my eyes. 'That idea you had, Leah, of offering this room out for local art groups. I really liked that. And with that in mind too, the obvious suggestion would be to bring the outside in. To make this a place where people will want to relax and linger, over their food for example, but also somewhere that leaves room for their own creativity to flourish. So, not a neutral canvas but not something that dominates either. Maybe soft greens and blues, like sea glass. But it can't all be pale because it's got to be practical after all, so you could have some darker tones for the flooring and furniture, but keep them natural in tone and texture; maybe jute, sisal, wicker even…' I grin. 'I'm thinking off the top of my head here, so feel free to shut me up.'

'And what about the bedrooms?' asks Robin.

'Again, simply because of where you are, I'd go with a natural theme. Think of a flower garden where everything goes together even though there are so many differing patterns and colours. You can apply the same principle here, keeping the background more neutral, but bringing some colour and pattern into the soft furnishings. Some warmer colours would be lovely in one or two of the rooms as well, so that in wintertime those seem cosier… ochres and splashes of burnt orange…'

Leah slides one of the pattern books towards me with a grin. 'So, we should think about how it makes us feel, just as much as what it looks like. Is that what you're saying?'

'Yes, as long as the theme has continuity, I think you can mix all manner of things together and they'll still look right.'

'I wanted everything to be super smart and sophisticated, and I think that's where I was going wrong,' says Leah. 'It's not very inviting, is it?' She wrinkles her nose.

'It can be, but I think it dates very quickly, and maybe isn't quite as… friendly.' I open up the book and begin to flip the pages, but I can see straight away that there's nothing in it that I would pick.

Robin's phone begins to ring as he slides me another book. 'Oh, it's David,' he says, as he pulls it from his pocket, turning away to answer the call. He wanders back out into the hallway.

'That's a friend of ours,' says Leah, coming to stand beside me so that we can go through the book together. 'He's in the business too and has promised to give us the contact details for some of the suppliers he uses. We want to source as much as we can from local businesses and there are some great ones around here, as you might expect. We don't just want to be one of those hotels that takes everything from tourists in the summer months, but then gives nothing back to the local economy. This is our community and we want to be a part of it too.'

'I think that's very wise,' I reply, marvelling at the change of heart my daughter seems to have had. 'And you can support in other ways as well, with the furnishings even. Buy things from local craftspeople if you can. They might be a little more expensive in the first place, but I bet they'd last a lot longer.'

Leah looks up and stares out of the window, and I know it's her future she's looking at. 'I was thinking that,' she agrees. 'There were some gorgeous things in that gallery we went into the other day. In fact, that might have been what got me thinking. Wouldn't it be lovely to choose a few pieces from local artists and display them here?'

I'm about to answer when Robin comes back into the room.

'What a star,' he says, holding up his phone. 'Dave's going to email us a list; there's rather a lot of people on it apparently.' He looks between the two of us. 'Right, where did we get to?'

'I think we need to just go for it,' says Leah. 'Let's make some decisions, otherwise we'll still be standing here in four hours' time.' She checks her watch. 'We've got all afternoon. Is that all right with you, Mum? Or do you want to get back to your book?'

I look at her eager face, energy buzzing around her like static electricity. 'Perfectly,' I reply. 'I'd got a bit stuck anyway, it can wait.' Right now, doing this with Leah and Robin is far more important.

I pick up the sample book I'd discarded a few moments ago and move it to one end of the table. 'I think we should try to whittle things down a bit, so why don't we have a quick flick through everything and any books that are a definite no we can put out of the way.'

'Yes, good idea.' Leah looks up suddenly. 'Hang on, I've just thought of something which might help.'

She disappears and returns a minute later holding her iPad. 'When we get to something we like, I'll take a photo of it. That way we can view them all at the same time, instead of flipping backwards and forwards trying to remember which ones were in which books.'

So that's exactly what we do. We discard about a third of the books on our first pass, and then by a constant process of elimination begin to whittle down our choices. The afternoon marches on, but by tea time we're beginning to see the wood for the trees. Leah uses some sort of note-taking app to write down a list of all the rooms or areas they need to decorate, adding all the designs we favour as little thumbnail photos. She can magically move them around, delete or duplicate them, and it soon becomes like finishing a jigsaw puzzle. Our excitement mounts as we all try to find the last few pieces, everyone talking at once, pointing at the screen, yelling, 'Put that there,' or 'No, in the conservatory,' but it's all good-humoured. The laughter and teasing feel just like a favourite dress you pull out of the wardrobe. One you haven't worn for ages, but when you try it on you can't remember why you haven't worn it more often.

Leah's eyes flash with exhilaration. 'Oh my God... I think we've actually done it,' she says. 'Look...' And she copies the last photo, adding it to the list of rooms, so that each now has a series of pictorial references beside it. Virtually the whole building can be seen at once.

Robin looks up, mirroring Leah's emotion. 'So, what do we think? Leah?'

'I love it! I absolutely love it. Oh God, Robin... this is going to be a thing, a beautiful, wonderful thing!'

And as he takes her in his arms and hugs her, she catches my eye over his shoulder with a smile that tells me everything I need to know.

It seemed inconceivable to me, even just one short month ago, that I could feel like this: full of happiness for Leah and Robin, and looking forward to a new life, instead of mourning the loss of my old one. I wipe a surreptitious finger under my eye as Robin's phone burbles with a message.

He pulls away from Leah, fishing it from his pocket and checking the screen. 'It's Dave... Oh, hang on, he's just emailed the list.' He taps another icon and pauses, holding the screen out for Leah to see. 'Here we go...'

She peers at the message. 'He wasn't joking, was he? Blimey, there's loads of people on here. Butchers... fish... oh, cheeses, cakes... even vineyards. Oh and—' She stops suddenly, pulling away. 'Wow, well we can have a look at that later.' She pushes the phone back towards Robin.

It's such a dismissive gesture that he frowns at her. 'What?' he says, glancing at the screen in puzzlement.

But Leah just flashes me a smile, before looking back at Robin, moving her head a fraction, lifting her eyebrows the tiniest amount. But it's enough. His eyes widen and, whatever it is, he's seen it too. His shoulders sag a little and I can sense their lightness of mood slipping away like air from a burst balloon. It's horrible.

'What's the matter?' I ask.

And although she tries desperately hard to hide it, the haunted look has returned to Leah's face. She looks at Robin, stricken. A cloud has just flitted across the sun and it's so obviously connected to what she's just seen that she has to say something.

But it's Robin who takes a deep breath. 'Leah, this isn't going to go away, and sooner or later it's something we're going to have to talk about.'

It's my turn to raise my eyebrows.

'When I got chatting to Dave about suppliers a couple of days ago, he mentioned several people locally. He's been in business a while now and knows a lot of folk hereabouts; hence the list. And one of the people on it is a guy he's been raving about, a local supplier who grows all his own veg and...' He trails off when he sees that I already know how the sentence ends. 'And I wasn't absolutely sure who he was meaning when we spoke, but this has just confirmed it.' He glances at Leah for reassurance. 'Louisa, it's Isaac...'

'Yes,' I say quietly, not sure where to look.

'I'm sorry, Louisa, but well, there's no getting away from it really. I mean, he lives here, it's a fact of life and everyone says...' He swallows. 'Everyone says he's a really nice guy.'

I nod, a series of them. 'Yes...' I agree. 'Yes, I know...' And then to my abject surprise and horror I burst into tears.

# CHAPTER TWENTY-THREE

It doesn't take long to tell them. There's not much to tell, beyond the fact that I've messed up.

'But I don't understand why you didn't say anything to us,' says Leah, not harshly, but disappointment sounds a discordant echo.

'I do…' Robin's face is full of empathy. 'Because, given the circumstances, how do you even begin that kind of conversation? Especially seeing as I've told Louisa how much you've been struggling with feelings about your dad recently.'

And instead of firing up like she would have used to, Leah simply nods. 'You're right. And I haven't made it any easier, have I? Making it all about me, as usual, and throwing your love for Dad back in your face like it was a bad thing. And I accused *you* of not being able to move on.' She shakes her head, annoyed with herself. 'That's rich, isn't it? Talk about the kettle calling the pot black.'

'No, please, Leah. It's no one's fault. It's just something that's happened without my really noticing it had, or why… And it's taken me so long to realise and admit it to myself, I think I was embarrassed to say anything.'

Leah lays a hand on my arm. 'You can tell us about him now, if you like.'

I give a wry smile. 'I'm still not really sure what to say,' I admit. 'Given that all this seems to have crept up on me, but maybe it's about saying that I think it's time I had friends, people in my life again. People who think like I do, or actually people who don't think like I do as well. Since meeting Isaac, my outlook on life has begun to change; I'm seeing things differently. Or maybe he's just been a reminder of how I *used* to see things. You said yourself about our home, how I'd filled it with all the things I loved, but somewhere along the line I'd forgotten I loved them.

'I want to live again, Leah. And stop fighting against the desire to do so. I've fought against all the things Isaac said, refusing to listen, but he's been right, every step of the way. And now, I can't imagine my life without people like Isaac in it.'

'Mum, maybe we're not the people you should be telling this to.'

I hang my head.

'I know… And this is where it gets even more complicated,' I reply, shame washing over me. 'I've written an article for the magazine, you see. About him.'

Leah's eyes widen and I can see the words 'You did what?' hover in front of her. It shows incredible restraint that they don't actually make it out of her mouth.

'I know… You don't have to tell me how stupid it was. But he'd accused me of so many things and I was so angry. Except in doing so I've made things much, much worse.'

'But can't you get the article back?' asks Robin.

'No, I've tried. Barbara's away. And you know how it is with her.'

Leah's brow furrows. 'But there must be something you can do. Does Isaac know you've written it?'

I hang my head. 'We had a furious row this morning. I tried to tell him, to explain what I'd done and why, but he threw me out and wouldn't listen. I can't say I blame him. I didn't know about Elena then, you see. I don't think *anyone* knows about Elena. She died not long before Isaac moved here and I'm pretty certain he won't have told anyone. He's just like Elliot.'

'Elliot?' Robin frowns. 'Who's he?'

'The man the cove is named after,' replies Leah. 'That's who you mean, isn't it? The one you're writing about.'

I nod. 'Everyone knew him but, at the same time, nobody did. They saw only what he chose to show them. And Isaac is just the same. And I knew this. I knew it from the minute I arrived and first met him. But even then, when I found out who he is, I didn't listen. I didn't act on what I learned about Isaac, I reacted to what I *thought* I knew of him. Like he was just another of my articles, his story black and white, and mine for the telling.' My eyes swim with tears. 'How could I even have done such a thing?'

'Mum, you weren't to know what had happened.'

'No, but I should have. The responsibility was mine and, of all people, I should have known better. I've always prided myself on getting my facts straight, never going to print until I was sure my story was watertight.'

I can see Leah looking helplessly at Robin.

'Then all you can do is wait,' she says. 'And try to explain.'

'He won't talk to me. I don't think he'll ever speak to me again.'

She frowns as a knock comes at the door.

'I'll get it,' says Robin, 'don't worry.'

She smiles sadly as he walks away. 'I know that's how it feels now, but once tempers cool, and a little more water has flowed under the bridge, it will be yesterday's news, you'll see. People will lose interest and maybe then you'll have an opportunity to explain.'

'But this will affect you too,' I say. 'Don't imagine for one minute that it won't. He is still the man who was involved in your father's accident and—'

I break off as Robin hovers on the threshold of the room, an odd expression on his face.

'Sorry… er, Louisa, there's someone to see you…'

He half-turns to reveal a figure coming up behind him. And whoever I'm expecting to see, it certainly isn't Francis.

I dash a hand against my cheeks. 'Francis…'

His face looks grave.

'I'm sorry,' he says. 'I wasn't sure who to ask and then I suddenly remembered you saying that you were staying with your daughter.' He looks at Robin and Leah, apology written across his face.

'No, it's fine… Is everything okay?'

He tries a small smile. 'Probably,' he replies. 'Just… Well, I wondered if you'd seen Isaac at all.'

Can he tell? I wonder. Can he see the pain already deep in my eyes, the anxiety creasing my face, still wet from my tears?

'It's a bit daft really,' he continues. 'But I was supposed to meet him earlier, just a quick pint after the shop shut, our usual weekly thing, but he didn't show up. You probably think I'm being melodramatic, but it's not like him, that's all. And yesterday, when…' He breaks off, looking nervous. 'I've never seen him looking so dreadful before and, perhaps I shouldn't say anything, but…'

'What do you want to say, Francis? Please, whatever it is, is fine.'

He nods. 'I should probably mind my own business, but do you ever get the feeling that Isaac is one of those people you never really know at all? Does that make sense?'

I can hear Leah's intake of breath.

'Go on,' I say. 'I think I know what you mean.'

'He doesn't really ever say much, does he? About himself, I mean. Have you noticed how you can be having a conversation with him and then, after it ends, you realise he hasn't answered any of your questions? And that somehow the conversation has turned back around onto you…' He trails off, unsure. 'Maybe it's stupid, but I'm a bit worried about him to tell the truth.'

Robin takes a step forward, flashing me a look as he does so. 'Do you have a number for him? Have you tried ringing?'

But Francis shakes his head. 'He doesn't have a mobile, doesn't like the thought of them. And I've been to all the places I thought he might be.'

'I saw him this morning,' I say, not sure what else to add. 'But you've tried the beach, have you? Elliot's Cove, I mean.'

'Yes, it's the first place I looked. A couple of walkers were there, but no one else. He's not at home either.'

'And the allotment?'

He nods. 'I've never been up there before but someone told me which plots were his. I knocked at his studio but no one was there, and on the way back the chap I spoke to told me he hadn't seen him since lunchtime.'

'Well, he was there when I left him, not that that means anything but—' And I realise what Francis actually said. 'Hang on… When you said you were at the allotment plots and knocked at his studio. Where exactly do you mean?'

Francis frowns. 'The shed by the path. The chap pointed it out to me; it's painted in bright colours.'

And I instantly see his mistake. 'Oh…' I give him a warm smile. 'That's not his studio, Francis. I can see how it would seem like it, but it's just his shed. His actual studio is down on the hillside below the allotment. I expect that's where he is; he's probably been there all day. He sleeps there sometimes too.'

I can see Leah watching me carefully.

Francis looks instantly relieved. 'Ah, well that explains it then,' he says. 'He probably just got involved in something and forgot the time.' He pulls an apologetic face. 'Sorry, I'll leave you to your evening. In fact, he's probably at the shop now wondering where *I* am.' He smiles at Robin and Leah.

But there's something about what Francis has just been saying, about what *we've* been saying; about Elliot… the similarities…

'No, wait a minute. Maybe we should just go and check. I can pop up there if you like. It does seem strange that he didn't turn up if it's something he doesn't normally forget.'

Robin is quick to come forward, sensing the direction of my thoughts. 'I can run you up there in the car if you like, it will only take a minute.'

'I didn't want to alarm anyone, I…'

'Better to be safe than sorry,' I say, smiling at Francis. 'It's not a problem.'

In fact, it takes four minutes to get to the allotments, and soon there are three of us making our way along the path towards Isaac's plot. Leah elected to stay at home, reasoning that it might look a bit strange for us all to turn up, and I'm already wondering how Isaac might feel having Robin and Francis show up too. Given how I left him, I'm not altogether sure how he's going to respond to me either. I'm beginning to feel a little foolish.

Francis indicates the shed where he's already been once this evening. 'I'll just go and give him another knock,' he says, moving off down the path.

It strikes me that I could let Francis go down to the studio on his own. I could easily give him directions and, after all, it's him who Isaac had arranged to meet. But as Francis comes back up the path towards us, it's clear he's been pondering the same question.

'Well, there's no reply,' he says. 'So, I guess he must be in the studio. Do you want to go, Louisa, or…' He stares off towards the sea. 'I'm just wondering whether it's a bit mob-handed if we all go. Where is it anyway, is it far?'

I shake my head. 'No, but maybe you're right. I don't mind going, it won't take long.'

'I'll stay here,' says Robin firmly. 'I don't really know the bloke, it will look a bit odd, I think.'

Francis nods. 'Yes, you go, Louisa, you know him better than us.'

I doubt that. If Isaac's been meeting Francis every week for goodness knows how long, I would have thought that they'd got to know each other pretty well. But I'm grateful for his tact, even if it is a little misplaced.

'Okay then, I won't be long.' And I set off towards the stile at the far end of the path.

My heart is in my mouth. If Isaac is there, what on earth am I going to say? I've been thrown out already once today, I could do without a repeat performance. But, by the time I've reached the top of the steps, I already know he's not there. There's something missing. A palpable emptiness in the air that swirls around me like the mist blown off the sea. But still, I carry on down.

I take the key from the jar and let myself into the space that I'd left so full of hurt this morning. And it doesn't look much different; the bed has been properly made, and some of the papers have been picked up, but others left, as if the task suddenly seemed pointless and was abandoned.

The ones that have been retrieved are stuffed into a colourful woven basket on the floor, which seems far too beautiful to serve as a wastepaper bin. My eyes flit from surface to surface and I suddenly realise that I'm looking for clues; anything that might tell me where Isaac has gone.

But the fact that he isn't at home, or here, or the allotment, or the beach, means nothing really. He could be out shopping. He might have gone away for a few days to stay with family. He might just be walking, stomping out the miles along the headland. None of us are his keeper. And yet as I see the rain start to blow against the window once more, I'm even more certain that he isn't in any of those other places either. And I don't know what to do.

The next instant I *am* looking for clues. Eyes raking the surfaces for anything that seems unusual. They stick when they come to the dark stain where my coffee spilled yesterday, but then move on... to pieces of glass, worn smooth by the tide, a lump of driftwood, a large pebble that has been split in two. My fingers explore the join as it falls open once more. Inside is the curled fossil of an ammonite, its segments distinct and beautifully preserved. And I smile at one of nature's building blocks; the golden ratio made manifest. Just like the shells on the beach...

My thoughts grind to a halt as I narrow my eyes. There are no shells on the bench. None at all. And the drawstring bag that is often filled with them is gone. Isaac's words from the other day come back to me. *Sometimes when you have nothing you have to look for the smallest things to give you hope…* And I'm pretty sure I know where Isaac has gone.

I look down at the key, still in my hand, and realise it's time to go. Besides, the rain seems to be picking up a bit and Robin and Francis have nowhere to shelter. I pull open the door, taken unaware by the blast of wind that hits it, almost snatching it from my hand. One of the papers from the floor whips into the air and slides back down towards me, slipping almost past my feet. I bend down to retrieve it, to put it back safely inside, when a line on the page catches my eye.

There's barely anything there, no more than a dozen lines drawn in charcoal, but each so expertly placed, so skilfully drawn, that the likeness on the paper is immediately apparent. The curve of a cheekbone, sweeping down to a chin, the curl of hair, lying against it. Intimate somehow, and I touch a hand to my cheek, the same cheek as that on the page. Because it's like looking in the mirror. The face in the drawing is mine.

*Sometimes when you have nothing you have to look for the smallest things to give you hope.*

# CHAPTER TWENTY-FOUR

I scramble back up the bank to the allotments as fast as I can. I'm now no longer kidding myself that everything is fine. And I can't believe I'm only just waking up to the fact that if I can acknowledge the effect that Isaac has had on me over the last week or so, that there might have been a corresponding effect on him… And today, I threw everything he'd given me back in his face. As if none of it mattered. As if I didn't care.

Robin and Francis are both standing, hunched against the rain, the wind blowing it in drifts across the exposed allotments. My face is full of apology as I hurry towards them.

'Sorry…' I pant, the climb up the hill rather swifter than I'm used to. 'I can't believe this rain. It comes from nowhere.'

Francis grimaces. 'That's the seaside for you.' His look is expectant, and I shake my head.

'He's not there,' I say. 'But I do think I might know where he is.'

'Oh?'

I'm torn because I don't want to tell them about the shell grotto. It was Elliot's special place, and now Isaac's… and mine too. I made a promise that I wouldn't tell anyone about it, and I can't go back on my word now. I've let Isaac down enough as it is.

'There's a place he goes to,' I say. 'Somewhere no one else knows about.'

Robin is watching me, a curious expression on his face. 'And you think that's where he is?'

I nod, indicating the path ahead. 'But let's get out of this rain first.'

Robin starts the car engine as soon as we're back inside, waiting for the screen to clear itself of fog. There's tense expectancy in the air. Francis is sitting in the front passenger seat and turns to me almost immediately, his beard glistening with small droplets of rain.

'So, what's your hunch?'

I pause for a moment, wondering how best to phrase my reply, but I needn't have worried.

Francis gives me a warm smile. 'Louisa, I'm aware, despite the impression he gives, that Isaac is a very private person. I'm also aware that there are almost certainly things which have happened in his life about which I know nothing. But if anyone is going to know them, it's you. So please, don't tell me anything that out of respect for him you'd rather keep to yourself. I value Isaac's friendship far more than I need to know the gossip, but it's obvious he hasn't been himself the last couple of days.'

I dip my head. 'Maybe that's just it,' I say. 'Maybe Isaac *has* been himself. Just the person that none of us realised he was. Let's find him first and make sure everything is okay. If he wants to explain, he will.'

Robin flicks me a glance in the rear-view mirror. 'So, where to, Louisa?'

'The beach – Elliot's Cove. But you may as well go back to the hotel, it'll be quicker to walk from there than trying to find a parking space.'

Robin peers up at the sky through the windscreen. 'I think you might be right.'

If anything, the rain is even harder as we turn back into the car park, but the streets are still busy. The town is full of holidaymakers and they have to go somewhere, even when it's wet.

'I'm just going to go and grab a jacket,' says Francis, as we clamber from the car. 'I've got one at the shop. Can I catch you up?'

We're all in tee shirts, Robin his usual shorts too.

'Good idea,' he says. 'We'll meet you by the beach steps, Francis. Louisa, let me get something for you too.' He can see that I'm anxious to be away.

I shake my head as, with a wave, Francis dashes off. 'I'm going to start walking, it's not cold.'

But Robin checks my arm. 'But it will be once you're soaked through.' He's studying my face. 'Another minute won't hurt… will it?'

I screw up my face. I can't explain the fear that is now gnawing at my brain, the feeling that something is very wrong. 'Probably not, but… I'm being melodramatic. You're right, it's silly to go without a coat.'

Robin holds my look. 'I'll be as quick as I can,' he says. 'Promise.'

I stand under the shelter of the porch to wait, anxious, though I don't know why, guilt filling every bone in my body. I push my hand into my jeans pocket, fingering the piece of paper that's folded there. And I hold the thought of it to me, like a warming blanket.

The door slams behind me and Robin is there, struggling into his raincoat as he holds out mine. 'Leah's keeping watch,' he says. 'And phoning a few shopkeepers she knows, just to check if anyone's seen him. Don't worry, Louisa.'

My shoulders sag. 'I'm sorry, Robin, this is all my fault, I should—'

But he silences me with a finger on his lips. 'No,' he says. 'No "what ifs", no blame.' He indicates the road beyond. 'Come on, let's get going.'

The beach has pretty much cleared of people, apart from those determined to enjoy their day; walking in the rain as opposed to just getting wet. But it's not pleasant; this close to the sea the wind has picked up and is whipping the sand about in stinging flurries. We pause a little way along to wait for Francis but I can already see him hurrying back along the causeway to meet us. He nods but says nothing as we start walking. Robin pulls out his phone, and I know it's to check if he's got signal.

And then time and distance do that strange thing they do when you're aware of them. They slow and lengthen so that our progress along the beach seems interminable, just like those favoured childhood destinations that take forever to reach but so little time to return from. I drop my head against the wind and the rain but every time I look up Elliot's Cove seems no closer. I have to fight the urge to stop and pick up the shells I see along the way.

It never even occurred to me to check the time, to think about the relentless march of the tide but, as we draw closer, I can see that the rocks closest to the sea are already underwater. I could cry. The tide is coming in and there's nothing I can do about it.

'Shit…' It's Robin, as he stands in front of the board which shouts the danger to anyone who'll listen. But I don't need it or him to know that the turn is well under way. My eyes have automatically sought out the red line of paint that Isaac daubed on the rock to mark the safest passage and it's almost hidden beneath the foaming waters that cover it.

I squint into the distance, trying to judge how quickly the sea is progressing, and I'm already walking past the board when Robin catches hold of my arm. 'Louisa, don't, it's too dangerous.'

'But I know the safest route,' I insist. 'Isaac showed me.'

Francis comes forward. 'And Isaac will have also told you, as he tells everyone, never to go through when the tide is turning. You'll get stuck, Louisa, it's too risky.'

I look back out to sea. There isn't time to argue. 'There's only one place I need to check and if Isaac isn't there then I don't know where he is. I'll come straight back, and if I can't get around then I'll stay until the tide turns again. I know where I can shelter.'

'No, Louisa, I can't let you.'

A wave crashes over the top of the rocks to land at our feet. Robin's eyebrows shoot into the air and he vents a breath. 'These signs are here for a reason, Louisa. No one is invincible, least of all you. I know you feel responsible for whatever this is, but for God's sake, we don't even know that anything is wrong. We could all be jumping to a massive conclusion here, and meanwhile Isaac is tucked up somewhere safe and warm. Don't risk your life on a whim.'

His eyes bore into mine, and I know what he's thinking. Just as I know exactly what Leah would be saying if she were standing here. And I almost don't go, but there's more than just our futures at stake here.

'Jesus, Louisa!'

I have one foot on the first rock when Robin pulls me back down again. 'This is ridiculous, please… What do I have to say to make you stay here and see sense? At least give me one good reason why you think you have to go.'

I stare at him and he groans.

'See! You don't even know yourself, do you?'

But I do know why. And I silently slide my hand into my pocket and fish out the drawing that nestles there. 'Keep this safe for me,' I say.

I see Robin's eyes widen as he opens up the folded sheet and then they lift to meet mine. There's an almost imperceptible nod. He folds it back up quickly against the rain and zips it into his jacket pocket.

'You promise me you'll stay there if it's not safe to come back,' he says. 'You can ring… and…'

He puts out a hand to steady me and I push myself up onto the rocks. My feet are already underwater.

I know I'm in the right place but the path to take is hidden from me, swirling with foam. I can't see the edges of the stones or judge their depth and within a couple of paces I realise that my past experience of traversing this area is no longer of any use to me. I edge my way forward, but it's a slow process.

Even being just a few feet higher than the level of the beach means that the wind can tear more easily at me, snatching at my hair, at the very air I breathe. And if there is any sound from the two men behind me, I can't hear it. I stumble on, almost falling as my ankle turns over and the arm I put out to save myself plunges me elbow-deep into the sea. The water is freezing.

I'm almost at the cliff face now and about to corner the headland, but already there is water sloshing off the edge of the rocks here, falling onto those below. This is a one-way ticket, I can see that now. But it will have to be enough. I stare down at the slope of rocks beneath me and try to pick up my pace as I head across those remaining. I've turned the corner now and can see the beach ahead of me.

And then I stop dead. Because in front of me is a crumpled figure, face down on the rocks. Isaac.

His name tears from my lips as I fling myself beside him. My hand on his shoulder elicits no response, nor my urgent shout in his ear. I shuffle backwards to give myself more room, crossing to his other side, trying to see his face, but I can't, it's hidden from me.

'Isaac!'

I'm shaking him now. Conscious that I need to move him fast, but which way? My frozen fingers burrow beneath his collar, seeking out the gap beneath his jaw where the soft skin hopefully beats with the pulse of his heart. But I can feel nothing. Or is it my fingers I can't feel? I withdraw them, rubbing my hands together, urging some life back into them, that I might find his. I try again, and I think there's something, faint and fluttery, like hope.

I stare at his unmoving form. Should I even try to move him? He may have injuries I can't see but if I leave him he'll drown. The thought closes my throat and a wave of panic sweeps over me. If we go onwards we'll be safe from the sea but alone. With no one to help us. And Isaac is unconscious, unresponsive. But if I go back… I can hear the sea behind me, the sound of the waves loud even above the howl of the wind.

I touch a hand against his cheek. I have to try. He needs help and there's only one place he can get that from. I thrust myself backwards and upwards, stumbling, shoulders crashing against the rocks higher above me. I climb, two, three… My foot splashes against water, the next deeper still. And as I look up I see that water is pouring from the edge of the rocks like a waterfall. By now the incoming tide will be creeping ever closer to the headland and once it does we'll be cut off.

'Robin!' I shout as loud as I can, hearing the echo coming back at me from behind. 'Robin…' I scream his name into the wind.

I turn back, praying that somehow Isaac will be stirring, that he'll be okay, and that with help he might even be able to get to his feet. Otherwise he's a dead weight, how will I ever be able to get him back?

The sea gushes hungrily over my hands as I seek to find purchase on the edge of the rocks, anything that I can use to pull myself back up onto them. And suddenly two arms reach down. Robin is on his knees before me, water pouring past his thighs. He's trying to pull me up.

'No, this way,' I shout. 'You have to come down. Quickly!'

He does as I ask, dropping beside me.

'He's here, Robin, on the rocks. Oh, thank God, we found him.' I pull him along.

'Wait… Francis is behind me too,' he splutters. 'We couldn't leave you.'

As he speaks, I see Francis appear, the water up to his knees. He takes Robin's outstretched arm and crashes down beside us.

'Come on,' I urge.

Robin moves past me and drops to his knees beside Isaac, his hand automatically following my action of earlier, sliding around Isaac's neck to feel for his pulse.

'Is he…?'

'He's alive…' He breaks off to look up. 'But he won't be very soon if we don't get him out of here. Francis, help me…' He slides one arm under Isaac's neck. 'Let's see if we can turn him. I can't tell what on earth's going on at the moment.'

I touch his shoulder. 'Should we even be moving him?'

But the look on Robin's face gives me my answer. Whatever injuries Isaac may have sustained are inconsequential compared with his possible death.

Robin wriggles his arm further forward, tugging at Isaac's shoulder as Francis supports his legs. Together they roll his body over, pulling him onto Robin's lap.

Isaac's eyes are closed and his face deathly pale, save for the single trickle of crimson which starts at his temple and curves a line across his cheek. And I'm felled by the emotion that surges through me. I never realised how familiar his face was, how I know every line, particular those when he smiles, the creases of happiness in his skin.

I look up into Robin's face. 'What do we do?'

But to my surprise it's Francis who answers. 'Give me a second,' he says, running his hands down Isaac's legs, first one and then the other. He's quick, methodical, as if he's done this before. And when he's finished with Isaac's legs, he does the same with his body, then his arms.

'Shit,' he mutters under his breath, a look of anguish crossing his face. He nods at Robin, and then I see it too. One of Isaac's hands is horribly swollen, the join where it meets his wrist puffy and mottled. 'We need to get moving,' he says. 'As far as I can tell nothing else is broken other than his wrist, but I'm more concerned about his head injury than anything else. He needs medical help, and quickly.'

Robin nods, his head swivelling. 'So which way? Do we get him down onto the beach, at least he'll be safe there?'

'No. The only access to Elliot's Cove for emergencies is the coastguard, and the nearest station is nearly an hour away.' His face is grave as he meets Robin's eyes. 'We have to take him back over the rocks. It's the only way. Louisa, ring for an ambulance and tell them we need them at Elliot's Cove headland. Ring Leah too and get her to meet them on the beach. She may need to guide them here.' He positions himself at Isaac's feet. 'Robin, help me get him down onto the sand.'

'But I thought you said we were going back?'

'Yes, but I can't lift him from this position… in fact, I'm not sure I can lift him at all.' He stares at Robin as if weighing something up. 'You're probably stronger than me, you'll have to do it,' he says. 'I'll show you how.'

Robin nods, wriggling out from underneath Isaac so that he can crouch beside him and take his arms. I can barely feel my fingers but I jab at my phone, praying that it connects. Leah answers just as they manage to lift him, grunting with the effort.

I jabber out my message, checking only that Leah understands. I daren't tell her exactly *where* we are, where Robin is, what's facing us…

'I have to go,' I shout. '*Please*, just ring for an ambulance now.' I hang up as soon as I hear her reply.

I'm back on the sand in seconds, to where Isaac is now flat on his back. Blood has seeped down his collar and onto the front of his shirt. I almost can't bear to look at it.

'We're never going to be able to lift him,' says Robin. 'Dear God, this is never going to work.'

'We have to try,' I urge. 'Please…'

I look at Francis who is standing by Isaac's feet.

'There is a way to lift him,' he says. 'But I won't pretend it will be easy. Going back over those rocks against the force of water is going to be one of the hardest things you've ever done, but you can do it, we can do it, *if* we work together. Robin, I'm going to show you how and then Louisa and I are going to help you over the rocks. Your job will be to carry Isaac, and ours will be to keep you on your feet, got it?' He doesn't wait for an answer.

My heartbeat ratchets up another few notches.

In one swift movement Francis slips his arm under Isaac's knees, lifting them upward so that they bend and he can get Isaac's feet flat on the sand. He turns slightly to his left, placing one foot over both of Isaac's and then, reaching down, grabs Isaac's right hand and pulls. Isaac comes up like Francis has stepped on the end of a rake and from there he drops his right shoulder, slides his arm between Isaac's legs and twists up and left. The whole movement takes less than two seconds and when he's finished Isaac is straddling Francis's shoulders, but I can see that he's held firm. My mouth drops open.

But before I have time to speak, Francis reverses the movement and slowly lowers Isaac back down to the sand.

'Your turn,' he says to Robin. 'Stand as I did. Now, are you right-handed?'

'Yes.'

'Good, because Isaac's busted his left wrist so we can only pull his right arm, and you'll find it much easier if you're pulling on your right too.' He repeats the initial movement with Isaacs's knees until his feet are flat on the sand once more. 'Right, are you okay with this?'

Robin looks petrified but he nods, watching Francis with ferocious concentration.

'Okay, so face slightly left, and stand just on the edge of Isaac's toes. Don't worry, that's the least of his concerns right now. Then you're going to reach forward for his right hand with your right hand… then pull, as hard as you can… Crouch and roll your right shoulder down into Isaac's belly as he comes up, slide your right arm through his legs and stand… and he'll come with you… Got that?' He places a hand on Robin's arm. 'Deep breaths,' he says. 'Get yourself ready, widen your legs, get them prepared to brace…' He holds Robin's look. 'And on three…'

With a roar that has as much to do with determination as effort, Robin does as Francis explained and, seconds later, he has Isaac over his shoulders. He wobbles, moves his feet, wriggles his stance, adjusts his grip and then nods grimly.

'Let's go,' he says. 'I'm okay, I'm okay…'

And he has Isaac's life in his arms.

Francis directs his attention to me. 'Louisa, you come and stand forward, okay? We're going to go first, as quick as we can but as surely as we can. We move, then balance, then support Robin to do the same. We're going to be his guide and his counterweight, okay?'

I manage a small sound, but it's snatched away by the wind. 'And let's go…'

The first few steps aren't too bad. The incline isn't steep here and the sea hasn't yet encroached the corner of the headland and so they're relatively dry apart from spray. But as we move higher I can almost feel the pressure of the sea behind me, clawing, seeking…

Francis is keeping up a near constant stream of chatter, talking to us both, but mainly to Robin. Small encouragements, confirmation that he's doing fine. And still we climb.

We're at the steeper section now, nearing the cliff face and the corner we have to navigate, one which will take us onto the flatter section on top of the rocks, but one which will also take us into deeper water, against the full force of the wind and the sweep of the waves.

The sea is now pouring off the top of the rocks, drenching us, blinding us as it splashes and foams. My hands flail for a series of agonising seconds before I feel Francis's grip firm in mine. I can't even see what's happening and spit out another mouthful of water, blinking furiously against the water in my eyes, but I keep going, one foot in front of the other as best I can.

The back of Robin's jacket is stained with Isaac's blood, bubbles of pink that form and are swept away. I have no idea how he's doing and long to take his hand, not even knowing whether he would feel it, but I can't. Not yet.

I plant my feet, finding my balance, as I flash a look at Francis. He scrambles upward on top of the rock beside me, holding us both steady for a moment as he glances behind him. I don't even want to look. I know it's bad. And any doubt I might have had about the validity of the signs back on the beach is gone in a nanosecond.

Francis has hold of Robin's hand and I his arm, and together we help him up the last section of rock, to stand in front of the cliff face, knee-deep in water. The wail of a siren comes in the distance as we exchange glances. There is still every possibility that this will end badly. If either of us lands up in the water… The waves are now crashing against the edge of the rocks that stick out to sea, sending great plumes of spray high into the air. All it would take is one slightly bigger than average wave to sweep us off our feet.

We make our way, inch by painful inch. My muscles are burning and I dread to think how Robin is feeling. His head has long since dropped and communication dried up beyond grunts of effort and hisses of pain and frustration. He's a runner, with strong leg muscles, used to enduring, but his burden is probably greater now than at any other time of his life. I strain to listen, shaking my head against the rain… There's something else I can hear on the wind, closer than the siren…

The others can hear it too, but we none of us dare alter our course, or turn around to see. It's a case of putting one foot down and then another, praying no one slips, praying we stay upright in ever-deepening water, and that for Isaac's sake we'll be in time.

And then I hear it even louder. A wild shout just behind us, from the direction of the beach, and suddenly we're no longer alone. A great bear of a man comes up behind Francis, and behind him another. Between them they lift Isaac from Robin's shoulders as if he were no more substantial than a bird. Robin sways, his burden lifted, as if released from it he no longer has anything tethering him to the ground. But then his knees buckle and Francis catches him, a strong arm around his back.

We're at the edge now but ahead there is only water, the rocks and sand beneath swallowed whole.

'Go!' a voice beside me urges and as I look I see a line of bodies stretching out to the shore, each one holding the other, a safety chain. The arms nearest to me stretch higher.

'I'll catch you!'

There's no time to think and, with my last remaining strength, I push off from the rocks. Shocking cold sweeps over me as I land, splashing and spluttering in the sea. It's dark and violent but I'm snatched from it and passed from one to the other, half-carried, half-stumbling so that the beach draws closer. Eventually I find my feet and stand on the sand, legs sagging beneath me as I tumble up the beach. I wave away the help that comes forward.

'I'm okay, I'm okay… Please, just get the others.'

I strain to see over the bodies in front of me, but I can tell from the movements that someone else is being passed to the shore. There's a flash of something pale and a cry goes up.

'Here! Over here!'

And there, suddenly, is an ambulance bumping over the sand towards us, people running alongside it. I close my eyes and sink back, shivering violently. A blanket is drawn around me, together with the tightest hug.

'It's okay, Mum.'

I cling to Leah, feeling her strength, feeling her love. 'Are they off?' I ask. 'Are they safe?'

She rubs my arm. 'I think so… I can't see, but I'm sure they are. I'm sure they are…' She's reassuring herself as well, I realise. It's not just Isaac out there, it's Robin too. 'I thought I was going to lose you, lose you all,' she says. 'Mum, please tell me you'll stay. With us. You can't move away now.'

I shake my head. 'I won't, I promise. I'm not sure how we'll do it but we'll make it work. I know where my home is now, Leah, I'm not about to go anywhere.'

The swell of voices gets louder and then, bursting from the throng towards us, I see the same two men who had come to our aid, carrying Isaac between them. The paramedics are moving forward and for a moment my view is blocked but, when it clears, I see both Robin and Francis, held firmly as they stumble up the shore, trying to make legs work that now fail them completely.

More blankets appear, pulled around their shoulders as they're led towards us and Leah scrambles to her feet to meet them. Her arms go around Robin and for a moment it's just the two of them, standing locked together like nothing will ever part them again. I force myself to my feet and reach out towards Francis, managing to smile as I pull him closer, and then we're clinging together, laughing at the fact that by some miracle we're all still alive.

'I don't know how to thank you,' I say, pulling away. 'If it hadn't been for you, none of us would have even known that Isaac was in trouble.'

But he shakes his head. 'No, he owes you his life,' he says, simply, looking to where Isaac is now lying on a stretcher.

'Do you think he'll be okay?' I whisper.

Francis smiles, but I know he can't answer my question. None of us can. Not yet. All we can do is hope.

I take his hand and pull him to sit on the sand, where I huddle beside him, oblivious to the rain that's still falling. I nudge his shoulder.

'How did you know all that stuff?' I ask. 'Lifting Isaac… We'd never have managed.'

Francis passes a hand across his face to wipe away the wet. 'A good pension wasn't the only thing I got from the RAF,' he replies. 'I don't think I ever told you, did I? What I did back then.'

I shake my head. 'No,' I say slowly. 'What did you do?'

'I was an instructor,' he replies. 'Survival training. But, Christ, am I unfit.'

'No more doughnuts for you,' I murmur, smiling as I meet the amusement in his eyes.

A man in green uniform is walking towards us and, as we pull each other to our feet, I instinctively look for Leah and Robin.

'Is he okay?' I ask, fear tugging at my stomach again as Leah comes to stand beside me.

'You can come and see him if you like,' the paramedic says. 'He's just regained consciousness. We'll know more when he gets to hospital but we're happy enough for now. His vital signs are steady so we're taking him in.' He looks between us. 'You three should also get checked over, but I can only take one in the ambulance.'

'Louisa, you should go with Isaac,' says Robin, as the others nod in agreement.

'Robin's right, Mum, you go,' says Leah. 'I can take Robin and Francis in.'

I don't need telling twice and finally let out the breath I seem to have been holding for the last few hours. The paramedic nods, holding out a solicitous arm, and, with a warm smile at them all, I let myself be led away.

'Louisa!'

I turn back to see Robin coming towards me, undoing the zip in his jacket as he walks. 'This is wet,' he says. 'So be careful. But you should have it. It's your turn to keep it safe.'

I meet his eyes, taking the drawing from him. 'Thanks, Robin,' I say.

The beach is clearing. Hugs are being exchanged and copious heartfelt thanks given. Until one by one people start to seek their own shelter from the rain.

The drama's over. For today.

But it isn't an end, it's a beginning.

# CHAPTER TWENTY-FIVE

## Two days later

'Are you going to steal all of those?' asks Isaac. 'Or do you think I might have one?'

The grape I'm about to eat pauses midway to my mouth before I guiltily lower it again. 'Sorry,' I say. 'I'm nervous.' But then I realise I can hardly put the grape back, so I eat it after all, surrendering the punnet when I'm done. I sit it beside Isaac's legs which are still tucked beneath the hospital bedsheets.

'Nervous?' Isaac says. 'Why are you nervous?' He fiddles with the grapes, trying to pull them from their stalks with one hand. His other sports a bright-blue plaster cast and is currently not much use to him.

'Well, because… aren't you?'

He grins. 'I asked first.'

I tap his fingers out of the way and pull a grape off the bunch, handing it to him and ignoring his question.

'So… Are you okay? What have the doctors said?'

'Well, I've a spectacularly busted wrist which, by the way, hurts like buggery. But otherwise, all okay. And, more importantly, not dead.' He holds my look. 'I think I have you to thank for that.'

'And Francis. And Robin of course. Leah… the paramedics, the crowd of people on the beach… those two blokes…'

'Louisa.' His voice is exasperated. 'I'm trying to say thank you here, and… you're not making it easy.'

'Well then, don't ask me questions like why am I nervous.'

He tuts, pretending to be exasperated.

'But everything else is okay, is it?' I peer at his forehead, and the neat bandage which now covers the left-hand side of it. 'There's no lasting damage?'

'Nope. And you never know, it might have knocked some sense into me.'

This time it's my turn to tut. 'Isaac, be serious for a minute. Falling down for no apparent reason isn't normal. Do the doctors know why it happened yet? Do they think… well, I just wondered, if it was anything like what happened to Elena.'

His eyes meet mine and he smiles, smoothing away my anxiety. 'No, nothing like Elena. Just me being a pillock… I seem to recall the last time we went to the shell grotto that I suggested you pause a moment before walking across the beach to get used to the change in light… Seems I should take my own advice on occasion.' He toys with another grape. 'I'd gone there, you see, because I was…'

'Angry with me?'

Another smile. 'Angry with myself,' he clarifies. 'For not saying what I should have done. For letting you go… And so, I'd been in the grotto, without proper light, working in the near dark, and in a right old funk as well. I lost complete track of time, was rushing to beat the tide, got dizzy, slipped and fell on my arse. Actually, I fell on my wrist and head but…'

'Ah… I see…' I let my words hover between us for a moment. 'Well, that's good then. Good that it was just a mistake as such, and not anything more serious.'

He nods.

I clear my throat.

'So, what was it you should have said?' I ask, feeling heat hit my neck.

His eyes search mine, weighing something up. And then his head drops and a slow breath is released before being sharply sucked in again.

'I promised myself I would tell you the truth but... Jesus this is hard.'

'Would it help if I promise not to run away again?'

'You didn't actually run away the last time, I threw you out... but yes, probably. There shouldn't be any more secrets between us, Louisa. But I'm sorry this one isn't going to be something you want to hear.'

But I *am* ready to hear it now. For the same reason that Isaac's just given and for the reason why I now need to be entirely honest with him. For the lines of a woman's face drawn onto a page...

'Go on,' I reply. 'It's okay.'

A pulse beats in Isaac's neck. It's strong and steady. It's beautiful.

He readies himself. 'On the night of the accident, everything happened exactly the way I told you. Except for one thing... We *were* celebrating Elena's news, her car *was* stolen, and I *did* drive her home, even though I'd had a drink. But I didn't cause the accident, Louisa. William took a bend too fast and was skidding out of control before he even hit me. There was nothing I could do to avoid him, and nowhere I could go. But, like an idiot, I jammed my brakes on too, and then there was even less I could do. He and I both spun; the road was icy, but he was going too fast and so when he hit us he spun off. I think you know the rest.'

His voice is quietly apologetic. Even when he has the chance to redeem himself, he doesn't want to take it. And Isaac is right, I do know the rest, but I also know what came before. I always have done. Because in my anger at William for leaving me on my own, I'd made him into the victim, reasoning that if the accident hadn't been his fault then he hadn't simply been careless with his life, but instead someone had taken him from me.

'But why didn't you say any of this? Not just to me, but at the inquest. You let yourself take the blame for the accident. Why?'

I can see the tussle on Isaac's face, but his eyes are the clearest blue as he meets mine. 'Because your husband had just been killed, Louisa. And by comparison I'd got off scot-free. But you, you'd lost everything that day, and even though I've told you what happened, there was still a chance that I could have saved the situation. Perhaps my reflexes had been too slow, perhaps my actions were the wrong ones, but more than anything I didn't want to take the risk that William be blamed for the accident. It was bad enough that he died, I had no wish to tarnish his memory as well.'

My nose burns suddenly as tears fill my eyes. That Isaac could do all that, for a perfect stranger. And even when Elena died he never once took the opportunity to lay the blame elsewhere. How much has he suffered, have we all suffered?

I push the grapes to one side, feeling for his fingers with mine. 'Isaac, I'm so, so sorry. Elena, she… I had no idea.'

'How could you, when no one knows?'

'But I've made things so much worse, I—'

'No,' says Isaac. 'Nothing you did made anything worse.'

'But the article…?'

'Louisa. All you did was make me realise that I'd not only been fooling everyone else, but myself into the bargain. I thought that all I had to do was stick a plaster over my grief and it would get better by itself. Which was just plain stupid. Stupid *and* delusional. The wound hasn't gone away. Because there's no magic cure that's going to heal it, just time and a little care. I know that now, and maybe that's half the battle. I was heading for a huge fall…' He pulls a wry face. 'So perhaps the one I had came in the nick of time. I understand now.'

His fingers squeeze mine, but I don't want to be let off the hook quite so easily. I have a lot to answer for.

'Don't be so hard on yourself, Isaac. I had no justification for writing that article when I did, and the fact that I didn't know about Elena at the time is no excuse. I brought back memories for you I had no right to, and worse I've exposed you. But I was angry, you see, and…' I sigh. 'Absolutely determined to prove you wrong.'

And much to my surprise, Isaac laughs.

'And I was absolutely determined to prove you wrong too… and look where that got me. Perhaps it's time we realised that we both have much to learn, from each other. I need to do a little more accepting and a bit less sweeping under the carpet.'

I smile. 'And I need to learn that the past is okay, but just as long as I have one foot in the future too.'

My hand is still in his, and his is warm, and soft, and… I hardly dare admit it to myself… but it feels like something I should hold onto and never let go. Reluctantly I withdraw it, meeting his eyes with uncertainty. There's one last hurdle left to jump.

I bend and fish in the bag at my feet. My fingers brush briefly against another paper that nestles there. It's a little worse for wear now from having got wet inside Robin's jacket pocket and then mine. But bent, wrinkled and a little crumpled, it's still the most precious thing in there. I find the folded sheets I'm looking for and withdraw them, only too aware how fast my heart is beginning to beat.

'I want you to read this,' I say, handing him the article. 'You were right when you said there should be no more secrets between us and, well, anyway, here you go.'

'Louisa, you don't have to do this.'

'No, I want to. I think you deserve to see what I wrote about you before things… well, before you decide where that leaves us.'

'Us?' he queries, but he's smiling. 'Whatever do you mean?'

I roll my eyes. 'Look, are you going to read the damn thing or not?'

Isaac takes the article from me, his hand trembling a little as he balances it on his lap, spreading the pages so that he can read them. He lifts the first page, eyes downcast as he moistens his lips a little, his mouth dry.

My hands are clasped beneath my legs, my knee jiggling as I wait out the minutes while he reads the first page, turns over the sheet and places it face down on the bed. He picks up the second… and then the third, and final, page.

*And so Isaac keeps watch over the beach, its unofficial guardian, looking out for the unwary walker or the plain foolish who take no heed of the many signs which spell out the dangers of Elliot's Cove.*

*That isn't even its real name though. Its real name is Eastwater Bay, but it's known locally for the man who used to fulfil the same role that Isaac does now. Little is known about Elliot, who died some ten years ago. Some say he was a drunk and unpleasant man, who chased people from the beach out of a selfish desire to have it all to himself. A hermit, vagrant, recluse – all names which have been applied to him at one time or another. But whatever the truth, it's fair to say that most people agree he was a bit of a character. Isaac, however, goes one step further than that. But then he would, because Isaac sees the good in everyone. He never knew Elliot, but he admires him; for having the courage to live his life the way he wanted to, unconventional possibly, but someone who managed something few of us do; to be at peace with himself.*

*It's no surprise then to learn that, in the time I've been here, for me it's very much become Isaac's Cove. It's beautiful, unspoilt, a little wild, but above all it shows us what's possible when the very best qualities are left to flourish. Much like Isaac himself.*

*I came here full of grief and anger, feeling bitter about my past, and despairing of my future. So, when I found out what part*

*Isaac had played in my life, I thought I knew exactly what would make it right again; someone to blame. I set about to tell his story as recompense for all those things I thought he'd taken from me.*

*Except that I was utterly wrong, because by thinking only of what I thought Isaac had taken from me, I neglected to see all the things he was giving me instead. I'm only glad that I realised just in time. And how different my life is set to be now that I know this.*

*You see, I've found that hope can be found in the smallest of things, in the darkest of times, but it cannot be claimed angrily or arrogantly, it can only come to you quietly, when you're ready to receive it. And when you realise it's a gift and not a God-given right. Whether you choose to receive it or not, that's up to you. But make no room for it in your life and it will always stay hidden. Lay yourself open to its possibility, however, and you'll see that hope is just one of the many things your heart can hold.*

Isaac's hand is still trembling as he lowers the final page to the bed. But his face is expressionless. Or rather I can't properly tell because he's staring straight out into the room, as if someone else is standing in front of him.

I can feel my heart thudding in my chest, even faster than the beats of time which stretch out between us. And I still don't know what Isaac's thinking. Whether I've done enough to say how sorry I am for ever doubting his integrity. And how thankful I am for letting me walk beside him on the path to my new future.

He makes a small noise in his throat and it breaks the surface tension of silence.

'Isaac…' I swallow. 'Please say something, I'm going nuts here…'

There's another pause before he turns to look at me. And I see the emotion in his eyes.

'I'd say things are looking hopeful,' he says.

And then he smiles.

# A LETTER FROM EMMA

Hello, and thank you so much for choosing to read *After the Crash*. I hope you enjoy reading my stories as much as I enjoy writing them. So if you'd like to stay updated on what's coming next, please do sign up to my newsletter here and you'll be the first to know!

*www.bookouture.com/emma-davies*

When I write my letter to you with each book, I always try to think about what has influenced each one, because they all have very definite personalities. And I realised that, incredibly, as the number of books I've written has hit the mid-teens, that this is my first book to be set beside the sea. Which seems extraordinary, given that it's my dream to live close to a beach, or preferably on it! Not in summer though – it's the wild wintry coastline I like best.

But I also wondered what made me choose to give this book such a setting, and I think that it was, in part, down to the situation we all found ourselves in during 2020 and 2021, that of the COVID virus and lockdown. I don't know about you, but I craved feel-good books and anything that carried a message of hope. Not surprisingly therefore, hope is probably one of this book's strongest themes.

I also spent hours looking at coastal towns in various locations, trying to decide where exactly Eastleigh should lie. I wonder if you can guess? As I wrote, I had multiple location photos and maps open on my laptop, to help me set my scenes, and at a time when we weren't allowed to travel, let alone go on holiday, I think I found it of huge benefit – allowing me my own series of awaydays, if only in my head. So I hope, having read it, that you felt transported to a lovely little town beside the sea, for a little while at least.

Of course none of this would have happened without the support of my wonderful editor, Jessie Botterill, who is so encouraging and supportive of my writing. Huge thanks to her and everyone at Bookouture for making this possible, but also to you, lovely readers, for choosing to read my books. You really do make everything worthwhile.

Having folks take the time to get in touch really does make my day, and if you'd like to contact me then I'd love to hear from you. The easiest way to do this is by finding me on Twitter and Facebook, or you could also pop by my website where you can read about my love of Pringles among other things…

I hope to see you again very soon and, in the meantime, if you've enjoyed reading *After the Crash*, I would really appreciate a few minutes of your time to leave a review or post on social media. Every single review makes a massive difference and is very much appreciated!

Until next time,
Love, Emma xx

@EmDaviesAuthor

emmadaviesauthor

www.emmadaviesauthor.com

Made in the USA
Las Vegas, NV
26 March 2021